OMNIBUS SIX

The Continuing Chronicles of Sherlock Holmes

C. Thorne

ISBN: 9798339987451
Imprint: Independently published

Cover and interior page design: L. Thorne
Library of Congress Control Number: 2018675309
Printed in the United States of America

To all who live in my heart, especially those no longer with me, I dedicate this book with the hopeful expectation that we may meet again one day. I will always love you!

CONTENTS

THE CONTINUING CHRONICLES
OF
SHERLOCK HOLMES

THE

YEW ALLEY
GHOST

C. THORNE

THE YEW ALLEY GHOST

That danger often comes from unexpected sources is a truth which has been driven home to me upon many occasions in my life, both as a soldier, and later through my involvement in the work of my friend, Sherlock Holmes, but I think never was that lesson demonstrated with quite so startling an effect as when it came from a source which I would never have suspected of being capable of such drastic violence.

The morning began like any other, with Mrs. Hudson bringing up a lovely breakfast tray, along with a pot of excellent tea, as Holmes and I discussed the day that lay ahead, I, seeing one of several patients I had acquired in those early days of my practice, Holmes mentioning some chemistry experiments he intended to conduct for the purpose of isolating certain compounds in blood stains.

Seated across from me as he was, far from the window, engaged in our light talk, I believe even Holmes was surprised to hear the ringing of the front bell at so early an hour, and when Mrs. Hudson showed up a slight young woman of perhaps twenty years of age, quite meek of visage and soft-spoken, the breakfast dishes were hastily cleared away and with courtesy the putative client was shown to the comfortable chair Holmes reserved to offer visitors to 221B Baker Street.

I saw that Holmes' gaze was fixed curiously upon the woman, evaluative but in no way troubled, nor did I sense any danger when I took a seat opposite her and opened the pad on which it was my custom to take notes, yet in retrospect I see there were signs from the first that there was a great tension in the woman, which at the time I put down to the strains often present in guests to Baker Street, tormented as so many have been by the very issues which brought them in to consult with Holmes.

"I am Helena Nichols," the young woman said, her accent northern and sharp, with a tone of agitation in it. She paused, as if the name should mean something to us, which at the time it did not.

"And how may I be of service to you, Miss Nichols?" Holmes asked courteously enough.

"*Mrs.* Nichols," she insisted.

"Ah, Mrs. Nichols then," said Holmes indulgently, though, like I, I am sure he noted that there was no wedding band upon her finger. "Pray, what brings you to Baker Street this morning?"

As we waited for her reply, the woman hesitated, and I saw her chest rise and fall with the rapidity of her breathing, which as seconds ticked past became something close to hyperventilation, and I wonder now, did I even then begin to sense the element of peril in her presence?

"You are known to me, Mr. Sherlock Holmes," she said at

last, a darkness in her tone. "Known to me from your work, and the actions you have taken against others…your intrusions, into their affairs….your *persecutions* of the righteous!"

At this accusation I saw Holmes stir, and I set aside the writing pad and was, myself, about to rise, for my every instinct had begun to call out to me.

"You have," the woman keened with a savage hiss, "sent my husband, Barty Nichols, to prison, and for that malice I shall strike you down!"

With those words of promise, before even Holmes with his almost preternatural speed could reach her, the woman's hand dipped into her purse, and with a violent motion she flung the contents of a jar toward my friend.

With his extended left arm, Holmes pushed me downward, crying:

"Stay back, Watson!"

I did not heed him, yet even as I grasped her arm a second too late to prevent her actions I saw a small black shape travel through the air and arrest its flight against Holmes' chest, where it fastened to him using tiny claws. With a burst of horror I realized it was a jet black scorpion, about the length of my middle finger, and its tail lashed downward, striking the detective with a thorn-like stinger.

Seeing the hideous creature stab her target, the woman cackled a gleeful cry and shouted:

"Sherlock Holmes is a dead man! Barty, I have avenged you!"

Holmes swept the scorpion from him with his left hand, and without hesitation smashed it underfoot with a violent stomp that gave off a sound like the crushing of a desiccated eggshell.

"Too late, fool!" Helena Nichols called, even as I grasped her in my strongest hold. "The sting of the Kaiser scorpion means *death*!"

Holmes' face showed nothing, neither anger nor fear nor pain, but kept upon it an element of unreadable blankness, even as he threw off his jacket and pulled open the front of his shirt, tearing the buttons asunder, and to my utter horror I saw a profoundly red welt the size of a dove's egg rising above a perfectly round hole in his flesh, where stinger had met his skin, and even as the foul woman keened with cruel laughter, I clung to her arm, and forced her down into the chair.

"Take heed, Watson," Holmes said, his words a grunt, for I knew he was already in considerable pain, "I perceive she is armed with a concealed dagger as well."

I took hold of her distant arm, so thin I felt the bones most prominently below the skin, and detected a blade strapped under her sleeve, so pulled that arm behind her as well and held it fast to the small of her back, aware even as I did so that my every instinct was to take care not to inflict pain upon a woman, so ingrained in me it was to conduct myself as a gentleman.

She had counted on that obsequiousness, and that is how she got to him, I thought ruefully, and tightened my hold on the writhing form below me.

I knew I needed to attend to Holmes, who, if the woman's claims of the creature being a Kaiser scorpion were true, bore a grave injury, but I could not get to him and yet restrain her at the same moment, so I shouted to Mrs. Hudson, whom I heard coming courageously up the stairs, summoned by the noises above.

"Pray, Mrs. Hudson," I cried, "do hurry and fetch a constable!"

She did so with much haste, and the knowledge that representatives of the law were coming caused the diminutive woman in my grip to fight still harder against me, her rage granting her a strength nearly paralleling my own as a man.

"He'll die!" she shouted up into my face, her teeth bared, all but spitting. "I know there is no antidote to the Kaiser scorpion's sting, for these last months I have worked for a chemist at university, who makes medicines from venoms. I have bided my time there, waiting for the deadliest of poisons to use against the cruel Sherlock Holmes, and when I saw the arrival of the Kaiser scorpion from German West Africa, and heard of its power, I knew I had found my means of revenge!"

I tried to recall of whom it was she spoke, and finally remembered a case from a year previous concerning a young clerk at a railroad company, Bartlett Nichols, who had sabotaged an engine there on behalf of a radical political movement, causing a collision which injured a dozen passengers, and closed a railway line into London for several days. Yet I also remembered that this man had had no wife, at least at the time of his conviction and the twelve year sentence it carried, despite this assailant's claims in the present that she was that person.

With admirable alacrity, Mrs. Hudson located a constable, and I heard the man's hobnailed boots stomping as he ran head-first up the stairs, and flung open the door.

"Mr. Holmes!" he declared with distress at seeing my friend's now-ashen countenance.

"Ah, Constable Murray," said Holmes with a small smile, his voice caught in a panting for breath which threatened to overcome him. "I am afraid you find me rather the worse for wear this morning."

"This woman is the assailant!" I told Murray. "Do restrain her while I see to Holmes!"

When Murray had taken hold of the so-called Mrs. Nichols —I still knew not the truth of her claim to be wed to the railroad saboteur—I rushed to my bedroom and snatched my medical bag off the floor.

"Dear Watson," said Holmes, now drooping into the chair behind him, his limbs trembling, "my condition is grave, as I feel the venom at work. She did not lie, I fear it was indeed that deadly tropical creature which assaulted me today."

He attempted a smile, then leaned back in the chair, and I saw with concern that even his lips were losing all colour.

Mrs. Hudson let loose a cry and shielded her face with her hands, overcome by the situation which had so suddenly unfolded upon us that morning, clearly afraid, as was I, that Holmes was beyond all help.

Mrs. Nichols, as she styled herself, cackled with delight to see her malice at work, and vowed:

"It is the hour of your death, Sherlock Holmes!"

Such an evil woman, I thought.

Out of the corner of my eye I espied to my surprise and, I uneasily confess somewhat to my satisfaction, Mrs. Hudson strike this Helena Nichols hard across the cheek with the flat of her hand.

"That's quite enough from you, villainess!" she cried heatedly, her face wearing an expression more stern than any I had ever glimpsed upon it.

It was a contest against death itself, I knew, yet I had a growing hope that I possessed a treatment worth attempting, for from my medical bag I drew a device I had kept on-hand in my time as an army surgeon in Afghanistan, where snakebites were not uncommon. It was a thin brass tube of some two inches in length, with a rubber bulb at the end, and by fitting this securely against the site of the sting, and depressing the bulb, it sometimes became possible to create a vacuum and draw out venom.

And so I attempted, crushing the bulb over and over in my fist, deflating and re-inflating it to create suction, wiping at the green-tinged fluid and thickened blood it drew forth. I kept this up for minutes unceasing, until with relief I cried:

"Holmes, I think it is working!"

My friend seemed to try to speak, then his mouth drooped and his face lost expression as he fell forward into a trembling faint, and Mrs. Hudson rushed to him and held him upright by the shoulders.

"Do keep at it, Doctor!" she cried.

And so I did for another five minutes, until my hand doubled into a cramp, and I wondered if I could possibly repeat the process even once more, yet just as I thought this, Holmes' eyes fluttered open, and he leaned back against the chair of his own volition.

"Watson..." he gasped, and Mrs. Hudson and I leaned

forward to hear him, "I feel cool death, once near to hand, receding into the distance, and think you have saved my life today."

The Nichols woman, in the process of being shackled by a newly-arrived second constable, while a third divested her of the dagger she'd concealed against her forearm, let loose a thunderous howl of anguish, and called:

"No, he cannot live! My beloved must be avenged!"

The savage outcries of the mad-woman echoed throughout 221B Baker Street as she was half-carried by constables toward a waiting paddy-wagon, and even from the street below, where a crowd had begun to gather, I heard her howling in disappointment.

For her dark wish that a fine man be taken from the world, was not to be granted.

<><><><><>

The long hours of that first day were still dreadful at times, for Holmes' breathing progressed only amidst struggles, while his body thrashed in bed as the remaining trace of venom burned through his bloodstream, and the foulest of hallucinations overcame him to the point it was twice necessary for me to apply all my strength to hold him in place, lest he flee raving into the darkness. With piteous regularity, he cried out to people who were not present, his deceased sister most of all.

"Water!" he would call out during moments of clear-mindedness, and would gulp down great quantities, which would soon pour from him in violent sweats.

Yet it was a testimony to his sheer strength that I report he was to survive the sting of one of Africa's deadliest creatures, and by the second day I judged the crisis had passed. Such a relief it was to see Holmes, though still pale and in pain, resting peacefully, and as the day went on, his complexion surrendered some of its gray tones, replaced by a healthy flush.

On the morning of the third day, he was able to sit up and ask that some parsley broth and well-crusted toast be brought to him, which Mrs. Hudson saw-to with the greatest of delight.

After taking his first meal in nearly half a week, Holmes looked at the many telegrams and letters of well-wishes that had come for him, sent by grateful clients, and even by Inspector Lestrade of Scotland Yard, who had called at Baker Street as Holmes lay in a stupor that first night.

"I will take a personal interest in that woman's case, Doctor, you can rely on that," he declared solemnly with a stony firmness. "An amateur he may be, and altogether too interfering at times I could mention, but many of us at Scotland Yard have formed a fondness for Mr. Holmes. That radical who attempted to take him from us shall neither be granted bail nor see daylight again for many years after *I've* given evidence against her for attempted murder, believe you me!"

I told Holmes of Lestrade's words, and though he showed no reaction, I guessed that the promise surely held value to him.

"It was but one token of the esteem with which you are held by many," I continued, as I sat in a chair beside his bed, a spot I had rarely abandoned in the days since the crisis began.

"But not universally regarded, it seems," Holmes said weakly as he sipped from a glass of barley-water Mrs. Hudson had brought up to him.

"No," I agreed, "only by the good people of London. Among evil-doers, you are justifiably detested as few have ever been."

He gazed out at me for a moment, then said:

"Watson, you must be exhausted past all endurance. Pray, do take to your own room and sleep a while. I can see to myself."

"I shall soon," I promised, "but I will stay a little longer, for I cannot tell you how marvelous it is to see you clear-headed and sitting up again. We were all deeply worried..."

"That woman, Watson..." Holmes began, interrupting my further declarations of concern and relief, "what news of her from the time of my incapacitation?"

"As we heard from her own lips, she calls herself 'Mrs.

Nichols'," I told him, "and claims to be the wife of that radical Bartlett Nichols, the railroad saboteur whose evil plots you foiled. He'd wanted to disrupt the railroads into the city to call attention to his dogma concerning the un-necessity of all institutions, social, religious, and political."

"Yes," Holmes said, still weak in his voice, "I remember him well, a clever plotter of mayhem, but too proud to hide his own rôle in the calamity he authored, and so he was easily bested. Though, Watson, I suspect you will find my assailant was no lawful wife to the man, whatever her claim."

"Exactly right," I agreed, unsure how he had deduced this there in his sick-bed. "Since taking over the case, himself, with great vigour I might add, Lestrade's investigations showed no marriage license between the woman and this Bartlett Nichols. Her claim is an anarchist's fantasy, part of her own rejection of the ceremony of marriage."

Holmes released a long sigh, and with bounteous self-reproach said:

"I failed to perceive the threat she posed, Watson. The fairer sex is often a source of peril, as I know full well, and yet I so docilely allowed this would-be Corday the very access to me from which she struck."

"You can hardly be blamed there Holmes," I said consolingly, "for I saw nothing in her to cause alarm, either, and —"

"Yes, Watson," Holmes sneered, "but I am hardly *you*, now, am I?"

It was the dismissive tone that heartened me, for however disdainful of my insights and intellect his response may have been, it showed he was fast-returning to himself, and so I smiled with relief at the slight, and said:

"No, my friend, you are unlike any other man in the whole of this world."

<><><><><>

Just as word had spread far and fast of Holmes' sordid brush with death, so the news of his recovery traveled rapidly as well, and though he was left weakened for some days after the attack, he bore his injury well, though his pride remained abashed over his failure to perceive the menace that had come before him in the form of a woman.

"I was as foolhardy as any rank amateur, Watson," he said more than once.

"I think you do quite well for yourself as a rule, Mr. Holmes," said Mrs. Hudson, who was upstairs in the sitting room with us, helping go through the letters that had come that morning.

"I thank you, Mrs. Hudson," Holmes said with the indulgent patience he seemed to demonstrate for her in greater quantities than was his habit toward anyone else on the planet.

When gathered into a stack, the letters bidding him a speedy recovery could have been set nearly a foot in height, with more brought in with each post. Despite his evincing scant emotion, or even approval, concerning these jotted well-wishes, I know the sentiment had to have pleased Holmes at least a little, for he looked over each note that either Mrs. Hudson or I handed to him, then mentioned with a word or two whom it was who had written.

"This card is from Mrs. Christensen, the Danish fishing heiress whose emerald I saw returned," he told us. "And this note is from Mr. Justice Fatherby, up in Nottingham, who hanged the murderer of the Bolton family on my expert evidence back in '78."

"A hanging? Well dear me," Mrs. Hudson said, placing a hand over her heart.

"Before my time," I said, having no idea to what case he referred.

"A well-deserved fate, I assure you," Holmes said, clearly relishing the memory, "for poisoners are the most odious of murderers, and to kill six at the dinner table over a minor argument is particularly repellent."

"And, look, Doctor Watson," Mrs. Hudson said, "a cable from America, from the Providence, Rhode Island Police Department, wishing Mr. Holmes good health and long life."

"Ah, that is Commissioner H. Treadwell," commented Holmes, "who has cabled me for advice a time or two in recent years. A fellow of excellent wisdom, for seeking out my aid."

Almost with awe, Mrs. Hudson stated:

"Do you see, Mr. Holmes, even so far as that news of you has spread?"

I knew she enjoyed having one of the more renown men in the city as her tenant, and Holmes, however much he may have pretended otherwise, enjoyed this tangible proof of the diffusion of his well-deserved fame.

It was a full week after the incident, and Holmes was nearly himself again, that there came to Baker Street a former client, one Colonel J. Basil Morley, retired from his long career with the 8th Surrey Rifles, whom Holmes had aided some seven months previous concerning a series of thefts from the armoury of the regimental headquarters. The Colonel had naturally wished to see the thefts stopped before his upcoming retirement, which was due in a matter of weeks, and Holmes had solved the mystery with alacrity, requiring but a few hours to see through to the heart of the matter and name the guilty party, a corporal who was selling munitions on the black market. The Colonel had been profusely grateful, and had proclaimed Holmes:

"The finest man I have met in these many a year!"

So it was that when the Colonel came up to Baker Street bearing a gift of expensive cigars, my friend took the time to sit with him in the parlour and enjoy a bit of conversation.

"Very glad am I, Mr. Holmes, to espy you looking so well," said Colonel Morley with his deep voice and tone of indisputable command. "Based on what was in the papers and spoken in the reports one hears swirling around even up in Suffolk, where I've retired now, I half-expected you'd be far worse off, for it was at death's very door that the reporters had you posed."

"My flame, as you see," said Holmes, "is rather difficult to extinguish."

At that the Colonel boomed out a hearty laugh.

"In truth he was not far from the Valley of the Shadow," I answered, smoking along on one of the excellent cigars myself. "It was a small miss, but a miss all the same."

"On fractions of inches do soldiers mark their lives," the Colonel declared soberly, "and count their blessings when in the path of fire the fickle dice of chance bounce their way."

A light of reflection rose in his eyes, as he perhaps recalled occasions from his own career when bullets had not missed their targets by those same proverbial inches.

"In that regard, I owe much indeed to Watson," Holmes told his guest.

"Then so do we all," the Colonel stated, lifting his cigar to me in a demi-salute.

"It was an old army doctor's trick," I said, "sucking out of the venom with a device."

"Ah, through the little rubberized bulb, yes," the Colonel remarked. "Fine work then, my good fellow. Seen it done a time or two myself off in the Himalayan Kush. So many vipers there among the rocks, you know. Our pickets were always getting stung along the ankles by those foul slithering beasts."

"The fault was mine in not perceiving the snake when it was before me that morning," Holmes stated, retaining that aura of frustration I had noted in him since the incident. "I should have known danger when it reared its ugly head."

But her head was not ugly, I reflected, *and that had been the problem.*

"Who can blame you there," claimed Morley, "for I ask you,

what man since the start of time has ever understood what roils within the female heart? You took that girl for what she seemed, and a dozen times more likely it was that she came to you a damsel in distress. Don't let yourself feel too badly about it all."

I knew the Colonel's words were meant as commiseration, but I also grasped that however sincerely spoken, they rankled Holmes, as they suggested there was a feat of discernment which lay beyond even him, a failing to which my proud friend would never admit.

"Well," Holmes said with finality, "I do not intend that such a thing shall happen twice, for I have learned painfully and well from my ordeal, and will never again be tricked by any woman, however meek her approach."

The words were spoken with such vigour that I caught in them the tone of a vow.

"Then all shall be well with you," the Colonel told him, "for I doubt not your powers of discernment. Thus let me then progress to the second part of why I come today to London."

Holmes gave him a nod, and the old soldier shifted in his chair and said:

"I take it that under the advice of the good doctor here, Mr. Holmes, you are to rest a bit longer and regain your fullest strength, and so I should very much like to extend to you an invitation to come up to the country and be my guest at the family estate in westernmost Suffolk, and let the open skies and good clean air work their wonders on restoring your famously Herculean constitution."

I knew the invitation was unfurled with the noblest of motives, but I understood equally well my friend's detestation of the countryside, for he saw London as his natural element, and the source of his native strength. In that as in so many things he was the opposite of most men.

Thus I was unsurprised when in the most polite manner, Holmes declined the offer, which to his credit the Colonel took in good form.

"I'll tell you, though," the retired officer said near the end of his stay, "it has been a rather strange stretch of weeks up at the old place just lately."

"Oh," I asked, "and why is that?"

I could tell Holmes, for his part, was now listening more closely after his visitor's declaration, for all varieties of strange goings-on of were always of interest to him.

"Well," said Morley, "to be candid—and mind you, this has no bearing one way or the other on why I offered my invitation —it seems the old ghost out in our yew alley has been making a reappearance this summer."

"A ghost?" I asked, and I saw Holmes' attention stray, for he held all ideas concerning such matters with at best ill-concealed contempt.

"Yes," Morley chuckled, "if you can believe such a thing. As a boy growing up there I heard all about the ghost from our old servants, who frequently claimed to have seen it, though I don't mind telling you I never did, and still have not. Accounts of the thing, though, go back to the 1300s, at least, and now after lying dormant for many years, it seems for whatever reason the spectre is again putting in appearances, around twilight, now, out in our yew alley, just beyond the house itself."

"What is it that people say of these sightings?" I inquired.

"Same now as it was in my boyhood," Colonel Morley told me, "a glowing golden figure, like a person, only rounder about the edges and floating rather than walking. Quite menacing, according to those who have encountered it, not at all the friendly sort of ghost one hears about in delightful campfire stories. It has been seen for the past fortnight now by several on staff, and more to the point, has captured the imagination of my eleven-year-old grandson, Barry, who is staying with us until the school term at Collinsdale begins in September. It is his absolute obsession that he see the thing before summer ends, so in his charming little mania the boy sits out in the evenings and keeps his eyes peeled from a vantage point near the edge of the yew alley."

"Indeed?" I asked. "And has young Barry had any success

in the matter?"

"Not to present he hasn't," the Colonel answered, "though I tell you, that is not from a lack of dogged determination."

"And what, specifically, is the legend concerning this phantom?" Holmes broke his silence to ask, though with a tone that suggested disdain rather than tremendous interest, as if he found all such ideas both tiresome and banal.

"Well," said Morley, "some say it is the ghost of a young nun from long ago, but others flip this claim onto its head, and in fact the way I grew up hearing it, it is the spirit of a man who lived on the property around the time of the Great Plague of the fourteenth century. They say he was a brute, somehow immune to the effects of the Black Death, and so he would rob the houses of the afflicted, and often the victims themselves as they lay dying, and in the lawless conditions of the catastrophe he grew wealthy, or did for a time, for it seems when the plague was waning, the surviving relatives of those from whom the man had thieved came and seized him, and shut him up inside a charnel house where the yew alley was planted some two centuries later, and there he was left until he perished from hunger."

"Such a ghastly tale!" I exclaimed.

"Rather an interesting one," Holmes said. Then with approval he added:

"It tells us of the prevailing morality of the time the story had its birth, for back then crime was met with stiffer punishment than today, as you see."

"Yes, well," said Morley, slightly ashamed, I think, to be confessing accounts of a phantom on his land, "the story is what the story is, and as I have said, I've never personally seen the thing, either as boy or man, and don't know what to think of this recent rash of reports of it being out there on any given night."

I'm sure Holmes could tell you his thoughts there, I mused.

"I'm certain if anyone can verify the existence of your resident spirit, it'll be your grandson, with the dogged efforts of boyhood," I said, offering my thoughts.

"He is unceasingly determined at that," the Colonel agreed, and I sensed he wished to dismiss the subject, so we did so.

In fact he stayed but a few minutes beyond the closing of this topic, and after once more wishing Holmes all the best in his recovery, took to the door, leaving behind the gift of the cigars, which I knew Holmes would put to good use.

"Fine fellow, him," I said once the Colonel had gone on his way and climbed into a cab out on Baker Street.

"Yes," Holmes agreed, "a most excellent former client."

"And dare I ask," I inquired, "what you make of his tale of a ghost seen on the grounds of his estate?"

"Absurdity, Watson," he told me, "for ghosts no more exist than does that great scaly monster in the waters of that loch up in your birth country."

"If you're predicating the spirit of the yew alley upon those terms, then I wouldn't be so sure it doesn't exist," I enjoined, defending our great national legend of the beast of Loch Ness, which every Scot took pride in championing when aspersions were cast upon the creature's existence...whether he truly believed in it or not.

"Eyewitness accounts are invariably faulty as a rule," Holmes told me, "and in the case of ghosts, more than a few tall tales are generally involved. Now, if you'd be so good as to fetch my Stradivarius for me, I think I shall try my hand at a little music for the first time since my inconveniencing by that sordid woman."

I went to his bedroom and returned with the requested case in hand, and was rewarded moments later by the ethereal sound of Bach's second violin concerto filing the cozy environs of Baker Street.

I felt a deep sense of peace that evening, and figured we'd see no more of Colonel Morley, amiable chap though the man was, and expected that in days ahead, as his strength returned, Holmes would find new mysteries to draw him away from Baker Street, but in at least part of that far-reaching assumption, I was to be proven humblingly incorrect.

<><><><><>

It was on the second morning following Colonel Morley's visit, and breakfast had just concluded, that a telegram was brought to the door of our Baker Street abode, soon to be conveyed upstairs by Mrs. Hudson.

"An urgent matter," Holmes noted, "judging by the alacrity with which she transports the cable to our door."

The mystery lasted no more than a quarter of a minute, for when Mrs. Hudson placed the paper in Holmes' hands, I saw my friend frown, as he informed me:

"This comes from Colonel Morley, late our guest. He writes that the grandson he mentioned in connection with the boy's ghost-hunting, has gone missing."

"What?" I cried, as a chill passed up my spine. "Does it tell anything else?"

"Not in his bed this morning, it seems, nor had the bed been slept in. Last seen yesterday evening when he claimed to be going upstairs for the night."

"This is dismal news, Holmes!" I cried out. "There are a score of ways for a boy of eleven to come to mischief in the country. Wells, ponds, perhaps even stumbling across an adder's nest in the woods."

"Not to mention *crime*," said Holmes. "Abduction for ransom…or for fouler purposes than that, for there are those, as you know, who prey upon children."

"The worst sorts of villains!" I said.

He leapt to his feet, showing the old, familiar energy that always overtook him when confronting a mystery. Though that forcefulness of stride had been absent in the days since his brush with death, it was fortifying to see it return.

"To the country, then!" he cried. "When is the next train to Suffolk?"

I consulted the schedule and gave him my answer as he ran to the bedroom to prepare for his journey, and then raced to the laboratory at the far end of the room, where he took from a shelf the case with which he sometimes traveled when out seeing to his investigations. I knew it contained a chemistry set in miniature that he had used a number of times with great effect.

"Forty minutes until the train, Watson!" he called. "We have not a moment to spare!"

When I hesitated, he demanded:

"Well, you are at liberty to accompany me, I presume?"

"I was only waiting for the invitation!" I replied happily, for after spending much of the past week fearing that my friend's days of adventuring were done, it was marvelous to receive this summons.

We were out the door in a trice, calling farewells to Mrs. Hudson in the kitchen, and were sent swiftly across London in a hansom cab driven by a tiny slip of a man, who smoked a stunted pipe, and squinted against even the light of the morning sun as he hunched over the reins in his leathery hands. A peculiar fellow to be sure, but he got us to Liverpool Station in good time, and a few moments later saw us buying tickets to Ipswich, and our journey of some ninety-five minutes up to Westerfield Station, in the heart of that distant city, was underway.

I reflected that I had been to Ipswich twice before in my life, both times in my days as a soldier, and on one of those had stayed at the Great White Horse Hotel, which Mr. Dickens had made famous in *The Pickwick Papers.* There'd be no such luxury for us today, however, and no sooner had our train bustled to a stop than Holmes had leaped outside, chemistry case in hand, and raced to find the first available conveyance to take us eleven miles to the town of Cottersfield, near where the Morley estate lay.

As we jostled along, and the cobbles of Ipswich gave way to the dusty lanes of the countryside, I looked several times toward my companion to see how Holmes was faring after his illness and recuperation, and upon my third such glance, he said to me:

"Though your skills as a physician are first-rate, Watson, you may safely take a day off in that regard."

"I fear you must allow me my worries, Holmes, for we nearly lost you."

"I assure you I have not only recovered from the consequences of that lapse in my instincts of self-preservation upon that lugubrious morning, but am entirely invigorated by thoughts of the case which lies before me."

"Good to hear!" I said heartily.

"I am never tired when working," he added, "only when swept up in the receding tides of lethargy and boredom. Indeed, the more hours a case requires, the greater my energies grow."

Yes, I thought, *but when the case is done, you all-but collapse in exhaustion.* My friend, I thought, medically-speaking, invested far too much of himself in his undertakings.

About half an hour into our ride, nearly halfway to our destination, I happened to glance over, and in a field off the roadway sat a caravan of Irish gypsies, their handful of little wagons, each merrily painted, spread out in a fallow field, where the inhabitants seemed to be less encamped than merely stopping for a morning break in their endless travels.

"Odd, Holmes," I remarked. "I did not think we'd be likely to encounter such a band up here this time of year."

"Well, they must always be somewhere, mustn't they?" he replied.

"I suppose so," I agreed, not letting his patronizing tone ruffle me.

"One finds them scattered across the countryside," he added, "and they are an odious lot as a rule, though I have had recourse to involve such as those in my investigations a time or two. For the right price they can be forthcoming with knowledge of a useful sort, and as strong-arm men for hire... well, one sometimes needs to turn to unorthodox means to achieve certain ends."

I did not know what to say to that, but as the caravan receded from my view and our coach rolled along far out in the quiet countryside of East Anglia, the Irish wanderers were soon out of my thoughts, replaced by the unavoidable question of whether it was just possible we might find Colonel Morley of the opinion that a ghost had played some rôle in his grandson's abrupt vanishing.

It was a silly thought, certainly, but still a thrill danced inside me when I remembered the tales I grew up hearing in Scotland, told me by an old neighbour woman from Fife, who claimed malevolent spirits sought out children in the dark hours of night, and that she herself had seen spirits many times. It was all nonsense, of course, the lurid imaginings of an old woman whose fanciful tales had delighted my brother and I in those days, yet I'd be lying if I failed to admit such deeply-instilled ideas vied against the logic of my better nature.

<><><><><>

It was a little before noon, and the warm summer sun was high overhead, when, despite him having been Holmes' client in the recent past, we arrived only for the first time at the estate of Colonel Morley. The grounds, I saw, were well-kept, with many mature trees above an immaculate and flourishing lawn, in the midst of which sat a sizable dun-brick manor house, and in front of that, somewhat out of usual custom, flew both the Union Jack, and the crimson and gold colours of his old regiment.

No doubt alerted to our coming by a sharp-eyed servant, we had only just drawn up before the house's great sandstone façade, an 18th century addition to a far older structure, I hazarded, when a rush of three figures came pressing through the doors. Colonel Morley led the way, but to the rear of him, a respectful few paces behind, was another, younger man, tall and with a distinct military bearing, the faintest traces of an incipient whitening at his temples, and to Morley's right was a woman of comparable age, whom I intuited must have been his wife. I noted that she was stout and graying, but from her expression of sober command guessed her to be an imperious sort who doubtless ran her household with the expected efficiency of the spouse of a career army officer.

"Mr. Holmes!" the Colonel cried, approaching us with haste. "Dr. Watson! I am so relieved you have come with such alacrity, sirs! You have my thanks, as matters here are utterly upended by young Barry's troubling disappearance!"

"Has the boy ever wandered off before, either here or at home, or at his school?" asked Holmes without undue preamble as he strode from the coach.

"Never!" Morley replied. "He is as fine and proper a lad as could be asked for, if at times rather too imaginative."

"He was happy to be spending his summer here?" Holmes demanded. "There was no one he unduly missed from home and with whom he might have set off to reconnect? Or anyone new in his life? A local friend perhaps?"

He was tossing these questions in a rapid-fire manner, but Morley took them in stride and answered:

"He showed every sign of enthusiastically embracing his time here, and just the other evening expressed his sorrow that the summer ever had to end, and he return to school."

A healthy enough sentiment for any boy, I thought.

"You have alerted the constabulary, I take it, and initiated a search on your own?" Holmes asked as he stopped at last in front of Colonel Morley and let his eyes pass over him and the others, pulling from their persons clues that would, I knew, have eluded the perception of even the most intelligent of ordinary men.

"Yes, all of that," Morley confirmed with an impatient agitation that he nonetheless held under a tight control.

"Tell me the steps taken, thus far, to locate your grandson," Holmes instructed him.

Morley began:

"Searches, as you said, have been made of all the places one might fear a boy could end up to his peril, and the constables are going around the countryside searching with our groom and groundsman in tow, along with some of the tenants, who are lending a hand in this worrisome hour."

"That is to the good," said Holmes shortly. "Then let us proceed indoors to—"

But here Colonel Morley burst out:

"Wait, Mr. Holmes, I must tell you, there is a new development just this last hour, and we don't know what to make of it, or what it signifies!"

Holmes set his case down on the ground beside him and, all attention now, demanded:

"New development? What is its nature?"

"Come, let me show you," insisted Morley. "It is quite peculiar!"

At this he hustled by us with impressive velocity for a man of increasing years, toward what I knew was the yew alley of which we'd been told, that scene so connected with the history of ghostly activity on the estate. We were at his heels and nearly there when he called:

"It is a *stain*, Mr. Holmes!"

"A stain?" Holmes demanded.

"Of some sort, yes, though highly unusual. Like nothing I have ever seen. It lies in the grass of the yew alley, precisely where the ghost has been seen. It showed up all at once this morning, a few yards from where Barry would spread his blanket and sit in wait for the spirit he was so determined to see."

Oh, surely this was not good, I thought.

"And you say this oddity was not there at any other time?" asked Holmes. "Nor even last night?"

"Never in the past, sir!"

It was Mrs. Morley, keeping pace with us from behind who answered this in her throaty tone of voice, breaking her weighty silence at last.

"I have never seen such a thing in all my days as this mark

on the ground," she stressed, "and I know not what it signifies, but connected as it surely is to my grandson's being taken there among those spirit-haunted yews, it tells of *something*, one may be sure!"

Her grandson's *being taken*, I thought, noting her words. So that was the mindset there, was it? That the boy had not wandered off into misadventure, as his grandfather, the Colonel, seemed to hope, but been deliberately transported away by someone... or some*thing*, I noted, thinking of her reference to the "spirit-haunted yews."

I knew Holmes had noted her term as well, though he said nothing.

We came to rest at a spot perhaps a dozen yards into the long yew alley, where the bushes, ancient and gnarled with interwoven branches, grew tall, and I saw plainly the mysterious marking upon the ground. It was dark brown, nearly black, perhaps the color of coffee left long-brewing, and was spread out in the shape of...

Oh! I hated to think so but the connection was absolutely there to be made, for it was undeniably in the shape of a boy of young Barry's age, limbs askew in what leaped out in my mind as...terror.

"We have not touched the stain," Morley told Holmes, nor have we approached it any closer than two yards, let us say, for we held out hopes that you were coming in response to my telegram, and knew you'd wish to see it untrammeled and in its purest state."

"Ah," said Holmes, "then you did well."

He knelt just beyond the long marking on the ground and set about opening the case which contained the portable chemistry lab.

To my eyes the discolouration looked like nothing so much as a shadow permanently suspended in time, in defiance of the sun, with the suggestion of arms outstretched in what was either defense, or absolute surprise.

"Again," Holmes asked, "you are certain this stain was

there neither last night nor at any time before it was noticed this morning?"

"Absolutely sure, sir," Mrs. Morley replied with a tone that left little room for argument. "We set out at first light to seek Barry, most of the household, I mean, and were this marking in the yew alley, then, we'd have seen it, yet we did not, nor did we until later in the morning, after many others had also passed near this spot."

"Yes, it was after my telegram had been sent," Colonel Morley added, "or I'd assuredly have mentioned it."

How very strange, I thought. *And how disturbing.*

Holmes drew exceedingly close to the stain, his face mere inches above its impenetrable darkness, before he removed from his case a flat wooden object, rather like a tongue depressor in my own medical practice, and used it to delicately touch the marking.

"It is dry," he noted aloud, then leaned low and carefully sniffed at it, before slowly raising up, and frowning. "And is not paint or any dye, nor is a burn mark, for the ground below is not charred by fire."

"It is not of this world," whispered Mrs. Morley under her breath, perhaps to herself.

Holmes frowned once again, whether in response to the woman's sentiment or for other reasons, then enunciating each syllable with care, stated:

"It is decidedly most peculiar..."

"It is clearly supernatural," Mrs. Morley said, now openly voicing her thoughts.

Holmes ignored this and from within his case removed a test tube and a scalpel, and a set of tweezers, and careful cut out a patch of the stain perhaps the size of a man's littlest finger. He dropped this into the test tube and sealed it, then stared a moment longer at the area before him, and I could read both contemplation and consternation in his eyes.

"What was your grandson's height and weight?" he demanded.

"I confess I do not know precisely," Mrs. Morley replied, "though he was an average-size boy, neither tall nor short, thin nor stout."

"That is fine," said Holmes. "The stain is not a precise match for a boy's figure, as you see, and there is, I do perceive, an overall foreshortening effect I find curious, but note that it does crudely approximate a suggestion of a human form. There is clearly a head, a torso, even limbs…which appear splayed, as if —"

He arrested his words, though I felt sure his thoughts were mirrors of my own in regards to what pose the shape suggested, and from where he knelt studied once more the darkening on the lawn, and appeared to sink into deep thought for a long silent moment before at last rising and announcing tersely:

"I require each of you to stand very still where you are and make no further intrusions into the yew alley. You were also wise not to touch the stain, and I advise you not to do so, now or in the future."

"Is it harmful?" Mrs. Morley asked.

"That, Madam, remains an unknown."

Holmes pulled a magnifying lens from his chemistry case, and assumed a pose and manner with which I was familiar from past cases, as he stooped low and peered intently at the ground all around him, proceeding at an exceedingly slow walk over the next quarter-hour, until he had covered the entirety of the alley, taking it in, then traveling around the entirety of the lawn in its vicinity, studying what looked to me each separate inch of the earth below. Finally he rose back to his full height and stood a moment staring into space itself, before he resumed his normal stride, and returned to us at last.

"What did you find, Mr. Holmes?" the Colonel demanded, unable to wait.

With a dissatisfied flatness in his tone, Holmes replied:

"I found nothing,"

"Nothing whatsoever?" Mrs. Morley pressed, as if unable to believe what she had heard.

"I saw neither traces left by the boy over the last day," Holmes clarified, "nor the tracks of anyone else whom I ascertained was not of the household. None of the tracks, so far as my methods allow me to say with certainty, were made overnight, based on the effect the morning dew would have in altering such imprints. There is no sign that any abduction at all took place within the yew alley. For our purposes, it lies as innocent as a lamb pasture."

While I was sifting out precisely what these findings indicated, Mrs. Morley, who was to my right threw up her hands and intoned:

"Then Barry has vanished into thin air! You see, gentlemen? It was the ghost! The ghost of that cruel man *has my grandchild!*"

I looked toward her, as did Holmes.

"You are a believer in supernatural phenomena, Madam?" I asked her, though it was clear that she was.

"A 'believer', no, Doctor Watson," she said with emotion, "rather a confirmed eyewitness, as I have seen the ghost on two occasions in my years of residence here. It is a glowing figure which hovers in the air itself, transmitting menace and anger, a cruel spirit in death, to be sure, as it was in life, robbing from the sick and dying as the man did, and meriting the punishment he received. I know the ghost to be real, and if, as you say, no human has taken my grandson, what possibility does that leave but his tragic encounter with the horrors of that which lies beyond?"

Beside her Colonel Morley appeared both embarrassed by his wife's words, and also moved by a desire to conceal the fact.

Holmes however, looked steadily at the woman and said:

"You misapprehend me, Madam, when I say there was no sign of any abduction within the alley, for this does not indicate that I attest to a supernatural authorship of the event, but rather that I am ruling it out."

"*Ruling it out?*" Mrs. Morley repeated. "How could that be so, when surely a man would have left behind traces of criminal actions?"

"For the simple reason," Holmes answered with forbearance, "that had the boy been taken in the alley, I should have seen the signs such an action would have left behind. Thus this can only mean that if an abduction has indeed occurred—"

"You can doubt that Barry has been taken?" Mrs. Morley demanded.

"I am not, shall we say," Holmes told her, "released from considering many possibilities, with hostile abduction being but one. As for the idea that the deed was perpetrated by the shade of a man centuries dead, if indeed such a person existed at all outside of local lore, that explanation I do not begin to entertain."

"Well I am not so closed-minded as you," Mrs. Morley said with a scoff. "For what evidence would a ghost leave when it snatched a living boy away into another realm? I suspect there would be none, just as you have discovered! So how does an absence of evidence rule out the supernatural, Mr. Holmes?"

"It is in the nature of a non-event to leave behind no evidence," said Holmes evenly. "And I rule it out, because the supernatural does not exist."

Mrs. Morley was stymied for a moment, as if unaccustomed to being challenged in this or any other regard, and Holmes went on, undeterred.

"To continue, I can now say that if there was an abduction, it occurred elsewhere, not in the yew alley itself. To this moment, that is what I have learned in the case."

"But the stain!" cried Mrs. Morley.

"I do not yet know what that signifies, but I have a theory, which I shall for the moment, keep to myself."

He turned, then, to his client and inquired:

"Colonel Morley, owing to our haste, I am lacking one introduction. Who is the second gentlemen in your retinue this morning?"

He spoke of the tall man standing to the couple's rear, who had emerged from the house at our arrival and gone to the yew alley with us, though he had said nothing to that point.

"I am sorry, Holmes," Morley spoke up to say, "the distress of these events has sent my manners flying. May I present my former aide-de-camp in the 8th Surrey Rifles, Lieutenant Terrence Peters, retired. He was away on leave at the time of your investigation into the armoury matter last spring, and presently works in the capacity of my assistant in the composition of my memoirs, for after three years serving under me, he knew my habits, sparing me having to break some new fellow into my stubborn ways."

"At your service, sir," said the Lieutenant, with a small bow to Holmes, before extending a hand toward me. "And you, Doctor, I could mark as a fellow army man, even had I not the advantage of foreknowledge."

I shook the proffered hand, finding nothing objectionable in the man, but Holmes glanced sternly toward Peters for an instant before asking:

"Where were you serving when you received the gunshot wound to your upper right arm?"

The Lieutenant gaped an instant, then demanded with surprise:

"Was the fact of my wounding previously known to you, sir?"

"Only by present observation," Holmes answered. "I perceive that you are, as is the case with most men, right-handed, yet there is a looseness to the fit of the sleeve of that arm, which with most men is usually present, however slightly, on the left side."

Here both the Colonel and Lieutenant Peters looked down at their sleeves for verification of the claim.

"Don't bother to seek out confirmation," Holmes said almost lazily, "it is only discernible to a uniquely trained eye, such as my own. I noted this fact about you, sir, and combined with my knowledge of your military career, it suggested that there is a degree of withering in your right arm, most likely as a result of a bullet wound while in uniform."

Peters' face took on an expression, somewhere between

embarrassment and distaste, and though I said nothing, I thought it rather an uncharitable observation for Holmes to offer, singling out the man in this way, given that his affliction had been incurred in Her Majesty's service.

"It was near the Hindu Kush, under the Colonel some years ago," Lieutenant Peters finally confirmed. "I was shot by a bandit while on patrol near the Jhelum River. Sent my assailant to Hell with my other arm, however."

Visible only to me, who knew his mannerisms so well, I noted something in the man's words seemed distasteful to Holmes, though quickly I told Peters:

"I can sympathize, as I, too, was wounded during my time in Afghanistan."

"Then we are brothers via the shedding of our blood for Queen and Country," Peters offered with a friendly smile.

Holmes, however, was not done with the man, for he stated:

"I perceive your spouse, Lieutenant Peters, is frequently away, and that matters are strained in your home life."

Oh, surely that was too much, I thought as Peters, offended, his theretofore pleasant expression slipping away, hotly cried:

"Now see here, sir!"

I little blamed him, and was wondering if Holmes entirely knew the rudeness of his last statement, when I caught the fact that he was giving the former officer a sharp stare of evaluation, as if seeking something in his unguarded reaction, though what this apparent exercise in deliberate provocation signified I could not guess, only grasped that for whatever reason, the taunt had not been accidental.

Whatever the motivation had been, Holmes turned back from Peters, as if finished with him and caring no more for him one way or the other, and said to Morley:

"Let us go now into the house, where I will speak with all of you, and perhaps others there on staff, if I require it, for I have many questions."

"Of course," Colonel Morley replied, hurriedly, before the

glowering Peters could give voice to his outrage.

Glancing over his shoulder at his now red-faced assistant, Morley added:

"We shall *all* grant you our fullest cooperation, as this matter supersedes any other considerations."

"Quite right, sir," Peters said, though with a final scowl cast at Holmes before he stepped off ahead of the rest of us, clearly putting all possible distance between himself and the detective's future offenses.

"Actually," Holmes stated, "Lieutenant Peters need not be present from this point forward. I shall not need him in future, as he is, incidentally, fully uninvolved in the disappearance of the boy, and therefore of limited interest to me."

"I never doubted his innocence there," said Morley, "but still I suppose it is good to have the matter confirmed."

"No," Holmes went on to add, startling even me, "on a habitual basis the man is a boorish lout toward his wife, but not an abuser of young boys. A boy, after all, might strike the coward back."

Every face, including my own, turned rapidly toward him.

Those who committed violence toward women were never looked on fondly by Holmes, I knew, whatever his recent outlook following one of the 'gentler sex' nearly killing him, but I wondered what clues he had seen upon the lieutenant to mark the retired junior officer as such a man?

"I cannot think that claim is true, Mr. Holmes," said Mrs. Morley, "for I know the lieutenant's wife, Violet, and have never perceived her to show any signs of fearing her husband, or being harmed by him. Had I seen these, I assure you, I should have spoken to my husband."

"There are many varieties of harm one might inflict upon another," Holmes answered, "and ways a victimized woman may conceal her state. Were I you, madam, I might speak closely with the lady upon this subject when next you see her. It is not unknown for a woman to confide only to another woman. And you, Colonel, might be wise to dismiss Peters from your service, for I do not judge you to be the sort who'd wish to be associated with a wife-beater."

These words had the effect of ending all talk for a moment, as each party considered what Holmes had said. Finally Morley answered solemnly:

"I will look into your claim, as I do value your insights, Mr. Holmes."

"I am glad to hear it," Holmes commented. "In the meantime I would rather not be unnecessarily in your assistant's presence."

Though his eyes widened at those words, Morley drew himself back to the case at hand, and as we closed-in on the house announced:

"It is possible the Constable-Sergeant from town, who is overseeing the official search for Barry, may join us, as he is due to check in and deliver his report. He came by not long before your arrival and promised another update before mid-afternoon."

"That is fine," said Holmes with a deep indifference that still managed to make it sound as if the decision regarding the constable's presence rested with him alone. In his hand he was conveying the case in which rested the chemistry set, with his sample from the yew alley sealed within, and I was most curious to find what he would learn of it.

We went up to the house, above which on the lintel stood an old carving of an owl with outstretched claws, swooping in upon a snake, and I saw Peters, who had marched ahead of us a little distance, stood waiting within the entryway,

There the Colonel said uneasily to him:

"Er, Terrence, would you mind perhaps going to my study and in my absence sorting through my writings from last night?"

Lieutenant Peters appeared surprised by this request, and gazed from his employer toward Holmes, as if aware the motivation for the directive had originated with him.

"Certainly, Colonel," he replied after an instant. "I'll be on-hand should you require me."

With a final belligerent glance at Holmes, Peters set off into the house, and was quickly gone from sight.

"I still think you are wrong about him," Morley said with a sigh, as he guided us into a vast and well-appointed drawing room on the ground floor opposite the yew alley, not at all the severe setting I might have expected in the home of a military man.

Not replying to this sentiment, the great consulting detective merely absorbed his surroundings with a roving eye.

"You entertained in this room last week," Holmes stated. "A gathering of military wives, perhaps?"

"Why, yes," Mrs. Morley answered, gazing around her in puzzlement, and I likewise saw no possible sign that such an event had transpired.

"The meager quantity of dust atop the Japanese-style partition placed in the far end of the room has recently been disturbed," Holmes explained lightly, "thus I intuited it was made use of not long before."

Facile enough, I thought.

Mrs. Morley offered us refreshments and proposed to ring for the butler, and in truth I could have used a spot of tea to pick me up after our journey, but Holmes pointedly declined, and announced:

"With your cooperation, before I analyze the sample you saw me take from the stain in the alley, I shall continue my investigation by interviewing you, Colonel and Mrs. Morley."

"Of course, sir," Mrs. Morley answered.

"In the previous day," Holmes began, "did you notice anything whatsoever unusual either here in the house or upon the grounds?"

"It was an ordinary day," Morley answered, causing his wife to nod silently beside him.

"Were there visitors of any kind?"

"None," Mrs. Morley replied.

"How did each of you spend it?

The pair answered, telling of unremarkable activities, such as replies to letters, going over household accounts with the cook, and the cleaning and oiling of shotguns in their cases, as the Colonel insisted be done once a fortnight throughout the year, whether or not the guns had been fired. Yet Mrs. Morley reported an incident which in its own small way did draw itself outside the mundane.

"I went unexpectedly to town," she admitted, "out of aggravation, I confess, for my cat, Wellington, he is of a mischievous nature, and I had come in from a walk with Barry out along the tree line—he wished only to speak of his efforts to see the ghost, a wearisome conversation, I say somewhat guiltily now—and had taken off my bonnet and laid it upon a table in the drawing room and was having some tea after my stroll, when I looked down to see Wellington had captured the bonnet in his paws and quite torn through it with his teeth. He ran from my scolding, and so aggrieved was I at my loss that I summoned my companion, Mrs. Drummond, who goes everyplace with me, and one of the house-maids as well, in case we stopped by the market and there was carrying to be done. We went into Cottersfield to see the milliner, Mrs. Ferguson and her daughter, and be measured for a new bonnet, identical to the one I'd lost."

"And while in Cottersfield," asked Holmes, "were you conscious of anything out of the ordinary? Did you see anyone who stands out in your mind as unusual?"

"Quite the contrary," Mrs. Morley claimed. "It was as staid and uneventful a trip as could be imagined."

"And where," Holmes asked, "was the boy, Barry, during the day?"

"Here," the Colonel supplied, "outside playing through the morning, and with me when I dined at noon. As for the rest of the day...well, boys will roam and find their adventures, won't they? He was back in time for dinner, which was later than usual that night, and if he made no especial mention of his activities, neither did he betray signs of anything out of the ordinary."

"Of what did he speak at dinner?" asked Holmes.

"We have raised our children, and they theirs, to keep silent at table," Mrs. Morley said, with a slight touch of pride.

"After dinner, then?" the detective pressed.

"We retired to the parlour," Mrs. Morley revealed, "and there we congregated for a while, and of course, as you might guess, it was his plans to see the ghost under the yews that was the subject which dominated his mind."

"Was he allowed to go out and seek the spirit?" asked Holmes.

"We had no objection if he did so a reasonable hour, and near the house," Morley stated. "It was his time to waste, as it were. It was, or so I thought, a charming little pursuit, one he would look back on in his dotage in the next century as a pleasant memory of a long-ago summer spent with his grandparents."

There was poignancy in this statement, and even Holmes was silent a moment before he asked:

"So he was back inside at the aforementioned 'reasonable hour'?"

"By 8.45, yes, and sent up to bed," the boy's grandmother confirmed. "I tucked him in myself."

"I presume he was not checked on in the night?"

"Certainly not," the lady answered, "he is quite old enough to be beyond such things, though it was generally I who would go in and see him in the morning, and so energetic a child was he that I never had to rouse him, he was always up and at the waiting to begin the day. It was abnormal, I felt at once, not to find him in his room, and to discern that his bed had not been slept in."

"How did you determine that?" Holmes asked.

"The covers were still turned down as I had left them, and the pillows plumped. The bed had obviously not been occupied in the night. Even my untrained eyes could detect that."

"So his disappearance, whatever the cause, was between, let us say ten last night, and six this morning?"

"Yes," Mrs. Morley said simply.

"What were your own specific movements last night, Colonel Morley?" Holmes next asked.

"I worked with Peters dictating my recollections of a skirmish in the hill country of northern India back in '62," came the reply. "Peters stayed on and dined with my wife and Barry and me before setting off for his home in Cottersfield, then I sat up alone after dinner, answering correspondence from an old friend, Brigadier Herschel Scott, also now retired, and living in Cornwall. Finally I went up to my room near eleven, and was asleep, I'd judge, by half-past."

"You sleep separately from your wife?"

"Yes, as it happens," Morley replied.

If he felt the question intruded into the privacy of his marriage, he did not show it, which I had long-ago decided was the best manner in which to handle Holmes' personal and often odd, inquiries.

"And when did you last set eyes upon the boy?"

"Just before I went into my office alone last evening," said Morley, "to see to the correspondence I mentioned."

"Did you speak with him?"

"For a moment."

"And what was his disposition?"

"He was his usual self, I would say. Neither agitated nor downcast. He spoke with me about his intentions to stalk the ghost if it did not soon appear, and I told him a little story about one of my staff officers in India, who lost a leg attempting to stalk a particularly cunning tigress in tall grass. Barry expressed sympathy for the man, and said he would have more care than the fellow did should he ever hunt a tiger, himself, one day, as I hope he shall."

Despite the gravity of the circumstances, the Colonel gave a fond little chuckle, and added:

"Ah that lad..."

"And you, Mrs. Morley?" Holmes asked next. "After seeing the boy to bed, what time did you turn in?"

"I am in the custom of an early retirement, and was asleep

before nine-thirty. I was among the first awake this morning, as I often am, and was about the house, as usual, just as the servants were first up seeing to the fires and taking on the rest of their duties. As I said I went up to rouse Barry, thinking he was sleeping oddly late, and I assumed it was because he had sneaked back outside behind my back to keep a watch for the ghost."

"Had you encouraged him to do so?" Holmes asked her.

"I had not," Mrs. Morley said firmly, "and intended to have a firm word with him if he had, though I did speak honestly with him and told him of the occasions I had seen the phantom, and I think these accounts did perhaps inspire some of his tenacity in that regard. I had seen the ghost, and he ardently wished to as well."

She added this with a defiantly raised eyebrow, as if daring Holmes to tell her again that the shade in the yew alley did not exist.

"You mentioned the staff were already about their duties upon your arising," he said. "Who are the persons in residence in your household?"

I supposed he posed this question to her rather than to the master of the place, for the reason that a woman might be expected to have a fuller knowledge of such matters, and indeed she answered at once.

"As for family," she began, "just Jonathan and myself, and of course Barry, who is visiting."

"And the others on-site?"

"The lieutenant, who is employed by my husband, does not reside here," she answered, "but there is Watkins, our groom, the groundsman, Clark, the cook, Mrs. Blithewaite, the scullery maid, who is a village child called Becky, the two house-maids, Ada and Ivy. There is also the butler, Hardy, and my ladies' maid, Mrs. Drummond, who alas, is indisposed, and has not left her room since last evening."

Now there was an aberration, I thought to myself.

Feeling the need to say more by way of clarification under the weight of Holmes' stare, she added:

"It is an unfortunate, recurring affliction, headaches that come upon her in several instances a year, and until their passing leave her nearly blinded by scintillating lights within her eyes. She is an excellent companion at all other times, and I do not hold the infirmity against her, for like a soldier she bears her suffering courageously and without complaint."

"A kinder attitude than many mistresses held toward their servants," I said.

"I am not illiberal by nature, Doctor," she replied.

I again wondered if this could possibly be a clue of some significance, the lady's companion being absent with a supposed condition coinciding with the boy's disappearance. I said nothing, however, and left it to Holmes to formulate his own perceptions. He said nothing of this, however, and simply asked:

"That is all who live here on the grounds?"

"That is the entirety of our household, yes," Mrs. Morley stated. "We have had no housekeeper here since the retirement of Mrs. Darrow some three years ago, as our family in residence had by then dwindled to just Jonathan and myself, our son and two daughters being grown and gone elsewhere. Also there is the matter of this place having stood empty of all save a minimal maintenance staff during the years we were in India, until our return in '73."

Holmes nodded and declared:

"That is sufficient for the moment, and I thank you. I now require a small room where I might conduct some experiments of a chemical nature. A place where it will not do damage if I require the lighting of a small flame, perhaps."

"I know of a place that should fulfill your requirements," said Mrs. Morley, who then rose and crossed the room to tug a velvet rope which dangled twelve feet from the ceiling, summoning the butler.

"In the meantime," Holmes said, turning to Colonel Morley, "I suggest the search efforts be kept up. As I cannot as of yet narrow matters down, this remains is the wisest course."

"It shall be," Morley said.

I saw upon his normally stoical features a certain dejection vying with the worry, and a vague consternation, for I think he had hoped that by some miracle Holmes would produce the missing boy within minutes of his arrival.

"Should the Constable-Sergeant you mentioned make an appearance to report on his attempts at progress," said Holmes, "do kindly inform me at once."

"Of course," said Morley.

It was then that the butler, Hardy, a lugubrious-looking stooped-shouldered specimen of the profession, cadaverously pale and dull about the eyes, came into the room and received his instructions to escort Holmes and myself to the far side of the dwelling.

"Very good, Madam," he intoned with a well-practiced bow, prior to showing us to a stone-sided mudroom off a side entrance.

Before he left us alone, Holmes stopped him a moment and asked:

"Tell me, Hardy, have you any thoughts upon the matter of the missing boy?"

"I am sure I do not, sir," Hardy answered without expression or emphasis.

Ah, I thought, *the stubbornness of all good butlers, who drain themselves of opinions and personality to show their dedication.*

"And what are your thoughts concerning accounts of the ghost here?" Holmes pressed him.

"I cannot speak with authority upon such phenomenon, myself, sir."

It was an odd turn of phrase, and indeed Holmes did not let it stand un-annotated.

"You *cannot*? Why is that?"

"I cannot speak of it, because I have not seen it, sir."

"But you have, of course, heard talk?"

"I have, sir."

"Moreso recently?"

"Yes, sir, particularly of late, for several on staff claim recent experiences of encountering the phantom."

This reflected what Morley had told us back at Baker Street two days previous.

"Was there any particular event which seemed to precede these sightings?" Holmes asked the man.

"Not that I am aware, sir."

"But the legend did pre-date these supposed manifestations of late?"

"It did, sir. I have heard tales of the yew alley being haunted since I first came into service here, well before the rash of claims made this present summer."

"Did these tales imparted to you in the past differ markedly from those ghostly intrusions reported in recent weeks?"

"Yes, sir, somewhat."

I was surprised to hear this and demanded:

"In what ways?"

"Well, sir," said Hardy, looking toward me with his blank eyes, "in most of the accounts I heard in the past, there was more than one ghost said to haunt the yew alley."

"How extraordinary!" I burst out.

"Tell me of them," Holmes instructed.

"There was said, sir, to be the ghost of a man, and the spirit of a lady. The former malevolent, the latter benign."

Somehow, though I could not think why, this revelation seemed unsettling.

"And do you hold that these tales have any merit in the world of reality?" Holmes asked him.

"As my mistress declares she has seen at least one of the ghosts herself, sir, it is not for me to contradict her."

A perfect reply for a loyal servant to offer, I thought, almost amused.

"And what did young Barry report of the matter?" Holmes asked with something of an air of finality to the question.

Hardy paused for the slightest instant, before he dutifully

answered:

"That when he met the ghost, he hoped he could go away with it into the netherworld."

<><><><><><>

"What are your thoughts thus far, Holmes?" I asked when the butler had departed, his last statement still ringing in my ears.

"That three elementary possibilities are supported by the facts, Watson: the child has absconded; the child has been taken; or the child has met with misfortune beyond his planning or control."

"Well, er, yes," I replied, "that is rather rudimentary, but I mean have you formed specific ideas, given the testimony and evidence?"

"None to speak of," he answered simply, looking away from me and beginning the work he had before him by opening the chemistry set.

"What was it that made you declare Lieutenant Peters to be...as you said he was?" I inquired, finding the idea of the brutalization of a woman so loathsome I could not openly speak of it.

"His knuckles bore signs of bruising," Holmes told me, "though I knew with his withered arm he was no avocational boxer, and gathered him to be a man who took his self-pitying frustrations out in other ways. Also the care demonstrated in his attire lacked a woman's touch, telling me he was deprived the attentions of a loving spouse. Furthermore there was, though I doubt you or the others noted it, a single scratch, nearly healed, upon his neck, just above his collar. It was made by the fingernails of a woman attempting to defend herself from an attack she should not have been obliged to endure. All this came together to paint an only-too telling portrait of that braggart's conduct in the domestic side of his life. Namely, he is one who beats his wife."

"I see," I said, feeling regret that I had shaken the hand of such a brute. "Fortunately you have planted the seeds of knowledge in Morley," I added, "and I shall take up my own interest in the welfare of this lady."

"As shall I," Holmes added, "when this case is done. Also I mentioned my knowledge of his wedded state to fluster him, as I find few men can manage both a concealment of guilt, and unexpected outrage at the same time, and I noted no hint that he was hiding undue worries where the boy's disappearance was concerned. Thus I knew he did not merit suspicion in that way at least. Now...on to my experiment. Let us see what the stain from the yew alley might tell us."

I fell silent and gazed on as Holmes turned to the portable chemistry set, and laid out certain items in preparation for the experiments he was clearly eager to undertake, for I could tell the stain in the yew alley had greatly roused his curiosity.

Carefully and precisely, he set a ceramic disk about the size of a tea platter down upon the shelving there, and un-stoppered the test tube which contained a sample of grass and soil from where the yew alley had borne a stain the colour of a moonless night sky, the entirety of it so suggestively shaped like a young boy. Using a scalpel, Holmes divided this into three parts, and then removed a trio of glass vials, two in liquid form, red and green, the third holding a grayish powder, a minute portion of which he skillfully combined with a small quantity of water, until it too attained a fluid state. Next I watched him take three separate droppers and drip a quantity of liquids onto the soil samples. In two cases there seemed no reaction, but in the third —upon which Holmes soon fixed the whole of his attention—a slight crackling was heard, followed by a boil of crystalline foam, reminding me of the effect of hydrogen peroxide poured onto a cut.

"Remarkable!" I exclaimed, though Holmes said nothing, merely looked on with total concentration, his eyes glued before him.

For half a minute the colourless bubbles continued to rise and expand before collapsing upon themselves, at which time Holmes withdrew a sample of the resultant liquid, steaming hot, and squirted it onto a petri dish, which he then heated still more over a low blue flame blazing upon a portable apparatus. This almost immediately began to simmer, then boil, and become thick, like molasses, so that what remained took on a tar-like quality, with a slight redness below its dark surface.

Holmes scooped away a little of the tarry material and spread it onto the tiny glass plate, which he slid in beneath a portable microscope he removed from inside the chemistry case. He placed his eye over the ocular and studied what he saw there.

"Fascinating, Watson," he said a minute later, almost with a sigh.

"What does it mean, Holmes?"

"It means, my dear Watson, that this is no ectoplasmic secretion from the darkness beyond the grave, but a rather moderately sophisticated compound made by someone who knows a little about the science of chemistry. Alas for this as-yet unknown person, I know a good deal more, and now understand how our supposed ghostly residue was formed."

"So it was a deliberate act?" I asked.

"Oh, yes, most definitely," he answered, sounding less focused and more contemplative, "which tells me a good deal more about this case than I could be sure of even half an hour ago, whatever my growing suspicions. Someone, you see, has plotted to throw off lesser investigators by making it seem as if a supernatural act transpired in the yew alley, when in the end, our 'ghostly shadow' came from a laboratory. I could create the same effect with half an hour's labour."

"A ruse, then," I exclaimed. "Someone has made use of the ghost as a smokescreen!"

"Indeed, and now we might cross two of the aforementioned possibilities off that little list I gave you, for I think it safe to proceed on the grounds that the boy has fallen victim to the dire crime of abduction."

"Even more frightening," I allowed.

"Astute, Watson, for there is nothing in any infernal realm darker than the human heart."

For a moment I was elated at his discovery, but then asked:

"But are we not now set back to square one in this matter? For knowing the cause is hardly the same as possessing the solution."

"Small steps, Watson, small steps."

He stood in thought for a moment, facing the windows that lay on the north end of the mud-room, while small summer breezes tossed the tops of the shrubbery beyond, and then a smile pierced his mouth, and a light seemed to spring up in his eyes.

"Of course," he said quietly. Then louder to me he repeated: "The perpetrator was delayed, and thus so was the effect of chemical formula."

"Holmes?"

Turning in my direction, he said:

"Though, you are correct, Watson, that the case is far from finished, matters now begin to unfold at a more rapid pace, for sometimes the falling of a single stone may lead to a great avalanche. It might interest you to know that the compound which was used to create the boy-size marking on the ground does not have an instant effect before the eyes of its user, but requires twelve hours to fully process once poured into place. However, once the chemical has begun its final reaction, the shape would manifest in mere minutes."

"What is the significance of that, Holmes?" I asked, puzzling through this information but not quite connecting it.

Holmes set about re-packing his chemistry equipment into the case, apparently having learned all he needed from the samples, then asked:

"What did the family say concerning the stain when first they set out on their search this morning?"

I recalled:

"That was not to be seen until mid-morning."

"And when was the boy discovered to be missing?"

"At first light."

"*Before* the stain had appeared. Tell me, Watson, do you think that timing was desired in our perpetrator's plan, or was it that party's intention that the stain should be seen by all immediately in the morning, thus adding to the appearance of the supernatural?"

"I see...yes," I said. "You've said the process required twelve hours to fully set up, so the timing of the application in the yew alley was somehow bungled!"

"Precisely! For some reason the placing of the chemicals onto that spot was delayed by roughly three to four hours beyond when I suspect the abductor—or his accomplice— wished it to be in place so that it could be seen in the morning, shortly after the boy was discovered missing."

"Yet, as this person was delinquent in laying down the chemical, something beyond his control interfered with the time-table!"

"What domestic action do we know of from yesterday, Watson, which was unexpected and took perhaps, three or four hours to complete?"

Instantly my mind fastened upon it. "The unplanned trip into town!"

With a hard smile, wholly predatory, yet also well pleased, my friend turned rapidly on his heel, the case containing the chemistry set in-hand, and without waiting for me, strode out of the mud-room and back toward the chamber from which we'd come forty-five minutes before.

<><><><><><>

Holmes entered the drawing room door, where Mrs. Morley sat with a woman of middle years, to whom she was conversing closely as we entered, the words—

"*...is it any wonder, then, that he shall perhaps prove*

irretrievably beyond our reach now…."

—were leaving her lips, and it was with surprise and, did I imagine something approaching guilt, that she pulled her head back from its proximity to the other woman, and looked up, her lips forming a startled O.

"Mr. Holmes!" the Colonel's wife said, rather in the way of an exclamation.

She recovered herself and demanded:

"Have you news?"

"I have not."

Disappointment showed on her face.

"May I, then, present my companion and lady's maid, Mrs. Drummond, who, blessedly, has recovered from her headache and its effects, and now has joined me to lend what comfort she may in this time of worry."

I bowed my head toward the woman, who rose and curtsied to me, but Holmes entirely ignored this polite exchange, and instead demanded:

"Mrs. Morley, you have said you went into town yesterday afternoon."

"To order a new bonnet, yes."

"And what was the time?"

Lifting a finger, he added:

"Precisely now!"

"We left around three o'clock. Closer than that I cannot be."

"And the hour of your return?"

"Sometime just after seven."

"You have told us you were accompanied by your lady's maid here."

"Mrs. Drummond," I said, using her name by way of demonstrating politeness, for Holmes was speaking of the woman as if she were not among us.

"Yes, naturally," Mrs. Morley confirmed. "I rarely go anyplace without her."

"Is that so?"

Holmes took a sharp step forward and looked at Mrs. Drummond in such an intense manner that she shifted on the sofa, and I saw a blush begin at her jawline, and spread up the soft flesh of her cheeks, for though it was not tactile, the stare he gave her was a thing of utmost intrusion, almost improper for a gentleman's eyes to probe a woman in such a meticulous evaluation. I could only guess at what Holmes was searching out in her, though I knew he never gazed at anyone but that he learned much indeed.

"Hmmph," he snorted. "This fails to surprise me."

And just as suddenly as his eyes had locked upon the woman's person, his gaze shifted, and a light which had been veritably shining there appeared instead to dull to nothing, for all at once Mrs. Drummond seemed of no further interest to him.

Turning back to Mrs. Morley, he demanded:

"And which of the two house-maids in service here was the third member of your party on the trip into town?"

The question seemed to surprise the woman, perhaps unused to outsiders taking an interest in her staff, but after a pause she said:

"Ada, the younger of the two, and the more recent addition to our household servants."

"Have the butler bring her here at once," Holmes said sternly.

Clearly in the habit of delegating rather than doing for herself, Mrs. Morley nodded to her companion, Mrs. Drummond, who stood from the sofa and went to the far corner, where the braided velvet rope dangled just above the floor, golden tassels at its end. She gave it a delicate pull, then returned beside her mistress.

There was something almost electrical in the air, like the atmosphere before a storm. I could discern it and saw the two ladies could as well, for Holmes had brought it into the room with him. There seemed almost an anger about him, barely suppressed and ill-concealed, whereas it was more usual for him to remain coolly detached when in the midst of an investigation such as this. I felt myself wanting to worry about him, and wondered if it might not have been too soon for him to end his recuperation at Baker Street, and be expending himself in this way. If so, as his doctor I blamed myself, for there was even the faintest gleam of perspiration upon his well-formed brow.

I was about to ask to speak privately with him in the hallway, to inquire how he was feeling, when he began speaking once more.

"Tell me of this girl," he instructed Mrs. Morley, and there was something so forceful in his voice that I felt once more that he was not quite himself. "How long has she been with you? What is her character? And what has she said of herself in relation to the vanishing of your grandson?"

Yes, I was quite taken aback at the fierceness which roiled within my friend's questions, and saw Mrs. Morley likewise recognized the forcefulness in his inquiries, for without preamble she docilely answered:

"Ada has been in domestic service here for ten months, and I have not had cause to complain about the performance of her duties. She...."

I saw her eyes go out to Mrs. Drummond, her lady's maid, before she continued.

"The unvarnished truth is, Mr. Holmes, that we took the girl in through a charity programme that finds domestic positions for fallen women, from the streets of London. Off Sultan Street in Camberwell, in her case."

"I see," Holmes spoke up.

Not a good district at all, I thought. I knew of such social improvement programmes, and had read of their notable successes in delivering women from the streets of the East End slums, and thought on the whole it was a meritorious undertaking. Even Mr. Gladstone was known to travel out into the poorer districts of London in the company of his wife, and invite fallen women to return home with them, in order to see them conveyed to organizations which would offer them training and the hope of a better existence.

It was then that Hardy, the Butler, appeared.

"Madam rang?" he intoned expressionlessly.

"Fetch the house-maid Ada and bring her here," Mrs. Morley told him in a manner which reminded me of a general ordering a soldier to the front.

Hardy betrayed no sign of any thoughts on the matter, simply bowed and set off to fulfill his command.

Mrs. Morley shifted on the sofa and asked:

"Am I to take it that you suspect Ada of playing some rôle in the matter of Barry's disappearance, Mr. Holmes?"

Smiling coldly at her, Holmes said sarcastically:

"A rôle? I had thought, Madam, that you were satisfied that the boy's absence had a supernatural cause?"

"I believe in the existence of the yew alley ghost, Mr. Holmes," she told him, "but—"

"Then why do you inquire as to a culprit, if you are convinced your grandson was swept away by a phantom from the Middle Ages?" he replied curtly.

"I assume you had me summon the girl for a reason..." the lady pressed, awkwardly.

"And so I did," replied Holmes.

This was inexcusable, and I felt a disproving annoyance rise in me, though I said nothing. Not so her companion Mrs. Drummond, however, who burst out:

"Sir, you are most rude, and it is unbecoming of a gentleman to speak so to a lady as careworn as my mistress is at this difficult time. Have you no feelings?"

Staring back at her with such frigidness that the woman, even amid her righteous indignation, was the first to lower her eyes, Holmes said firmly:

"I only voice the lady's stated opinion, and echo it back to her."

Before anything further could be said, he turned on his heels and went to a window, before which he stood regarding a small stand of decorative trees at the perimeter of the lawn.

I went over beside him and said in a whisper:

"Why this discourtesy to your client's wife, and her companion? I do not understand, Holmes."

"Do you not," he replied disdainfully, in a slightly louder tone than I had employed, though whether within the hearing of the women I could not say. "I have recently been lead to death's very doorway by a woman because I deferred to her on the basis of what she was, Watson, and I shall not make that mistake twice. Not when spiders abound among that sex, and I suspect one of them is guilty of much in the matter at-hand."

"A woman has taken the boy?" I asked, startled.

"I did not express that sentiment," he corrected. "In truth we are in the midst of more than one act of crime, however much one may serve to overshadow the other."

"I doubt Mrs. Morley would harm her own grandchild, Holmes," I protested. "Yet you speak to her in a tone that lacks all mildness and courtesy, despite what she is enduring."

"Mildness and courtesy, you say? I have treated her with a directness warranted by the urgency of this matter. I saw no rudeness in that, and in future intend to converse with women without the nearly fatal deference shown the would-be assassin at Baker Street. How you speak to others I leave you to decide, but I tell you this for your own edification—Watson, once again a woman is to blame for a degree of the malice which has played out here. After reflection these past days, I begin to see how much evil in the world comes from the feminine half of the society, and often passes little suspected, and much excused."

I shook my head at this, and as a doctor knew I was seeing the effects of the wound Holmes had received that recent morning, not to his body, which had healed, but to his once towering self-confidence, which had clearly been shaken to the point that it had left this alteration in him. I only hoped this effect, and the exaggerated mistrust toward women that it revealed, would not prove lasting, yet the moods and reactions of my friend, I knew, were not like those of other men.

A few minutes passed with a web of silence spun about the room, until Hardy returned with the summoned house-maid,

Ada, behind him.

My first thought at turning toward her was that this Ada was a strikingly pretty young woman, perhaps in her early twenties, and I felt some surprise at this, for I knew it was the usual custom of ladies of the house to select female servants of plain features and humble dispositions, but it seemed Mrs. Morley owned sufficient confidence in herself—and her husband—to not make this a disqualifying factor.

"The house-maid Ada, Madam," Hardy said in a sepulchral tone.

"Madam?" the maid asked in her turn, dipping into a curtsey, her eyes averted with full propriety.

"Er, Ada, yes," Mrs. Morley said uneasily, "this is Mr. Sherlock Holmes, from London, here to investigate Barry's disappearance, and he has some questions he would like to put to you."

"Yes, Madam," the girl replied, evenly.

Ada raised her eyes to gaze full-on at Holmes, neither challenging him nor wilting away. If I'd expected Mrs. Morley's announcement to discommode the young woman, I saw that the words had no discernible effect on either her expression or the steadiness of her voice, and realized that she was possibly a person with some confidence about her, and this realization brought to mind how difficult survival must have been in the life she'd once led on the streets, and the effect it may have had on instilling self-reliance into her.

Holmes showed no sign that her steadfastness impressed him, and immediately launched onto Ada a question that caught me very much off guard:

"What did you tell the boy to lure him outside last night?"

Ada's eyes widened, but her face stayed much the same, save that she blinked twice before demanding:

"Sir?"

I caught the Cockney in her accent, out of place there in the fens of Suffolk, and saw that though she gave every sign of being puzzled by the inquiry, she lost none of the confidence she projected.

"Ah, are you to feign puzzlement then?" Holmes utterly sternly, as he advanced on the woman and began to circle her in predatory fashion, moving around her side, and then coming forward again until he stood very close to her, his piercing gray eyes locking on her own, of a delicate sky-blue.

"Your question of me, sir, I do not understand. I led no one out of the house last night or any other night, and if you are referring to young Master Barry, I will tell you I have never spoken to him upon any occasion here or elsewhere."

She said this with such a mingling of bewilderment and earnestness that I realized I very much wanted to believe her. With a start I recalled the words Holmes had just imparted to me about how easy it was to fail to suspect in a woman what one might be only too willing to believe of a man, and a wave of guilt washed over me.

Stay impartial, John, I told myself.

"Then I ask you, *Ada,*" Holmes continued, "or whatever your name originally was before your supposed reclamation in the London charity-house, to think for a moment....of your neck."

"Sir?"

"Oh, yes, such a lovely little neck. I see it is slender and pale and doubtless an endowment of some pride to you, as it is a feature which has certainly drawn the admiring eyes of men often enough."

"My...my neck, sir?"

Ada appeared at a loss for words, and with a face as innocent as a lamb, she gazed almost helplessly toward her mistress, who likewise seemed swallowed-up by puzzlement. Beside her, though, the lady's maid, Mrs. Drummond, sat silently, though clearly, I saw, frowning her disproval of Ada, and I guessed what her own sentiments had been concerning a young woman from the reclamation project coming into employment in the Morley household.

"I mentioned your neck, Ada," said Holmes, "because I ask

you to imagine how it shall feel when a hempen rope is fitted around that delicate bridge between head and body, and you drop through the floor to hang until you are lifeless."

There came a gasp from Mrs. Morley, and from Ada a momentary curdling of her once-placid face, and against this Holmes threw out:

"For hang you shall, girl, spinning and kicking in the air, if this is a case of murder!"

The words were abrupt, and spoken with such force that I almost felt struck in the chest by the intrusion of so macabre a subject there in the sedate drawing room. Yet the exercise had its effect, for almost as if beyond her self-control, Ada burst out:

"Murder? No, he said he'd never hurt the boy!"

Her mouth flew open, realizing the confession which had slipped from her.

"And so swiftly as that we have an admission of guilt," declared Holmes, a look of blackest triumphant taking over his pale face, his eyes almost feline in their menace.

"Mrs. Morley sprang to her feet and cried:

"Jezebel! We took you into this house on charity and gave you a chance at self-redemption, and this is how our kindness is returned! What is it you know?"

I believe she would have advanced on the guilty maid had not I held out a restraining arm, and said:

"Pray, Mrs. Morley, do leave Mr. Holmes to his work."

After peering at me for an instant, the lady nodded and sat back onto the sofa, where Mrs. Drummond touched her arm and said:

"She is a viper, Madam!"

"Well now," Holmes said triumphantly but also in a quieter tone than he had used a moment before, "the truth leaps out as guilt confesses itself."

Ada now lost her look of self-mastery and her eyes flew about the room, realizing how in her lapse she had revealed herself, and was now trapped. She also looked chagrined to have been jolted so easily.

"It wasn't me, Madam," she declared, gazing toward the sofa, and I saw that like some stage actress, she was attempting to force tears into her eyes. "That man, he made me do it. I was so frightened by him, and I had no choice. I was scared, and that's the Gospel truth!"

"Tsk, and now you compound your crime with lies," Holmes said with mockery, still standing very close to the girl. "To abandon this charade and tell me everything is the only hope you possess, and quickly, for the hangman's rope is closing in around you."

Ada opened her mouth and seemed about to speak, then shut it, and when she next spoke, her voice was entirely different, no longer the façade of the meek country-house servant, but the brassy tones of a streetwise woman of the East End, as stubbornly she said:

"What can you do for me if I rabbit on him?"

"Come clean with me," Holmes said, his voice divided between sternness and indifference, "and when the hour comes I shall testify in front of the law that you have claimed yourself coerced beyond your capacity to resist."

"Not good enough," Ada said sourly. "It's barrels and eels, and I know it. See I'm given a deal and I'll talk straight away, here and now."

If I expected Holmes to throw her words back at her with a ferocious threat, I was surprised, for he became almost gentle when he said:

"It is well known that I have friends within the police and the courts as well, and I tell you I will speak to them about you, but you must show yourself worthy of my intervention."

I saw the swirl of deliberation in Ada's mind, but still she hesitated.

"I know," spoke Holmes, "a great deal more of what has transpired here than you might suspect I do."

"You don't know me at all," Ada boasted.

"Oh, but I do. I know that you are ambitious, and a far brighter girl than you want the world to know, as playing the rôle of the meek, contrite sort has served you more than once. It impressed the simple Christian folk of the reform society, after all, and got you out of London, where so many of your fellow *demimonde* of a less determined disposition remain behind. It brought you here to a fine country estate, where you were just biding your time until the next opportunity for self-advancement arose, and you thought you'd found it."

He paused and added:

"I know that you steal candies from your mistress' dish in the parlour at every chance, for look, there is a little smear of orange left behind on your left fingertip, even in the midst of this crisis, showing how recent your misconduct has been."

Ada's eyes dipped to her hands.

"I know that you have bullied the little scullery maid with whom you share an attic room here, so that she sleeps on the floor each night, no matter how cold the weather, so that you might occupy an entire bed by yourself. Oh, such a luxury for you!"

As if her fate had just been told by an oracle, Ada's eyes widened with wonder at how this shameful fact could possibly be known to Holmes.

"And I know your mother," he continued, "is still alive in the East End, and that the scarf you keep tucked inside your pocket is the one gift that pathetic soul ever gave you."

Here Ada's eyes both hardened and took on the first look of true hurt I'd seen in them.

"Don't you dare speak of my mother!" she seethed.

Holmes gave her a smile that had little of kindness in it, and promised:

"With or without you, Ada, I'll have him soon enough, and knowing this, a wise girl might begin to assist me, while still the chance remained, by turning on her benefactor....this would-be master of a daring crime. Your..."

Leaning closer still to the girl, he added at a whisper:

"....*lover*."

At that word, normally forbidden for a gentleman to utter

in the presence of ladies, Mrs. Morley closed her eyes, though I could not discern whether it was in shame or anger that the woman she had taken into her house should so deeply betray her.

Yet heedless of the lady's reaction, Holmes pressed on.

"Far from being of benefit to you, Ada, the man I seek has set you down a dreadful path, and your involvement in the plot in which he has embroiled you as his accomplice out in the yew alley—oh yes, I know what it was you did there in crafting the stain—can only lead to your ruin. Even your death. If you do not aid me, I promise you I shall see that it goes as hard for you as I can make it, but if you tell me all that you know, so that I might put right the terrible wrong against an innocent boy and his family, I will do what I can for you."

"And what would that be?" Ada asked, her eyes going sharp once more.

"A much better deal than you'll have if I act against you," said Holmes, with a jaunty snarl. "So I give you one chance, and one only, to earn your reprieve, by telling all."

The pretty housemaid stood unmoving for just another moment, then nodded, and without asking Mrs. Morley's permission, pulled out a chair and fell back into it in a most unladylike pose.

"It is true, is it not," stated Holmes, "that the unexpected trip into town to see the milliner with Mrs. Morley, delayed you from the schedule laid down for you? It was your mission, I believe, to slip out in the late afternoon and pour the chemical he gave you in order to make the suggestive shape in the yew alley?"

"Yes," Ada confirmed ruefully. "He said it would need half a day to set up, so wanted me to pour the liquid there in the rough shape of a boy, so that it would be spotted at first light, when the party had just started off looking for the missing child."

"The idea being to suggest, amid the fertile climate of so much recent talk of the supernatural, that it was a ghost from local legend who had taken the boy?"

"Yes."

"A ghost," said Holmes, glancing toward Mrs. Morley, "that despite rumours has remained unseen upon the estate this past fortnight, save in the imaginations of those here. And all of that was set in motion by your own false claims to have crossed paths with the entity in the yew alley, was it not?"

"But I tell you, *I* have seen it!" Mrs. Morley cried out before the girl could answer.

"Lately?" Holmes demanded of her.

"No," the lady admitted.

"And when you did, was it perhaps on full-moon nights, after a rain-shower, when the yews leaves, noted for holding water long after a storm, would have shone suggestively in the moonlight?"

At this question, Mrs. Morley fell silent, clearly offended, and ignoring her in any case, Ada said:

"He told me to begin spreading the rumours of my encounter two weeks before the boy arrived for his summer holiday, and said others would fall in line and claim they'd seen it as well, a 'contagious hysteria of the imagination,' he termed it, if I merely got the ball rolling. And so it did! I made my claims, pretending to be all scared and mystified, and the second night took my room-mate, the scullery girl, little Betsy, out into the darkness with me, and played at seeing the ghost chasing after us, and so simple was Betsy I soon had her reduced to tears, convinced she'd seen it, too, and had even felt its cold touch against her back while we ran from it, though of course that was really me clutching at her in the dark, and there was never anything there at all!"

She gave a haughty laugh.

"The stories among the servants took off with a life of their own," she bragged, "and I admit I was rather proud of what I'd set in motion. Within a week half the staff were saying they'd seen the thing, bunch of fibbers. Mr. Hardy, that sheep-faced old butler, tried to hush us up, but it was far too big a story by then, and some of the claims they made, oh, you should have heard the inventions. All I could do to play along and keep a straight face!"

"Maybe they weren't all inventing, you foul girl!" Mrs. Morley thundered from the sofa. "For many have seen the ghost going back five hundred years!"

Ada stared insolently at the woman, and again let loose a giggly sort of laugh. "So stupid," she said without a trace of shame.

"Whatever the truth of the ghost's reality," I offered, with I hoped a diplomatic nod toward Mrs. Morley, whose anger, I noted, was quickly blooming toward rage, "I think we can safely presume there never was a ghost apparating during the time young Barry was here on holiday, or even a thing legitimately mistaken to be one."

"Of course not, Watson," Holmes declared. "A tale of a ghostly encounter invariably tells us more about the claimant than it does the nature of any life that may follow this one. An interest in a swirling rumour of the preternatural can be forgiven in a boy of eleven, but for adults to have fallen for such nonsense is worthy only of castigation."

To Ada again, he stated:

"I presume you made opportunities to place yourself in the boy's path throughout the summer, and tell your nonsense concerning the phantom?"

"That was my mission," Ada said with a smile of pride, "and I done it well. Had him eating out of my hand, wanting my stories about the ghost told over and over, and it wasn't hard to prime him to be outdoors last night, when the man was ready to come for him, leaping out of the shadows like a jungle cat with knockout drops on a cloth, grabbing him from behind on the cobbles of the patio... Weren't no trouble at all to get to that boy. Over and done with in a second, and he was gone, easy as pie in the sunshine."

This causal admission of how she had betrayed the child and lured him outside into the clutches of a heartless plot made revulsion swirl inside me.

"And now," Holmes said, showing no reaction to her

confession, "it is time to tell me the rest. Describe for me the appearance of this mastermind behind the abduction. How did he approach you, and what was it that he promised for your sordid cooperation?"

"That last bit's easy," Ada said proudly. "He *liked* me, you see. Men usually do, because I'm not old and fat and ugly like some I could name around here."

She cast a glance at Mrs. Morley, and Mrs. Drummond said: "You are a fiend!"

Ada next revealed:

"He promised to keep me in finery when he had this house."

"That's absurdity," I voiced, less concerned with the girl's feelings after her unwarranted swipe at Mrs. Morley's appearance. "A landed man with even the merest pretentions of being a gentleman wouldn't take to consort a woman raised off the streets of London."

Ada laughed. "Oh, think me a mad little fool, do you? I'd never want to be wife to one such as him, no, but there are ways a girl can live right well off a man's feelings for her, better than a wife, even, and he promised to set me up in town, and keep in fine style, whatever else was going on back here at this house, once he owned it."

"Own this house?" Mrs. Morley burst out.

"Oh, yeah," Ada taunted. "Always has wanted it, ever since he was here as a little boy. His dad, you see, used to work on these grounds doing something, he never said what exactly it was, and he fell hard for this place, did my fella, so when he come back from America, where he went over as a boy, and soon his fortune made good 'n proper, it was all he wanted. Knew you'd never sell, though, not unless there was a good reason."

"Like the tragic memory of a grandson disappearing from the grounds," I said.

"Yeah," Ada agreed, "not to mention the tainted history of the place, a ghost being on-site? One that snatches away children, never to be seen no more? Who'd want to live here then?"

It was a diabolical plan, almost absurd, and yet in its daring it had threatened to succeed, and still might.

"And the schemer himself," said Holmes. "What was his name?"

"Said to call him Peter, but I knew, of course that weren't his real name, no more than mine's really Ada."

"And his appearance?"

"Good looking bloke, ain't he? Regular height, light brown hair what falls down over his forehead in the wind, eyes brown as a stag's, strong as an ox, and brave, so brave..."

It was the description of a smitten woman, I knew, despite whatever claims of disdain for the institution of wedlock Ada might have professed.

"Nevermind all that, you cunning little rodent, where, is my grandson?" Mrs. Morley demanded in a rage.

"That is the one thing I cannot tell you," said Ada, staring with hate-filled eyes at the woman who had provided honest employment for her, despite her chequered past, "for it is the one thing Pete never told me."

"It might interest you to know," Holmes began, "that your 'Pete' has left you behind, and has no intentions of ever seeing you again."

"Now there you lie," Ada laughed.

"Do I? I confess you know the man more intimately than I, but think, girl, what further use for you, has he? Would you return for a loose end in your scheme? You might consider yourself quite lucky he didn't invite you along in his act of absconding, and do away with you in some convenient hollow between here and town."

At this charge Ada showed a considerable diminution in her haughtiness, and fell silent in rueful thought.

"I've told you everything, just like you asked," she said after a moment. "Now you'll help me out, right?"

At this Holmes replied with but a cold smile, and it was at this precise second that there was the sound of the great front doors opening, and the noise of heavy footsteps in the entryway, making all our eyes turn there, as Colonel Morley trod inside with his military bearing, trailed by a country policeman in uniform.

"Ah, the Constable Sergeant of whom I have been told," Holmes remarked, turning away now from Ada, and seemingly putting her from his mind.

"Constable Sergeant Welkirk at your service, sir," the man said with a nod of his head. "You are known to me, even out here, with much admiration, Mr. Holmes."

"What news, gentlemen?" I called out.

"None, I am afraid," answered the Colonel.

"None indeed," Constable Sergeant Welkirk confirmed. "We have hunted high and low around the countryside for miles, and there is no trace of the boy."

"Then you will be cheered when I deliver the tidings that I have here before us one of the culprits in what I can confidently tell you, Colonel, was indeed the abduction of your grandson."

"What? Her? The house-maid?" Morley thundered. "What have you done with the boy?"

"She is of no further use, Colonel," Holmes interjected, "and I will tell you all. In fact having wrung all the information from her that she has to give, your timing is excellent, for I was just about to inquire from your wife if there was a secure closet in the house where I might lock the villainess away until the police could take her, but as you are here, Constable Sergeant, I commend her to you."

Taking Sherlock Holmes at his word without asking questions, Welkirk crossed the room and slipped handcuffs around Ada's slender and truly lovely wrists.

"I think one of our cells in town might fit the bill a little better," he remarked.

"Wait," Ada barked at Holmes as the Sergeant walked her to the door, where another constable waited, "you promised you'd aid me!"

"Ah, yes, so I did," said Holmes. "Constable Sergeant, this

woman claims she was coerced and compelled into acting on behalf of the abductor, with whom she had formed a romantic attachment. There, Ada, you see, I have spoken on your behalf, as I promised. Now address me nevermore."

As he turned from her, the girl was pulled from the room cursing Holmes' very name, and loathsome though I found her, I did feel my scruples somewhat disjointed at Holmes' lackluster efforts to further advocate for her, as he'd indicated he would. His words had been weak at best, evidence of deceit at worst. None of it was in keeping with the man I knew, and once more I reflected that the sickness that had overcome him following his narrow escape from death had left him changed in ways I marked as no improvement.

Holmes seemed not at all chagrined at his deceitfulness, however, as he told Morley of Ada's revelations, and asked the man:

"Think back, who in the past meets the description she has given? Here as a boy many years ago, let us say twenty or more, and of the appearance she gave?"

The Colonel's eyes took on a distant cast as he ran through the fields of memory, and then all at once burst out:

"Why it must surely be Tony Turner's son, Willie!"

"Tell me of him!" Holmes commanded.

"Turner was the engineer who saw to the dredging of the fetid pond one summer, '60 it was, and being a widower, he brought his son with him. I found him a likely boy, good-natured and quick to smile, but moody and spoiled and audacious, as well. I always thought the army would bring out the best in such a solid lad, and chip away the bad, though he was gone from here long before coming of age. Got into fisticuffs with my own boy, Evanston, and got the best of him, though Evanston was no weakling. I liked the Turner lad despite the flare-up, and often saw him walking in our woods, and once climbing the tall oak that used to stand at the property's edge, before the big storm in '73 felled it, a hundred feet up he went, and laughed down at us, sure-footed as a mountain goat, and fearless to his very heart."

"I remember him differently!" Mrs. Morley exclaimed. "A ruffian, that child, no good at all, and glad I was when the work was done on the pond, and he and his too-indulgent father were gone."

"It seems, Madam, that he has returned," Holmes told her, ironically.

Leaning out toward Holmes, but for some reason finding my own eyes, Mrs. Morley added fiercely:

"He bloodied my Evanston's mouth and blacked both his eyes! The wild gypsy-child, I used to call him."

"To think," said Morley, "these twenty-three years this house and the grounds has stayed so strongly in his mind, apparently every moment of his life. I heard that his father had gone off to America to do engineering work in the fortifications being built during that nation's internal war, and after that went on into the growing west, to Denver, I heard it was, and the boy went with him. It seems he has come back after somehow making his fortune off in that wild land, and still with his eye on this place..."

It was all strange, I thought, a man's determination to claim a place he'd been but once in his youth, but as a doctor I knew how compelling the force of obsession could be, and clearly this Turner must have set his mind on becoming master of the house, through whatever means were required, even so bizarre and criminal a plan. An unrestrained force, I judged him, and wondered how it must be to possess so fearlessly determined a heart, undeterred by laws or their consequences.

"Now you know his name, arrest him!" Mrs. Morley shouted.

"I am afraid it will not be so simple," said Holmes. "I doubt very greatly that the man calls himself by his father's surname any longer. He might go by any name, and be passing himself off as nearly anyone. Furthermore, he will soon learn that his scheme has failed, and slip away, most probably back to America, where one might hide til the end of time itself."

"And my grandson?" Morley asked.

"I do not think it is in the nature of a risk-taker such as this Turner to keep a stolen boy with him," Holmes stated. "Too dangerous, given the police are out in force searching for him. No, assuming he has scrupled at murder, and left young Barry alive..."

Mrs. Morley exhaled rapidly and loudly.

"As I believe he has," Holmes said, an eye on her, "for killing the boy would have been far simpler than abducting him, yet he spared him, demonstrating to me that Turner has that many principles at least. So I must now think, where would the boy be deposited, in safety, but kept out of the way? And in not too distant a place, at that, for time was a great factor in arranging all of this."

"There is a small cave near the creek," suggested Constable Sergeant Welkirk.

Holmes looked toward him, interested, until the policeman added:

"But we searched it thoroughly and found no sign of anyone having been inside for ages."

"Where else have you searched?" Holmes inquired.

"Every barn in this section of the county. Outbuildings, under the bridge over Bishopsgate Creek, haystacks, everywhere the mind could conceive of to look, my men and I did, as did the parties who have volunteered, and are still out now combing the countryside."

"Then it is likely Turner has somehow spirited the child away," said Holmes, whose eyes were deeply reflective of the churning seas of his mind, "most probably with the aid of a confederate."

"Another like Ada somewhere?" Morley suggested.

"You are sure that Lieutenant Peters played no rôle whatsoever?" I asked Holmes.

He told me:

"Peters is a coward who brutalizes his wife, not one to nebulously gamble on a long-term reward promised him from a child-abduction plot. He is a fruitless prospect, and upon his ignorance in this entire matter I would stake my professional reputation."

"Then we are at a standstill, even now after learning so much?" Colonel Morley asked, his voice mired in misery.

But I saw that Holmes was walking slowly away from him, toward the window, his head bowed, his mind churning, and I held my breath, for I sensed that he had fastened on to something of significance. And I was right, for an instant later he whirled back toward us all and, his eyes blazing like torches, exclaimed:

"'The wild gypsy-child'!"

He roared this so loudly that the ladies on the sofa flinched, and Morley demanded:

"What?"

Suddenly, though, a light went off in my own head, and I knew the reference.

"The Irish gypsy caravan we spied coming in from Ipswich!" I cried.

"Of course!" Holmes shouted. "So focused was I on arriving at the culprit, I gave little thought til now of the means by which he might have secreted the boy away, but as you say, Watson, it is the most likely connection. Irish gypsies are notorious thieves and confidence men, hated across the realm for their predatory ways, and even, I fear, their involvement in the abduction and sale of small children, for there is a sordid market for such, even here in England, let alone on the continent."

At mention of the sale of children—into ghastly fates, I did not doubt—I shuddered, and said:

"And to think, we may have rolled right by him this very morning!"

A great rush of activity then burst upon the house as Holmes unfurled his plan and the Constable Sergeant cooperatively accepted it as stated, mentioning only that without a warrant he could not enter the gypsy's wagons, to which Holmes promised to provide him with the legal grounds to do so, should he find the child to be present.

Upon hearing this, Welkirk sent one of his men into town on the double, to bring back three other constables, and their two fastest wagons.

In the meantime, Holmes retrieved his chemistry case off the floor, and as I trailed him into an empty side-room, he told me:

"In among my chemistry apparatus I keep effects by which I might transform myself via disguise."

"And this will benefit the infiltration of the gypsy caravan?" I asked.

"Immeasurably."

I watched as Sherlock Holmes vanished from the world, and in his place came a tramp, down on his luck, shabby in hat and heels, weary of eye, stooped of back, and four inches lesser in height than Holmes' towering six feet, a man whipped by life, and more than a little crazed around the edges. In short, perfect prey for the ruthless gypsies.

The transformation complete, Holmes returned to the room where Colonel and Mrs. Morley and the Constable Sergeant stood waiting, and told them all:

"In this guise shall I approach the caravan, while you, Watson, you, Colonel Morley and you, Constable Sergeant and your men, shall wait concealed in the woods, not to approach until I signal for you by raising my arms above my head. Then you must rush in, expecting resistance, I doubt not, and retrieve the boy, if I am correct about him being kept concealed within one of the wagons."

"Ah," said the Colonel, an old military man, "a pincer action! My personal favourite for overwhelming a foe!"

"Precisely," Holmes agreed, "but do remember, the assault must come only at my signal, for I will get farther in this disguise than would the police devoid a warrant which might require many hours to attain, and by engaging in conversation with the thuggish wanderers, and I shall learn what I may. If they have the boy, they will not be able to deceive me upon the subject, and he will soon be home again."

"Oh, sir, let that be so!" Mrs. Morley exclaimed, placing her hands above her heart. "And all of you, do be careful…"

<><><><><>

We were off no more than twenty minutes later, with such great alacrity did Constable Sergeant Welkirk assemble his fellows, and set off at a nearly break-neck pace back across the country road down which we'd come, and an hour saw us at the spot where we'd passed the caravan trespassing in some farmer's meadow, though I was little surprised to see it had since moved on.

"Now," said Holmes, "we come rapidly to the part wherein finesse shall play its rôle, for we must proceed to the point of spying the caravan ahead in the distance, but not draw so close as to be seen in return. Carefully now, and with greater slowness let us proceed!"

And so we did, progressing at a lessened pace, and it was another full-forty very long and weighty minutes before Holmes' sharp eyes became the first among us to sight our quarry, nearly half a mile distant atop a hill, where the gypsies appeared to be taking another break, spread out as they were on a tree-lined expanse, allowing their horses to graze, sitting together at several small foldable tables, each lined with teapots and light fare.

"Hold here, at this low point in the woods, Sergeant!" Holmes said urgently, his blood high, the thrill of his work upon him, however dangerous what he had planned might have been.

"It is the same band of vagrants?" the Colonel asked hotly, desirous of the battle ahead.

"It is, sir," Holmes told him. "And Fortuna is with us, for a thick wood surrounds the clearing upon the hilltop, ideal for concealment. Keep to the plan, all of you! I shall go forward on the road, giving the impression of being a wanderer, and shall approach the caravan with a story that will be of interest to those there."

"It sounds dangerous, Holmes," I said, knowing nothing else to add.

"It is, Watson," he confessed without qualification. "Now, creep close, all of you, but stay concealed, and should I raise my arms in the signal, sweep in like a storm and be ready, for when cornered Irish gypsies are known as fierce fighters. If I am right, we shall have the boy home with you before sunset, Colonel. To your places now, and stick to my plan with precision!"

"You heard the man," said Constable Sergeant Welkirk to his officers. "No deviation, now, and no mistakes. Have your truncheons at the ready, for a fight may be coming, and Heaven help the man who lets himself be spotted early by our quarry!"

And so as Holmes walked on apart from us, raising my worries for him, his stride unusual, as if weary or partly lame, his back bent, the rest of us stayed low and proceeded off-road into the woods, creeping up the near-side of the hill which was playing host to the gypsies. We were able to reach a spot behind where a large plane tree had fallen in the last year, and lined up there, within easy sight of the group, and in an unexpected plus, even within hearing, for the curve of the hillside acted as a natural amplifier of sound, like an amphitheater.

It took Holmes many minutes to follow the curve of the dusty country lane, moving as he was in a world-weary shuffle, a stick in his right hand, worn boots upon his feet. He paused at the roadway's crest, as if just seeing the caravan for the first time, and several among that group, an older woman with steel gray hair and burning black eyes, and two younger men, perhaps her sons, spotted him as well and paused, standing rigidly as they stared out at him.

A fission of fear went through me, thinking only now of the calamity should the gypsies, thinking themselves alone upon the fens, no witnesses, simply decide to try to rob Holmes rather than listen to him, yet I also thought surely that would provide the necessary legal grounds for Welkirk to rush the encampment, would it not?

Holmes gave the wanderers a broad wave with his left arm, and set off toward them at the same low-key and unhurried shuffle, giving the impression of a man in no haste to be anywhere, for being homeless, he had nowhere to go.

"Ahoy there!" he cried to the gypsies. "Might a weary traveler upon these same roads approach and be among you for a moment?"

I saw the wheels within the gray-haired woman's mind turn as she sized up this newcomer and measured him against her perpetual hopes that she might exploit him, as she made a practice of doing to all outsiders she encountered.

"And fer what purpose might that be?" she called back, her accent thickly that of Connaught, in the far west of her native island.

"If a man might set his hopes on sharing a cup of tea with you, he might find himself most glad indeed," said Holmes.

"We don't give away what we own, man," said the woman, "though we might sell you a cup, or make other arrangements."

"Fine, fine," said Holmes, whose advance had never slowed during the tentative conversation. He was now within the perimeter of the caravan, and a look of simple, slightly wary good-nature was set upon his dust-smudged face.

No one among the tribe spoke words of welcome, and the eyes of the nine within the group turned toward him, hard with suspicion.

As if unconscious of the group's reaction to him, Holmes walked up next to the woman and removed a ha'penny from his pocket and held it out.

"For a mug of tea, mayhaps, and a bite of bread and cheese, if you have it."

The woman looked a moment upon the ha'penny, and then took it from his fingers.

"Sit," she said, pointing to a three-legged stool. "Saoirse," she called to a young and somewhat cowed girl who had been standing back by the most distant of the brightly-painted wagons, gaping at the interactions, "fetch this one a cup and something to eat. Be hasty!"

The girl, Saoirse, surely no older than twelve, scrambled to carry out the instructions, and I could spy worry in the green-gray eyes of the girl, very thin, she was, and with her great mass of auburn hair, long-unwashed by the look of it, left tangled loose about her shoulders. I told myself it could have been a projection of my imagination, but something in my instincts as a physician told me that she was an oppressed soul, the lowest among those in the caravan, and that fright was her main lot in this world. She moved quickly, and in a number of seconds had the demanded items set on the tiny fold-up table before where Holmes stood.

I saw his eyes flash out to her, sweeping her from head to foot, and then go back to the food.

Though the bread looked stale and its grain coarsely-ground, Holmes plopped onto the three-legged stool and set about shoving the offering into his mouth, and gulping the tea to wetten it down his throat all the easier. He then pushed a mouldy rind of some questionable cheese in behind all this, and wiped his lips with the back of his arm. The unappealing meal, such as it was, vanished in an instant, and Holmes leaned back, as if staring at the sky itself in thanks.

"First food I've had since the night afore last," he claimed.

"Well, you've eaten, so now be on with you," said the matriarchal gray-haired woman, clearly the leader of the group, she being the only one to have uttered a word thus far.

"Hold now, hold a moment," said Holmes, humbly with less a tone of challenge than supplication. "Having paid a ha'penny in the matter, mightn't a weary old fellow sit just another few moments and enjoy the good fortune of his meeting with such fine people as yourselves?"

The woman stared back before saying:

"A moment."

As if incognizant of the suspicion and ill-hidden hostility arrayed around him, Holmes slumped upon the stool and appeared to sigh away a great weight on his shoulders.

"A cruel life it can be when a man lives upon the road," he said, his accent unrefined and rural, with perhaps a hint of the Midlands in it. "I thank you, missus for easing my way even this much."

"Where is it you're heading?" the gray-haired woman demanded, less conversationally than with some covert shrewdness to her question. Behind her stood two strong-looking and nearly grown boys, and I did not like her or them, and I did not like the situation in which Holmes had placed himself, a hundred yards off and alone.

"Where am I heading, missus?" he replied. "Wherever the road may take me. To Canterbury, mayhaps, or mayhaps in the opposite direction, to Liverpool. In fact..."

He leaned out and fixed the woman with his eye.

"....mayhaps it is providence itself that moves in my life today, for I have met your people before, and never once have I been done wrong by their advice when they've consulted the unseen oracles through the cards."

Now the woman's gaze changed, no less unfriendly, but perhaps with a purpose, sensing that the winds may have shifted and were blowing a chance to profit her way.

"I can tell you what awaits in either direction," she promised, "Canterbury or Liverpool, for I, myself, know much of the future, and the cards know all!"

"Bless you, bless you!" Holmes said, then coughed, as if his lungs had borne much to distress them in his wanderings. "You see," he said, as if confiding a secret, "I do not wander these roads of fair England without purpose, no, no, in fact..."

He looked around him carefully, as if making sure no one else was there to hear him.

"I know of Danish gold," he told her, "a hoard of treasure, long-buried, for I saw it in a dream, and it was no regular dream, I vow, but so vivid that I left the life I had, and have taken to wandering these three years in search of it."

Now a great many heads turned his way, the eyes

interested, curious, rapt with attention, for the Irish gypsies were well-known for being a superstitious lot, given to placing great store in dreams.

"What was it you saw?" the woman demanded.

"A battle!" Holmes replied. "From long ago, when tall dragon ships sailed the coasts, and terrible men in mail slew all they found, taking away what was never their own. A great jarl, as the Danes called their kings, buried his loot in a place, and in my slumbering state I stood beside him and watched him do so, and then that same day he was set-upon by soldiers of a Saxon king, and slain before he could return to his loot."

"And how will you find this treasure?" the woman asked, avarice in her voice.

"That is why I wander, searching," Holmes said, "for so burned into my mind is the memory of that spot, that when I see it, I will know!"

Whether the woman thought him mad and sought to exploit him, or was overcome with desire to know more, I could not say, for I sensed that she was in her own right something of a skilled actress. She said:

"I can tell you much, perhaps all, of what lies ahead for you, traveling man, but I do not read the cards without due recompense."

"Oh, bless you, good lady, and fear not," said Holmes, who took half a sovereign from his coat and held it gleaming in the sunlight. "I am a poor man, but this coin has traveled far with me, for I have saved it for the day it would serve its purpose and point me on the way to the fortune I seek as my own!"

Her hand a blur, the gypsy woman snatched the coin from his fingers and just as rapidly set it down inside the neckline of the billowing white homespun blouse she wore.

"Sit then!" she intoned, pointing back at the folding table. "You have bought my attention for a little while, and caught the notice of the spirits which are always near a seer such as myself. I shall certainly tell you something of your future, though it may not be what you wish to hear."

"A future where I find my treasure, I pray!" Holmes said with the illusion of great hopefulness in his voice.

"We shall see," said the woman, "we shall see, but first tell me what you saw of this location, and how you will know this place."

"By a tall gray rock jutting below three mountains beyond it," said Holmes, and I knew he was describing a site in Cumberlandshire where I had gone with him that spring on a case.

The description meant nothing to the woman, and a small sneer of disappointment crossed her face.

"That is all? Perhaps you are a mad-man," she said, "or perhaps you, too, have something of the seer in you. The cards shall tell me which it is...."

I could almost have forgotten at that moment why we were there, so fascinating was the theatricality of the woman's taking of the cards from the hand of the downtrodden girl, Saoirse, who'd fetched them from the lead wagon, and her lifting them high above her head toward the sky, and my ears rang with the trilling syllables of whatever it was she cried out in that ancient language known as Gaelic:

"Leis na h-uilebheistean agus leis na h-uile dhiathan, nochd dhomh dè a thig a-màireach!"

She shuffled the deck and then laid the cards on the table as she commanded:

"Divide them into three."

The fact that Holmes did so made me wonder if he had not yet discerned the signs he sought of the boy's presence, and I watched as his long white hands cut the deck into three, and at the woman's instruction he tapped the top of the middle pile, which the woman then fanned out, reversing the cards there.

She placed the cards back into one stack, and one by one turned nine cards over and laid them out in the shape of a tall, uneven cross.

"Poor man," she said, frowning, "you have never known love, and never shall, though much else will you possess, for you will live many lifetimes before your death. In your past I see much loss, and much...."

She swallowed as her frown deepened and her eyes darkened.

"....deception."

As she hissed this word, several of the men near the wagons shifted and I saw their poses tighten, not liking her revelation.

"There is much animosity surrounding you," she went on as she turned over an additional card, "for you are a man with many foes who would seek to harm you, including a great adversary, unknown to you now, but who shall come for you in time."

Holmes said nothing, and showed no reaction which I could discern. His eyes were not taking in the caravan, as I expected, but were riveted on the woman. Surely, I thought, *he* could not truly be interested in her words?

"You have but three souls in this world you trust, though one of them less than the others. You are loved by a woman, not your mother, but maternal all the same... And your mind is never at rest, but churns like the sea in storm, never content, always hungry for more...like a gluttonous fire, consuming, seeking..."

"I seek the treasure, yes," said Holmes. "I will not rest until I find it."

The woman looked up from the cards and stared harshly at him in a way that reminded me of an expression I had often seen Holmes wear when he was evaluating another, seeking hidden signs of significance. I had the strongest sense that something had changed, that no longer was this an exercise in theater, that the woman, a shrewd old con and survivor of much in a hard life, had grasped some telling revelation she had not put to voice.

The tension around us all became very great.

There was a moment of silence broken only by the wind, and when Holmes next spoke, and he said in his own voice, not the wheezing humble imprecations of the tramp.

"And my future, Madam?" he asked with unaffected clarity.

"To die twice," she said.

Then so under her breath that I barely heard her, she whispered:

"But you will never truly fall."

All time stood still, and then:

"You should never have accepted the boy last night," Holmes said to the gypsy matriarch, then very rapidly he stood and thrust both his arms above his head.

The signal!

Moving as one, shouts issuing from their lungs, the force of constables surged out of the wood and swept into the field, Colonel Morley, seeming all at once far younger than his years with them, and I beside him.

Atop the hill, the men of the caravan leaped to action and rushed to meet us, violence erupting, just as Holmes had predicted.

Stepping around the gray-haired woman with her dark eyes—she was "Black" Irish, I judged—Holmes closed in on the tallest and strongest of the young men, and ducked the man's roundhouse swing, only to rise up fast as a cat, and strike him thrice with hard jabs to his stomach and ribcage, before sending him earthward with a last great blow to his temple. The man collapsed like a sack of sand, unconscious.

The battle was swift and not without bloodshed on our own side, for one of the constables was soon to be found rolling in agony, full-length on the ground, his nose and jaw broken by a flailing *shillelagh* made of knotted blackthorn.

I made to rush to him and offer medical aid, but a swift Irishman, reedy and powerful, was on me, grappling, an adept wrestler, and he soon had me onto my back, arms locked in a hold, while he raised his skull above my face, meaning to smash it down onto me like a hammer.... Only for my assailant to be thrown headfirst through the air, as Holmes, with his sinewy might, chucked him from me, and set upon him with a series of blows that quickly left the man out of commission.

"Are you injured, Watson?" he called, turning to lend me a hand.

"I am well enough," I answered, though in truth was very much shaken up.

I was just reaching to take Holmes' hand and rise, when I spotted a movement to his rear, and realized with horror that the gray-haired matriarch had pulled a dagger from up inside her blouse-sleeve and was plunging it downward at Holmes' unprotected back in a killing strike.

Yet just before the blade met its target, an earthen vase exploded into pieces over the gypsy woman's head, and she fell to the ground, limp as a rag doll, eyes white and rolling upward in their sockets.

The girl, Saoirse had come up behind the would-be murderess and stuck her down, her eyes going out to Holmes while her breath came in panting gasps audible from several feet away. Staring at us, she burst into tears and ran off on her bare feet, finally crawling under one of the brightly painted wagons, where she rolled into a ball, sobbing wretchedly.

After the fall of the matriarch, the battle against the Irish ended quickly, and the police had the entire band, save the girl Saoirse, in shackles.

"Do forestall clamping that one in chains," Holmes had said to Welkirk, as he drew near to the wagon under which the girl cowered, "for I think you will find she is not of this tribe, but its slave, and that her unfortunate story will prove not unlike that of Barry Morley himself."

"She was herself taken by this heinous group?" asked Colonel Morley, who approached us now, panting, winded, but with his soldiering spirits in high form from the skirmish.

Holmes looked toward the cowering girl with something like tenderness in his eyes, the first such look I had seen from him since the morning of the attack back at Baker Street, and nodded his head.

"They took me from my family's farm in Cornwall last year," the girl said, gazing up, frightened.

"Those devils," Morley intoned.

I looked at her more closely now, and saw bruises covering her arms, and it struck me that the treatment she had doubtless received her at the hands of these criminal wanderers, thieves and much worse that they were, was surely appalling.

"Yes, poor child," I finally said.

As I stared at the dagger gleaming upon the ground, I reflected that twice in recent days women had nearly succeeded in killing Holmes, and yet today one of the fairer sex had also saved him. I hoped he might see this, and lose some of the harsh sentiments toward women that had descended onto him since the initial incident, for I did not approve of the distrustful statements about women he had recently made. Therefore I was quite cheered by what he said next.

"You saved my life with your action, Saoirse," Holmes told the child. "And for that I thank you, and shall see you done right by, and returned to your family in Cornwall. Now you can further help me by saving me the trouble of a search and pointing out which wagon holds the boy who was brought to these people in the night."

"The red wagon," she said, sitting up and pointing.

The Constable Sergeant, his eye already showing the bruising it would soon evince, nodded and went to the wagon with Colonel Morley walking swiftly beside him, as I knelt beside the injured constable on the ground, and set about examining his broken nose.

"You did not know yourself which wagon it was?" I asked Holmes, once we were together a little distance from the others, and I was feeling at the unconscious man's face in order to set his jaw.

"Of course I did," Holmes stated, "for I knew it was the one the men guarded most closely. The one I saw each of their eyes repeatedly go to."

"And yet you asked the child, Saoirse," I pressed him.

"The girl has borne many abuses, Watson, and there is empowerment in contributing to the downfall of a foe. I allowed her to tell me so that she might feel less powerless, as surely she does to a healing degree after striking down the witch-woman who was clearly her most ardent tormentor."

It had been an act of kindness then, on Holmes part, and I approved deeply of his show of concern toward this girl to whom he owed much indeed.

A moment later a bellowing outcry of sheer joy split the country air, and showed Saoirse's words correct, for inside the wagon, bound hand and foot, a rag over his mouth, his eyes red and puffy from crying, young Barry Morley had lain the entire time.

His grandfather soon had him free of his bonds, and a soothing banter spilled from him as he patted the boy's cheek to revive him, saying:

"Barry, my boy, you are all right now, lad...come on... wake up a little more...that's it. Let's get you home to your grandmother, and your bed."

"Grandfather, is it you?" the child asked sleepily, dazed.

"It is, my boy, it is I come at last with the help of these fine men, and you are safe!"

"I finally saw the ghost last night," the boy mumbled, "just before that man grabbed me and put the cloth over my face...I saw her...the lady in the yew alley..."

"There's a lad," Colonel Morley said, paying his grandson's claims no heed. "It's all well now, boy, as you're with me among friends and the law, and we'll soon have you home right as rain."

"She glowed, Grandfather," the boy said as a false sleep once again overcame him, "she glowed so very beautifully in the dark...."

I left the constable, who despite his injuries was standing and doing his best to shrug off his pains, and knelt on the grass beside where Morley had laid the boy down upon his own overcoat. His pulse was slow but regular, and I was relieved to tell the Colonel he'd soon he feeling more steady.

"He's plainly delirious," said the Colonel. "Poor child had so wanted to see the family ghost that he'd let himself be misled by the venal and horrid housemaid, Ada, and even now in his dreams he speaks of what I suppose never truly was."

"Plainly," said Holmes, who stood a moment looking on, before walking over to offer the other child present, Saoirse, a drink of water, and speak with her in low, gentle tones, much as one might a skittish horse.

Half an hour later Barry Morley was awake and walking on his own power, and I looked closely into his eyes and asked him to follow my finger as I moved it about. I asked him several questions about himself and his treatment by the gypsies, one of which I whispered in his ear and felt relief when he answered in the negative, for no child in the world deserved an ordeal such as the one I feared may have been his, yet all too many endured just such vile assaults, I knew.

Two of the constables went off to bring up the police wagons, while the others stood guard on the gypsy band, whom Constable Sergeant Welkirk had ordered to sit upon the ground, pending transport back to the station.

Reviving slowly from her injury, her coal black eyes bleary and focused only on Holmes, at whom she glared with a viperous intensity, the gray-haired matriarch began to venomously chant what I took for some arcane incantation:

Gun òl uisgeachan na mara thu sìos! Na sluig an talamh do chnàmhan agus nach spìon e a-mach iad gu bràth! Gum b' fheàrr le do nàimhdean thu, fàgaidh na friogais thu, bidh do luchd-gràidh gad bhrath. An losgadh agus an losgadh thu, nàmhaid mo chridhe!

"It'll take more than rhymes to daunt me, woman," Holmes told her with a laugh, "for if being cursed could kill a man, I'd have been in my grave long years before this, done-in by far more menacing villains than you."

He turned away and paid her no more heed, as the constables lead her and all her kind, three women, the remainder men (for I had heard of immoral polygamy being the norm among this kind) to the prison-wagon, and the rest of us went into another, bound for the Morley estate.

We were back in town in good time, and after we left the station, Holmes detoured a moment, bidding us wait for him, as he led Saoirse to an inn there, the Four Keys, and paid for her to have a room.

"Lock the door and wait for me here," he said to her, "and I shall soon return to obtain details from you of where you previously lived. I'll see you sent back home by train at first morning light."

It was a second and more unexpected righting of past wrongs connected to the Morley case, and as the sun was lowering in the west, we were back at the family house, Welkirk, the Colonel and Barry, Holmes, and myself.

Hearing the wagon pulling up outside, Mrs. Morley and her companion rushed outdoors, and upon seeing her grandson looking safe and returned home again, the Colonel's wife let loose a great cry, and ran to sweep the lad up into her arms.

"Barry, my little soldier-man," she sang out, "I was so wretchedly worried for you! I'll never let go of you now, I think!"

She half carried and half led the boy indoors, speaking of a warm bath and a filling supper before bed. At the doorway she paused and turned and smiled warmly while expressing a brief but clearly heartfelt thanks to Sherlock Holmes.

"You are a worker of wonders," she said, before disappearing inside her home.

Though his emotions were more contained, the Colonel likewise let loose a long breath where he stood beside the wagon, and reached out to shake Holmes' hand, and my own.

"Mr. Holmes," the Colonel boomed, "this is not the first time I have sought your aid, and never have you left me disappointed! You are a true wonder-worker as my wife has said, sir, and any reward I might offer, in addition to your fee, you shall have!"

Though I may have questioned the timing of what he was about to say, I saw Holmes' eyes go past the Colonel to those of Lieutenant Peters, who now stepped out from the house to stare at the assembly outdoors.

"Do not dismiss that man from your service," Holmes said nodding to the lieutenant, "for the loss of income would see him relocated elsewhere in search of employment, and his much-troubled wife would lose the safeguards I hope might soon be in place for her. Rather monitor him as regards his marriage. Look out for Mrs. Peters, and should your assistant continue violence against her, summon Welkirk, who shall deal with him in short order. Will you not, Sergeant?"

Welkirk, who had known nothing of any allegations of wife-beating, nonetheless took on a stern visage and replied:

"Most definitely I shall, Mr. Holmes, for I do not countenance any man's cruelty toward a woman."

"I thought not, as I perceive you were raised by a widowed mother, unless I mistake the signs, and know you have sympathies for women in general."

"I do at that, sir," the Constable Sergeant agreed, fixing a hard, albeit well-blackened, eye upon Peters, though saying nothing further.

I was cheered by these words, as I had hoped I sensed a lessening of my friend's anger toward both women in general and himself in particular, the latter for having let down his guard that fateful morning.

Yet he was not done, for to Peters he said in a serious tone:

"You have heard what has been said before you tonight, Lieutenant, and know that I, too, shall be keeping an ear open, for I have many sources, as you might imagine, and should I hear that you have resumed the persecutions of your spouse, I shall most assuredly deal with you."

It was a short declaration, but one that so dripped menace that Peters merely swallowed hard, his face flushing, and after an instant, he took to his heel and marched back inside the house.

Mrs. Morley took Barry upstairs, to see a bath run for him after a light supper, and put him to bed, where she promised him she'd stay in his room with him through the night.

Just before he left the drawing room where we were all assembled, however, Barry turned back, and to Holmes he asked in a small trembling voice:

"I was sure I saw the ghost among the yew shrubs last night, but you say it was just pretty Ada tricking me, sir? There never really was a ghost at all?"

"There was not," Holmes told him firmly but by no means unkindly. "For ghosts are merely stories, misunderstandings, and most usually, lies."

Somehow, even more than the relief that also occupied the boy's eyes, disappointment filled them more deeply still as he turned back to the hallway, and his now-silent grandmother.

"You have certainly done well by us, Holmes,' said the Colonel. "More than I could have asked."

But there a minute smile played out on Holmes' lips: a smile of anticipation.

"I do thank you, Colonel," he said, "and have seen your matter to its conclusion with the return of the boy, and the revelation of the faithless servant in your home, but, ah, I think you overlook the fact that the entirety of my work is not done."

"The perpetrator, Turner," Morley agreed. "The scoundrel who caused all of this."

"Indeed," said Holmes. "He yet eludes my net, though not for much longer."

"Clearly he is an audacious and daring foe," the Colonel said. "And while I cannot imagine he shall ever trouble us again, and surely shall know this house will never be his for any price, he remains at large, as you say. However will you be able to find and apprehend him, Holmes?"

"That plan, Colonel," the detective said, his smile broader now, the look of the hunter I knew so well writ large upon him, "is already fully-formed, and even now my net slowly begins to close around him."

With those cryptic words, which revealed no more to me than they had to the Colonel, Holmes accepted a cheque for his services, and we set off toward town in the Colonel's own carriage, conveyed by his driver, Watkins.

And now I must add a detail concerning an incident which I have ever-after struggled to explain, for ere I tell the remainder of what unfolded in this far-reaching case, I pause, strictly in the interests of truth and full disclosure, however you might receive what I shall write next, for as we set off into the blackness of the country night, Holmes and I, amid the sound of crickets chirruping in the grass, I happened to turn and gaze over my shoulder for one last look at the house which my friend had restored to happiness, and for the merest instant, like the after-flash in the eyes that comes after seeing a strong light suddenly shining out in darkness, I saw a glowing form, human-sized, human-like, golden and bright, not menacing, no, but sad, lonely, weak, and trapped, there and gone again faster than the duration of a blink, so rapid from its beginning to its end that I told myself perhaps I had never seen anything at all, yet I knew despite the doubts of rationality, it had been there, whatever it was, female and forlorn, hovering in the shadows of a deserted yew alley.

<><><><><><>

We returned to Cottersfield, to the Four Keys Inn, where Holmes had rented a room for the girl whom the gypsy matriarch had called Saoirse, and he asked me to go upstairs and check in on her, and have her come down and join us in a late supper, which I did, finding her timid, and worried about the eyes, and much pity did I feel for this child, stolen by people whose own lives embodied so much evil, and I tried not to think of the abuses she must have known ever since.

"You will be all right now," I promised her. "As my friend Mr. Holmes has said, we'll have you home again as swift as we can."

"Thank you, sir," she said simply, her little hands protectively folded together in front of her waist.

"You were very brave today," I told her, "and what you did there on that field this afternoon most likely saved Mr. Holmes' life."

She sat with us at table, and at first seemed reluctant to eat, but once she began, she ate heartily, and Holmes kept her plate filled, as he gently asked her questions about her family and the gypsies.

"Saoirse is the name your captives have set upon you," he said. "Tell me, what is it you are truly called?"

"My name is Rachel," said the girl. "Rachel Webber."

"Then that is what I shall call you," said Holmes, "and nevermore shall you ever hear that other name spoken."

And so young Rachel Webber told of being taken from her own bed in the night, through an open window on her family's farm, and carried off with a blade at her throat, and then turned into the servant of the tribe, with one of them, a tall red-haired fellow named Cathal, promising he'd have her for his wife in due time.

The girl trembled to recall this, and when she closed her eyes, I gave my head a little shake, telling Holmes he should ask her nothing further.

It was a horrid situation, and I wondered how many other bands of gypsies there were crisscrossing England, bringing such miseries onto the innocent.

"There is a nurse for hire in town," Holmes finally said at meal's end, "who enjoys an excellent reputation according to inquiries I have made, and I have sent for her. A kind woman, she will stay with you tonight, Rachel, and sit with you on the train to London, and from there upon a second train that shall take you to Cornwall, where she'll see you returned to your family."

"Thank you, sir," little Rachel said. Then a worried look came into her eyes, which had for a moment brimmed with happiness. "But, sir...what if they come back, and take me again."

Holmes looked steadily at the child and said:

"I ask you to trust me when I tell you, those villains shall not see freedom until long after you are a woman grown, and

I find it likely they shall one and all be expelled from England after their time in prison is done."

"Good," was all the girl said, though fear was still in her, alongside great relief.

The nurse, a plump and soft-faced woman called Mrs. Dowsey, arrived shortly after, and once she had spoken to Holmes, went upstairs with the girl, and I felt a happy warmth, knowing my friend had done right by the child.

"Goodbye, Mr. Holmes, Doctor Watson," Rachel said just before she vanished from sight. "And thank you."

"Child," said Holmes, "it is I who owe you my own thanks."

Yet when she was gone, everything changed.

"Now, Watson," Holmes said, a seriousness upon him, the fire I'd seen earlier blazing again in his eyes, "ours shall not be the delight of warm bed tonight, for much lies ahead. Are you with me?"

Though I was tired, and could never match Holmes' seemingly unending vigour while upon a case, I replied:

"Of course."

"Splendid," he said, "for in the interior world of my being, I have been diligently at work on our next step, and know my course of action."

"What shall that be?"

"Clearly our man, Turner, or by whatever name he goes, has had to spend some not inconsiderable time locally while setting his snare for the Morley child. I considered that he was staying with the gypsies, but as you saw, I looked inside each wagon, and discerned no traces that he had ever been there. Which left the probability of accommodations in town."

"And this is the sole inn!" I said excitedly.

"Precisely! He has been here, I'd stake a pound against a shilling on that!"

He sprang from his chair and approached the landlord, a Mr. Prescott, who was behind the bar wiping out newly-washed glasses in preparation for closing down for the night. He was a wide-shouldered man with a heavy mustache, and a part down

THE YEW ALLEY GHOST

the middle of his well-oiled black hair, probably dyed, I judged, for he looked well past fifty. I imagined he was a man who had laboured long to reach the point of owning the establishment, for I saw in his build old muscles, still strong from days of strenuous work.

Holmes was on him with his questions, asking if a man meeting the description we had of this suspect Turner had stayed beneath his roof.

"Normally I don't discuss my guests, a matter of confidence and privacy, you see," said the landlord, "but from what I overheard said to that girl at table with you, I think in this case good should better be served if I would, for I think you are a man about the work of justice, are you not?"

"I seek to right a deep wrong against a child and his family," said Holmes, to which the landlord's eyebrows raised, "and to reel in the villain who brought about this injustice, and stop him from committing other offenses of like kind, for he is, I have deduced, a man of great energies, who enjoys his plottings and his misadventures rather as a drunkard enjoys gin. He is ambitious, and does not scruple at upending the lives of others for his own amusements."

"I can tell you, then," said Prescott, "that the only guest meeting that description we've had here at Four Keys called himself Longbrook. Not like to forget him, sort of a strong-natured, memorable fellow, I'd say. Good-looking, with a deal of flash to him, if you like. Touch of American in his words, somehow, but just a bit."

"Interesting..." Holmes muttered, his eyes alive with the electricity of rapid thought.

The landlord turned the registration book around to us and pointed out the man's signature, which Holmes leaned close to and peered at for a longer time than I might ever have guessed a mere scrawl merited.

"There is much to learn from another's handwriting, Watson," he voiced, as if intercepting my thoughts. "See how he strikes his t's with such force, yet loops the bottoms of the letter 'y' with sloppy disregard for making its ends connect? Vigor and impatience! And this confirms all I have heard of this man, for he is an energetic type, filled with bravado, yet also somewhat careless, and confident to the point of being recklessly headstrong. Women are likely to be fascinated with the attentions and flattery of this schemer, but also to soon grow angry with him, and feel themselves mislead and ill-used, as we have seen with the maid who so readily gave him up under the mildest pressure. Which for our cause is all excellent, for a cautious man is apt to be wiser than a gambler, and one who long-holds the affections of a woman is less likely to be betrayed by her, as this fellow was by his paramour back at the Morley house."

"He promised Ada much, but would ultimately have delivered nothing," I said. "A villain in full, in other words," I summed-up.

"Quite."

Without asking for the landlord's leave, Holmes quickly and carefully tipped out a quantity of charcoal residue onto the space around the signature in the ledger, and nodded with satisfaction when several fingerprints showed up. These he soon lifted from the page using a strip of thinnest foil, which he dropped into a glass jar no larger than his thumb.

"His prints," he explained to Prescott, the landlord. "They will be unlike those of any other man in the entirety of the world, as are your own, or mine or Dr. Watson's here."

"Remarkable thing, that," Prescott said.

"From these," said Holmes, "I can now identify the fellow who stayed here, no matter what he may call himself, or by what disguise he should seek to conceal his appearance."

The landlord then offered:

"He stayed in room number four upstairs several times in recent weeks—"

"Always the same room?" Holmes interrupted to inquire.

"Yes, sir, always asked for it special, on account of the view out into the fields. In these parts on business, said he was, taking orders for roofing repairs on behalf of a company in Birmingham, and was back again this week, spending the last three nights here, but he left last evening with a jaunt in his step, I noted, and never returned. My daughter Molly, who acts as our maid here at Four Keys, knocked on the door to bring him up his breakfast tray, part of our service here, you see, and said his bed had not been slept in and all his possessions were gone."

"Indeed!"

The landlord shrugged. "Thought it odd, but none of my concern, I figured, how a guest conducts himself. He'd paid up to morning tomorrow in any case, so no loss on my part whether he was in the room or not, was how I figured it."

I nodded.

"Tell me, has Molly cleaned the room?" Holmes asked him, and I caught a hopefulness in his voice.

"Not as yet, since the man paid to tomorrow, as I said, and we don't intrude on a guest lest services are asked for particular, like."

"Mr. Prescott, I thank you, sir," said Holmes, "you have been of immense help to me in my cause. I bid you, though, might it be possible for me to see the chamber he previously occupied? This room four?"

Not waiting for a reply, Holmes set coins on the counter, paying for lodgings there, though I doubted he had any intention of spending the night within the Four Keys.

"I reckon no harm in that ambition," said the landlord, his bulging walrus mustache bouncing with the words. He did not touch the coins, though his eyes focused on them. "Just so you know, though, sir, I'd have said yes to the request without you needin' to pay for it."

"I know you should have," said Holmes, "and that is why I presented the money. A generous spirit is rare in this world, and deserves to be rewarded."

Only then did the landlord give him a grateful nod, and pocket the offering.

Key in hand a moment later, Holmes bounded up the

stairs and soon had room four opened.

"Careful where you step, Watson," he told me, "in fact stay back near the door, lest you disturb something I might find to be a clue."

"What are you looking for?" I asked.

"His whereabouts," Holmes answered stonily.

I let loose a little laugh and jested:

"Holmes I do not think you will find him concealed in this chamber."

"Oh, there you may be more wrong than you know, Watson!"

What? I had been joking but could there truly be some hidden chamber?

I gazed about the room and as I could see the entire space, even under the bed, and found it empty, I thought Holmes was barking up the wrong tree, but stayed back in the doorway as he instructed while he stooped low and slowly made his way across the room, the lens he'd pulled from his overcoat in hand and pressed up by his eye, methodically taking in its every board, wall, ceiling, and corner of what looked to me a tidy and well-kept little room.

"Does he know you are on his heels, Holmes?" I asked. "If so, might he have left some trap concealed here, in wait for you?"

"Unlikely, though I am proceeding with such an eventuality in mind."

Had he grown more cautious after the incident at Baker Street? I wondered.

Holmes continued to take in his surroundings for another long moment, before he turned to a small table with a single wooden chair before it, and then he let loose such a throaty exclamation of sheer glee that I admit I stared bemused before the sound of it.

"Holmes?" I cried.

"This is marvelous!" he shouted, so rapt by some discovery I think he was completely heedless of others in nearby rooms hearing his yell of exultation. "Look, Watson, the ash tray!

It is full!"

I did look over to see that several days of ashes lay within the unadorned tin dish, though how this merited the great detective's manic glee I could not understand.

"In such a well-attended establishment as this," he said delightedly, "I mark there is no possibility that the landlord would allow a new guest to find a dirty ash tray in his room, so these all must date to the time of our suspect's occupation!"

"Yes?" I asked, putting much confusion into the syllable.

"Ah, Watson, as you have never, despite my not infrequent encouragement, read the manuscript for my monograph *Upon the Distinction Between the Ashes of the Various Tobaccos* you fail to appreciate what a gold mine lies before my eyes."

He leaned toward the ashes, careful with his breath, I noted, lest he scatter them with each exhalation, and examined them first visually, then under a magnifying glass he still clutched, and finally, after removing a small microscope from within the portable chemistry case, in that manner as well, painstakingly brushing through the sample under the lens with a single toothpick.

"It is wonderful!" he cried. "More than I could have hoped for!"

"Yes?" I demanded.

He rose to his full height, suddenly transformed into the very image of beatific joy, like some saint upon a stained glass window.

"I'll have him, Watson," he smiled. "I shall definitely have him."

He thundered past me and galloped down the stairs toward the front door, case in hand, I at his heels, as ever the slower man of our pairing. Calling a farewell to the helpful landlord, he was almost instantly outside in the dark running toward the house of the man I knew to be the driver who had transported us to the Morley estate that morning.

As under the dark sky of night he knocked loudly and with rapidity at the man's door, I demanded of him:

"Well, are you going to tell me what it was you found in those ashes to merit such a display of manic exuberance?"

With a great smile beamed less at me than the world entire, Holmes threw back his head and barked out a laugh:

"It seems during his years in America, our man Turner acquired a preference for a specific variety of tobacco, and now shuns our domestic varieties in favour of a broadleaf grown in the commonwealth of Kentucky! I saw none other below my lens, and a most useful clue that was."

"Because…" I said aloud as I worked this matter out, "not every tobacconist would sell imported Kentucky broadleaf?"

"But a few, in fact outside London," said Holmes, "and none hereabouts in the countryside of Suffolk. No, I think Turner is to be found in the nearest city large enough to provide him with the fulfillment of his acquired vice, and yet be sufficiently close that it is not a thing of overbearing inconvenience to make frequent journeys to this little town by Morley estate he covets, so that he might oversee the unfolding of the cruel plot he has set in motion!"

"Norwich!" I cried.

"None other!" confirmed Holmes.

At that moment the door to the house opened and the face of the town's drive for hire peered out.

"'Tis after dark, gentlemen," he said, frowning, but with a civil enough tone in his words. "I keep daylight hours."

"Even for triple the fare to the station in Ipswich?" Holmes inquired, and enticingly held a bank note out before the man.

The man stared at the money with almost a physical hunger in his eyes, and said:

"I'll get my coat, and fasten up the team."

Back went we across the same country roads that we'd twice hastened down that day, though in the blackness, lighted only by a single lantern hanging out before the wagon, nothing seemed familiar to my eyes at all. The branches of trees, perhaps almost majestic in the sunlight now seemed like clawed hands, bedecked by talons, reaching down for us in the dark. To the driver's credit, he earned his exorbitant fee, and had us in Ipswich just before the clock struck midnight, and, duly paid, was on his way home again without an excess of words.

Within a few minutes, Holmes and I were aboard the final train of the night from Ipswich to Norwich, one county over, the city lights flashing past, to be replaced by more unbroken rural darkness, the interior of the train dim as well, and silent of the usual conversation of daytime hours, the main noise the clacking of the wheels on the tracks below. I had to battle a sense of drowsiness that threatened to come upon me in such an environment.

"I do not think we will find any tobacco shops open before eight at the earliest," I said, "so why the haste tonight?"

"I doubt not that Turner is keeping an ear out for how his plan unfolds back in Cottersfield," Holmes claimed, "and though he may not yet have heard of the arrest of the Irish gypsies, or the return of young Barry Morley from the slavery that should have been his fate, he shall in short order, likely sometime on the morrow. After that, the world will be wide open to him, and he will flee elsewhere, probably back to America, his hopes dashed, his conspiracy foiled, and a new plot will take root to stimulate his mind and fulfill his ambitions, as I doubt not many others have before this. I think that is how he made his fortune, less by some lucky strike out in the broad spaces of America, but via his machinations at the expense of others."

"All with an eye to obtaining the estate he coveted as a boy?"

"Not entirely, though that would have fulfilled much in the heart of this confidence man and adventurer, for it would place him into a sphere of legitimacy in society's regard, and for all his audacity and daring, that is something he has heretofore lacked."

"So time is limited, then," I said, understanding.

"It is, and the moment I step out in Norwich, I shall be narrowing down the shoppes at which I shall inquire, and if luck be with me, Watson, I shall confront this doer of black deeds before the sun is far above the rooftops."

My friend's words would turn out to be a prophetic remark indeed...

<><><><><>

The train ride between the cities was not long in duration, being but a forty mile trip, though the late hour narrowed our options as to how to spend the intervening hours until dawn. I thought we were either to linger in Thorpe Station, or perhaps seek out a hôtel for a few hours slumber before the trials of the morning, but Holmes had an entirely different idea.

After obtaining a penny-directory of Norwich from a stand, he set off into the sleeping city which surrounded us in all directions, and announced:

"Come, Watson, tonight we walk!"

"With an eye to locating tobacconists?"

"Indubitably. Let us survey the area while we wait for the sun, for time is precious."

Armed with his guide and the map printed within, Holmes set off toward the city's main thoroughfare, and passed several tobacco shoppes, studying each a moment before discounting them via some qualifying equation carried out in his head.

"No," he muttered before one, "decidedly not prosperous enough to import tobacco from the subtropical fields of faraway Kentucky."

Before another he declared:

"A definite possibility, Watson, but the housing around it...I cannot see our man Turner residing hereabouts, however briefly he intends his stay in Norwich to be."

"Holmes, do you feel you know him so well that you can hypothesize as to where he might live?"

"I have formed a portrait, let us say, Watson, of his type, and can deduce with some acuity what such a man might undertake when about his existence, and what he would not."

"I see," I conceded as we walked on.

"Somehow I think you do not," Holmes said, challenging my statement. "Man is, by an almost invariable rule, a creature of habit, and is far less prone to originality in behavior than we might like to imagine. Give me a few germane facts about an individual, and I can reduce him to a member of a herd and tell you what he is likely to think, to do, to *be*. This Turner is not only no exception to this rule, but falls, I think, quite plainly into a very broad type, which for my purposes I dub 'the audacious criminal.' In perpetrating crime for the thrill of the act, he thus differs markedly from, say, one who commits wrongdoing out of some necessity, as would, let us say a starving man, or a penniless drunkard desirous of gin. In fact I would go so far as to note that all criminals, regardless of any other details which may be singular to them, invariably fall within seven categories, and once identified within one of these orders, proceeding against them becomes a more uniform matter."

"Fascinating," I admitted. "I had never thought of categorizing criminal behavior in such a way."

"Yes," Holmes mused in closing, "I really should compose a monograph on the subject one day, for I think it should aid police forces immeasurably."

We continued our progress through the sleeping city, coming to several shoppes of interest to Holmes. As we did so, I worried about being stopped on our perambulations and questioned by a suspicious constable, or perhaps encountering street thugs who surely prowled about at night no less here than in London, but Holmes proceeded with a buoyant and preoccupied confidence that I thought may well have dispelled all intrusions.

I followed along trying to hold myself up in a like manner, tired though I was by this time, and quite drooping with hunger: the penalty for accompanying a man who seemed to forget to rest or eat, or recall that anyone else had those needs. I had also learned almost from the start of our association, that though I was not lacking in vigour by the standards of most of my contemporaries, when upon a case, I could not match my friend's limitless energies.

After we had walked on for some not inconsiderable distance, Holmes paused to smoke, and remarked:

"I have marked two prosperous and entrepreneurial-minded establishments on this map, Pennyworth's, and Sutton's by name, as likely being worth a visit at first light, and as you see, in making our rounds tonight I have saved us several hours that would otherwise have been spent on the undertaking in the morning. I further noted another tobacconist, Howard's, on Price Avenue, that stands within the realms of possibility for supplying Turner with his uniquely-identifying preference."

"That is excellent," I said.

"Of course, and yet, Watson..." he began.

"Yes, Holmes, what is it?"

He thought a moment before finishing:

"And yet, my good Watson, my instincts, which I trust as a sailor does the sails above him, tell me I have not yet located our target."

"Have you anything upon which to base this?"

"I have not, and yet..."

Holmes once again removed the map from his pocket and studied it, for unlike London, wherein I knew he could call to mind the details of every alleyway from Seven Dials to Grosvenor Square, Norwich was not so precisely known to him.

"King Street is a possibility...yes," he muttered at last. "The area is one I could see Turner occupying, judging it worthy of his pretentions, for I'll wager he owns himself to be a man equally at home in the rough conditions of the American West, or among things of a finer nature now and again. And, ah, I now see there is listed a large and fine tobacconist there, one Spencer and Son, near some fine properties available for short-term lease. I cannot say why it is, Watson, but at times my instincts veritably sing out to me, and though I cannot always justify this testimony by any logic, I have profited much in the past by heeding its call."

"So to King Street then?" I asked him.

"At once!" he agreed.

Scenic even in the dark, parts of it quite Medieval, other sections modern and pricey, King Street sprawled silently around us, its cobbles wide and old, true cut stones instead of the cheap brick underfoot in much of London, and I found my tired jaws yawning just as the clock struck the last hour before dawn.

"Five o' clock," I muttered.

"The final hold of night," Holmes affirmed, and I noted that somehow he sounded even more vigorous than he'd been before we'd started our explorations of nocturnal Norwich.

We located the shoppe Holmes had remarked upon, and peered in through its great front windows to a display area decorated with elaborate pipes and smoking jackets and the accoutrements of its prosperous proprietor's trade. I also saw with leaping heart, for it seemed a significant detail, that there was a wooden statue of an American Indian in the lobby, right inside the door. It was as tall as a figure from life, dressed in carven buckskins, and with a vast headdress full of feathers above a stern visage and hard wooden eyes. *Chief Red Owl*, read the name carved by its moccasin-clad feet.

"Look, Holmes," I cried, "surely seeing the trappings of western America like that would appeal to Turner in some way, owing to his time spent there, for I have heard cigar stores there often display carvings of Indians in just such a manner!"

"*Yes*," Holmes drawled with keen satisfaction, "he comes here, Watson. I have no evidence to support my suspicions, but tell you all the same that my theory shall shortly be proven true."

"I do not doubt you," I said my flagging spirits bolstered above my bone-deep weariness.

"And look, Watson," Holmes added, "again fortune stands with us, for the owner is an early riser."

He pointed to a notice-board against the glass of the door, which gave the shoppe's opening time as seven rather than eight, or even the nine 'o clock hour that some London proprietors gave.

"How wonderful!" I said. "Time shall be with us!"

"A distinct advantage," Holmes called it.

And so it was, but the time for the owner's arrival seemed to extend out like days, until at last I spied a gentleman in gray tweed, sportily dressed, almost dapper, coming toward us down the way, a brass-topped ebony-wood walking stick in hand, which he tapped against King Street's great Medieval cobbles.

"Surely that's him," I said quietly.

"It is plain enough to the eye that he is a native of this city, married, for he, of course, wears a ring, is a near-constant smoker of cigarettes, for there is the tell-tale yellowing of the fingertips that practice produces, and look, he holds a half-smoked cigarette now. I further see he is a lifelong player of cricket, for I note the callus between his right thumb and forefinger, which long involvement in the sports leaves almost like a trademark. Furthermore he sleeps on the right side of a double bed directly below a broad window, which is often left open at night, though not, I think, due to his own preference, but rather a concession to his wife, who perhaps suffers from claustrophobia."

Exactly how Holmes deduced these last declarations merely from the approaching man's person I was never to know, for when this fellow spied us standing outside his shoppe's door, he became the very soul of the merry proprietor, calling over as he approached in a bouncing stride:

"How now, gentlemen, is it the case that you find yourselves out of tobacco so early in the morning, and do not wish to face the day smoke-less?"

He gave a little laugh at his own wit, and came near, his smile bright and jolly as he pulled a ring of keys from his pocket.

"Indeed, my most excellent fellow," Holmes replied, "I am but a visitor in your fair city and have a preference for a variety of tobacco which I am given to believe you carry?"

The man unbolted the door and pushed it wide before stepping back so that we, his first customers of this bright and early morning, could enter before him.

"I doubt that not, sir," he replied with his rolling East Anglican accent, "for I have made it a point of honour to carry a great variety of man's noblest plant, as you shall see if you look around you."

He did not lie, for along the walls of his broad and airy establishment were many shelves, all well-made of oak, and deeply varnished, telling of the money that had been invested in such a shoppe. I judged there must have been a hundred types of tobacco, more than was carried by plenty of noteworthy London stores I had visited, and I wondered whether he was the father or the son the sign outside spoke of.

"And what sort of tobacco is it that tickles your fancy this morning, sir?" he asked, once he had placed his coat upon a stand at the far end of the room, behind the counter.

"I seek a fine Kentucky broadleaf," said Holmes, "cultivated in the Bluegrass region, and most ideal for a relaxing smoke."

"Ah, yes, indeed, my good man," answered the proprietor, pleased to hear of the request, "you were not misinformed, for I have just such a high-quality variety which I import through a brokerage in Paris, Kentucky, in the Bluegrass hills of that corner of ever-sprawling America. Each plant is carefully nurtured throughout its growth under the warm, even rainfall of that state, which permeates the limestone below the rich southern soil, fed by a degree of sunlight so perfect, the result has never failed to please even the palate of the most refined connoisseur such as yourself!"

Holmes nodded, seeming satisfied, and ordered a quantity of the prized commodity, and paid the rather steep price asked for it, then opened the tin and sniffed deeply, before giving what I felt was an honest sigh of approval.

"It is a masterpiece of cultivation!" he declared at last, making the proprietor break out with a wide grin.

"I am pleased that you find it so, sir," the man stated, appearing happy indeed.

"And now," began Holmes, "I think there is one other

matter with which you might be able to help me today."

"Indeed?" said the man affably and with no small curiosity. "If I can, sir, I certainly shall."

"My friend here and I are newly up from London, arriving just yesterday, and were told much about you and this fine city, by an acquaintance of ours, who is the only soul known to us in the entirety of Norwich. He, too, smokes excellent Kentucky tobacco, and was in fact the very individual who suggested that were we ever here, we should call upon you."

"I am grateful the gentleman thought me worthy of such a recommendation," said the man, humbly. "I do strive to please all my customers, and leave them with a favourable impression."

"Seeing as he is a customer of yours," Holmes continued, "we thought you might know him and could direct us his way. We, I must admit, have lost track of him in the time he has been here, and would be most interested in paying him a call while we are here in Norwich, which I dare say would be a very great surprise to him, indeed."

I alone caught the ironic humour in that last remark.

"That does sound like it would pleasant," the man agreed with a nod. "What is your local acquaintance's name?"

"Ah, better still, let me describe him," said Holmes dancing around the name, as he knew it was likely Turner called himself something different. He gave a detailed description, the one provided by Ada, and before he was done, the tobacconist was nodding forcefully, his polite smile even brighter.

"I know just the fellow!" he confirmed. "You are surely referring to Mr. Herrington, of Tanner Alley, just off King Street here, not four blocks up. A fine chap he is, Mr. Herrington, and an excellent customer. Why the stories he tells me of his life, young though he is, I declare, sirs, they do so dazzle, being about America and—"

But having gotten what he came for, Holmes did not invest further time in listening, and instead strode quickly toward the door, not thinking upon his rudeness, leaving me to call over apologetically to the bewildered tobacconist:

"We thank you, sir, but as you see, my friend is in quite a rush to see our acquaintance, he..."

As I did not know how to finish, I, too, hurried out of the shoppe, feeling awkward at the way we'd repaid the man's geniality with brusqueness.

"Tanner Alley, just off King Street!" Holmes cried. "So near to our quarry these past two hours! Hurry, Watson, keep up, there is not a moment to be lost when Turner might learn of matters at any instant through one of many means."

And hurry I did, but drew no closer to my onrushing friend than half a block, his Ulster trailing him in his extreme haste. He located Tanner Alley, and dashed onto it, and as I turned a corner, I saw him halt before a door to a residential structure through which a businessman of advancing years was exiting. Pushing into the door before the other man could close it, and eliciting an outcry of disapproval from the fellow, Holmes burst into the building, and I heard him stomping up the stairs, and only just caught the door in my own hands before it was shut.

"Beg pardon!" I called to the older gentleman as I passed him with much rudeness, but did not wait to hear his reply as I likewise sped up the stairs, my side aching but my tiredness momentarily dispelled by my urgency and excitement, for surely we had closed-in upon Turner at last.

There was a great crashing sound ahead of me, and I mastered the final set of stairs in time to see Holmes shoving through a doorway that marked the left-hand flat on this, the fifth and highest floor of the building.

Had he truly shouldered his way in? I marveled.

Seconds later I too was in inside the flat, aware we had broken and entered into a private dwelling, but trusting Holmes must have had his reasons, as indeed he had, for he cried out to me, even as he was making his dash toward an open window above the street some sixty feet below:

"The instincts of this man are keen, Watson, for somehow he was tipped to our coming, and I heard him making his flight out this window, and toward the rooftop!"

"And so you shoved through his door!" I confirmed.

Holmes hefted his way out the window and onto a metal fire-stairway bolted in place there, and I lost sight of him as he vanished like quicksilver up the clanging steps, I close on his heels, my breath coming rather hard, but was only in time to see the swirl of his coat tails as he took to the roof, eyes now on his target.

Across the roof itself, Turner was fleeing, Holmes directly after him, until his quarry leaped atop the yard-wide ledge which encircled the building, and dropped down from its farther side, Holmes doing exactly the same. I ran across as well, stepping up onto the ledge and lowering myself onto a second metal staircase affixed to the building's distant side, and followed the pursuit I spied underway several yards below, proceeding down this staircase just as previously it had been run up the other.

Turner was now mid-way down this second set of fire-stairs, Holmes hot on his heels, one landing behind, and yet his next action startled me greatly, for instead of re-entering the building through a window, as might be expected, Turner leapt flat-footed up onto the metal railing at the staircase's outer edge, barely an inch wide, landing with precision, and there he stood perfectly balanced still thirty feet above the alleyway.

At once, Holmes stopped and stood in place, staring expressionlessly at the other man, two arm's length between them. As for me, I felt my heart freeze, for I saw that in his desperation, this Turner intended to make a leap toward the far side of the alley, where one floor down a sort of balcony lay jutting from an adjoining building at least ten feet away.

It was clearly too far for one to leap.

Turner paused balanced on the rail under his feet, and Holmes for his part drew no closer to him from where he stood on the stairwell itself, his footing much more sound.

When Turner shifted so he was facing his purser, to my surprise I saw it was a vast smile that he wore on his young and handsome face, quite suntanned and with an easy charm in his every aspect.

"How's that for a lucky leap up onto this railing?" he asked, genially.

"It is the best I have yet seen," replied Holmes.

"I think I know who you are," Turner said in a conversational tone, his accent partly that of America, partially that of his native England, a strange but not displeasing mixture of the two dialects, representing the best of each. "You are, I think, that Mr. Sherlock Holmes, of London, the detective I have read so much about of late since coming back over here, whose adventures I have enjoyed so thoroughly."

"I am the same," Holmes confirmed, and I thought what a strange conversation this was, one man balanced like a tightrope walker on a narrow handrail still a dozen or more yards above the alleyway below, the other standing a little a distance off, seemingly content to stay there and speak a moment.

"I thought so," said Turner, "because you fit the description. When I happened to see you coming down King Street, all quick and sneaky, while I was fixing to fry up some bacon for my breakfast, I got a flash as to why you were here, and lit out, like you see. But not quite fast enough, it looks like."

"That is why you fled," Holmes inquired, "because you happened to see me? You were not tipped off?"

"Who would tip me off?" Turner asked. "I keep my associates at arm's length. Not sure how you found me, and somehow I doubt you're going to tell."

"It was through your tobacco ash back at the Four Keys Inn, in Cottersfield," Holmes replied, causing Turner to raise an eyebrow.

"Well that doesn't explain much," he laughed.

"Perhaps you'll have time to read my monograph on the subject while you are languishing in a well-deserved prison cell," said Holmes.

"I wouldn't take odds on my ending up in any prison," Turner said with a boast that somehow still ended up sounding friendly enough in his cockiness. "I always keep a few extra cards up my sleeve."

"You are not as skilled an opponent as you think yourself to be," Holmes told him levelly. "If you had not by chance spied my approach, I should have had you in the flat."

"Yeah," Turner agreed, "I just caught a break there, but that's the way I am, lady luck's with me as a rule. The stories I could tell about my luck would fill a magazine in themselves. I escaped a furious mother bear once out in Colorado. Another time I talked some Cheyenne out of taking me prisoner. Had the wife of the mayor of Kansas City fall in love with me just from my smile. And I once won a carriage off a riverboat gambler down near Natchez while playing with his own crooked deck. Sure, I'm a rogue, but my fortune is made in the stars. My, oh, my, I am living quite a life."

He paused his boastful musings and said:

"Guess you know my name, don't you?"

"You are Turner," confirmed Holmes, "late of America, originally a wanderer of our own island here, in the company of your father, an engineer, whose travels took him across the nation."

"That'd be me," Turner answered, and to my utmost shock, I saw him, still balanced on the handrail with a jaunty air, remove a cigarette from a gold case in his pocket, and set about smoking."

"Kentucky tobacco, I perceive," Holmes stated.

"Only the best. Got a taste for it over there, you see," Turner confirmed.

"Then I think I shall join you in partaking," Holmes stated, dipping into his own pocket. After a moment he had rolled out a cigarette, and in a truly bizarre spectacle, smoked along with the man from where he stood.

"Now you'll be spoiled," Turner laughed, "and never want to go back to plain old tobacco anymore!"

He was an exceedingly self-confident young man, I thought, and yet I despaired of anyone maintaining footing on such a small surface for long. A fall from the height would surely be fatal.

"Why don't you step down from there?" I urged.

He looked at me and a grin soon occupied his face.

"And you'd be Dr. John Watson," he said, "writer of those stories about Holmes." He gestured at me with his cigarette and said, "Pleased I am to make your acquaintance."

"I wish I could say the same," I replied.

To this he only chuckled, showing no shame, no fear, no hurry. Such a friendly if audacious sort he seemed, entirely out of keeping with the brooding villain I had expected. He was, I felt, a taker of risks, as Holmes had said, but I was not prepared to find such a daredevil as this.

"You took the Morley boy," Holmes said simply, as if discussing the weather.

"That I did," Turner confirmed. "couldn't see any other way around it."

"You make light, sir, of a vile misdeed," I charged.

"Well," Turner said ruminatively, "history is full of ambitious men and those that get shoved aside in their pursuit of what they want. I'm no exception to the type."

I recalled how smitten he had rendered the maid Ada back at the Morley household, and began to understand how such a man might hold great appeal to women, yet also realized such a man as he would see women as there for his own use, to be bent to his will as pawns in his machinations. Oh, he was a scoundrel, I knew, but an exciting one to know, I doubted not.

There were not yet many out upon the street, not at this early hour, but from the all-but deserted alley below I heard a woman gasp and looked down to see her pointing upward, one hand over her mouth, in shock.

Turner waved down at her with a grin, and as he did, I noted his balance on the railing did not alter. Seeing my noting this, he said:

"When you've climbed as many mountains as I did across the ocean, you learn how to keep a solid footing. Don't be worrying about me there, Doctor, I am not going to accidentally fall."

Accidentally, I noted.

Holmes, who had made no effort to approach Turner, now said:

"You know, of course, however pleasant it may be for you to show off your skills as you have a smoke with me, I must bring this matter through to its necessary conclusion, however it is fated to unfold."

I did not detect regret in his words, but there was something like a grim truth in his statement.

"That seems the situation," Turner agreed. "You caught me flatfooted this morning, and the shame is mine. Another hour and I'd have heard about you on the case, and lit out for America and not been back for years, and then under a new identity, whole new ball game, as they say, but you got the jump on me."

He tossed his half-smoked cigarette toward the alley and watched it fall to the cobbles.

"What now?" I asked, though I was unsure as to whom I addressed.

"Yeah," said Turner, "that's the big question, isn't it, Doc?"

"It is," agreed Holmes, "and the choice I leave to you. Submit to me, or gamble upon a highly uncertain outcome."

"Step down!" I urged, sensing the matter racing now toward a conclusion I knew could go very wrong. "Let us take you to the police. You'll be given fair treatment."

Turner laughed. "You have to admit, 'fair treatment' doesn't favour me much."

He looked across the alley at the distant balcony a floor below on the other building and noted:

"I make it a ten foot leap, and a story drop after that to reach the other side."

"Which even then shall not be a conclusion to the chase, but only its continuation," Holmes doggedly promised, tossing the remains of his own cigarette down into the alley.

"And even if you make it, you may be too injured to flee far on foot," I told him. "Medically, I can say you are more likely to shatter bones in landing on the balcony than to walk away unscathed."

I swallowed at the thought and added:

"In my estimation, it's probable you shall miss your mark and plunge to your death."

Turner did not reply for a moment, but stayed poised on his perch, his body ramrod straight, almost like some Greek statue of a proud warrior-youth.

"Yeah," he said, sounding more the American at that moment, "that seems the situation, doesn't it?"

I felt some relief to hear him agree, but lost the comfort when he added:

"But as Mr. Sherlock Holmes could tell you, I've always been a gambler."

I watched with horror so profound that an involuntary shout left my lungs, as with those words, Turner leapt outward from a flat-footed pose, flinging himself through the air, arms reaching, sailing like an arrow in human form.

Holmes looked on impassively, and said:

"Unwise."

Yet what happened next was unexpected and amazing, for Turner cleared the distance and reached the far-off balcony, though as he landed with a roll, his trailing foot clipped the railing there, and he fell violently forward, his impact audible even from where we stood.

There was a pause which seemed interminable as I stood riveted and staring, til finally Turner rose, his breathing hard, the life or death thrill heavily upon him, and he grinned back at us with a carefree audacity, and gave a wave as he yanked open the doorway there and disappeared, but not before I noted he was limply badly.

"Holmes," I called, as my friend broke into a run down the fire-stairs, "I think he has broken a foot in his landing."

"I mark the same!" Holmes noted.

"He will not move quickly now!"

And so this proved true, for we had no sooner reached the cobbles of the alleyway and turned the corner to the fore of the building opposite, when we saw Turner sitting there on the outside stairs, lighting another cigarette, one leg outstretched, calmly waiting.

When we appeared, he raised his hands, palms upward in a self-deprecating gesture and announced without obvious rancor:

"Took a bad landing, as you saw, and find I can't walk much beyond a limp, so no sense in trying to run off from the likes of you, Mr. Holmes. I'd have made it, though if I hadn't gotten busted up just then."

To me he added:

"I think something shattered good and hard in my foot, Doc. You mind taking a look?"

He flipped a coin to me for my services, which without thinking I caught in mid-air, then tossed it back to him.

Turner laughed and to Holmes he announced:

"Your prisoner now, sir."

"Indeed you are," Holmes agreed, "as I promised."

As I had given my oath to heal where I could, I did take it upon myself to kneel and lift the roguish criminal's swollen foot gently into my hands. I saw at once from the angle that he had incurred a bad break, and told him so, yet despite my inner condemnation of the crimes this darkly charming man had authored, I told him:

"That was the most courageous and foolhardy leap I have ever seen. I never would have imagined it could be made."

Turned basked in this praise, though I read much pain in his eyes.

"Funny what desperation will drive a fellow to do, isn't it, Doc?" he asked me.

"You hit upon the story of the ghost and shaped it to your plans," I said.

"I did," Turner agreed. "Worked well, too, up to the point

your friend there got called in. Yesterday morning that would have been, I reckon?"

"Almost from the first," Holmes told him, as a small crowd gathered around the scene, and I knew it was only a matter of time until a constable appeared to see what was the cause of the conglomeration.

"And the gypsies? Your confederates?" Holmes inquired.

"Old friends from my boyhood, those. Always did like their sort. Useful, because they know a lot more about what's going on than most people would credit, since they travel and see everything while they do."

"Utterly true," Holmes agreed. "I have often used them, myself. But they failed to penetrate my disguise before it was too late, and I retrieved the boy from their clutches, and saw all your associates, them and the house-maid you left so smitten, in irons before sundown."

"*All* my associates, you say?" Turner replied with a mysterious grin.

"A not unexpected boast, but you know no others remain at large," Holmes told him.

Odd, I thought, how my friend seemed to bear Turner less ill will than was usual in his apprehensions of the guilty. Was it possible he admired the quality of daring that was so clearly within him? My thoughts, though went backward and came to rest upon another matter.

"Mr. Turner," I asked, as I finished binding his foot with a makeshift bandage, "what made you seize upon the legend of the ghost instead of abducting the boy through other means?"

He looked at me with a degree of evaluation that seemed almost probing, then with a small smile answered:

"You saw her, too, out in the yew alley."

Holmes looked sharply at me, and though I wished I could say otherwise, and stand with my friend's confident belief that the supernatural did not inhabitant his reality of purest logic, I nodded.

Turned smiled and confessed:

"Then you might understand, that's why I wanted the estate. I saw the ghost many times as a boy that summer my father and I were there, and after a while it got so she didn't vanish as soon as she appeared, just stayed there floating near me in the dark, beautiful and serene and shy, and being the age I was, I fell in love with her. It was the most profound experience of my life. They got it wrong, you see, in saying there is only the ghost of a scoundrel from the Middle Ages, because if there is one like that, I never saw him, no, just that beautiful and lonely lady I've spent every day of my entire life thinking of, and wanting to see again."

Holmes frowned then, a deep, grave, and final judgment on Turner and his account, and the supernatural as a whole.

But as for me, I remembered what I had glimpsed for that merest instant the night before as we'd left the estate, and the sense I felt radiating out from the apparition, if indeed apparition it had been, was much as Turner had said, so despite myself I understood how the experience could have had so deep an impact on a boy of just the right age to feel such things, and how such a memory might continue on, even in the man Turner became.

Poignant and tragic, I judged it all.

My thoughts were interrupted when Turner called:

"The police at last."

He gazed past Holmes and me, beyond even the gathering crowd, where a blue-uniformed constable was approaching with an uncertain expression on his whiskered face.

"Now," Turner said, almost with amusement, "we'll see how my luck holds in court, for a good lawyer, gentlemen, can work true wonders. Might be I walk free after all this yet."

"Not after my testimony," Holmes boasted back.

"Then it'll be a contest between us," Turner replied.

He released a hearty laugh, tinged with pain, and nodded a goodbye to us both, as the constable elbowed through the crowd, and reached us with an inquisitive stare.

<><><><><><>

After giving our statements at the police station, and leaving Turner in their custody to roll the dice on the expertise of lawyers, Holmes and I were soon at Norwich-Victoria Station, to catch a London-bound train.

"Watson, I have had more than enough of pristine East Anglia," my friend said, "and look forward to nothing so much as a return to the familiar grime of London."

Tired as I had been throughout the night, I found that sleep was elude me on our two hours' journey back to the south, my thoughts returning to what I believed I had seen in the yew alley, and Turner's claims concerning his experiences with it. And then there was young Barry Morley's words on the subject as well, his assertion that he was seeing the ghost even as his abduction unfolded. So what *was* the truth...?

Thus I sat in the compartment with Holmes, more wide awake than I wished to be as verdant fens, brimming with herds of spotted dairy cows, sped by, and across from me the masterful detective smoked contentedly, returning from the elevated energies the case had brought to him.

I knew the slumber I needed was to prove in short supply when I returned home to 221B Baker Street, as I had a patient to see in the afternoon, and a pleasant obligation I had to fulfill that evening, escorting Miss Mary Morstan, toward whom I had come to harbor deep feelings, out to dinner.

It was as I brought to mind the woman who would become my first wife, that I finally put my thoughts into words, and broached a subject which had lingered in my head throughout this case, indeed ever since the morning of the attempt on my friend's life.

"Holmes," I began, "it is true a woman nearly took your life earlier this month, but I believe your self-anger over having failed to foresee her intentions has hardened your heart toward all women in general. Yet I remind you in Suffolk, a young woman likewise *saved* you when the gypsy matriarch would surely have stabbed you through the back. Does not one deed in some fashion nullify the other, and ease your sentiments, at least that much more?"

Holmes inhaled from his pipe and let the smoke linger long in his lungs, before he answered:

"Women have their natures, Watson, and it does not do for me to disregard this truth. Yet I confess, for me to hate the fairer sex for doing what comes naturally to them is likewise a shortcoming on my part, and a disservice to women as a whole."

"So you have softened the harsh regard you seemed to evince after the incident at Baker Street?"

"No, Watson," Holmes said carefully, "rather I have come to recognize a valuable truth arising from recent matters."

"Which is?" I demanded.

"That a woman," he said leaning toward me, utter seriousness in his every word, "is every bit as dangerous as a man, and both warrant the same caution."

I stared at him a moment, then turned away, and looked again out the train window.

THE CONTINUING CHRONICLES OF SHERLOCK HOLMES

THE ADVENTURE OF THE ARTFUL DODGER

C. THORNE

THE ADVENTURE OF
THE ARTFUL DODGER

My working day having been completed in rather rewarding fashion, discovering that a case of measles had left my young patient little worse for wear, I took longer than was my usual wont on that lovely afternoon to walk about Paddington Street Garden, before heading home to 221B Baker Street, where I shared a residence with my esteemed friend Mr. Sherlock Holmes.

I was in particularly high spirits that day, for I was very much a man in love, and was in fact due to wed Miss Mary Morstan in about a fortnight's time. As such I beamed my delight out at the world, my walking stick tapping out a frolicking tune against the pavement underfoot, my medical bag swinging in time to my steps, and all in all life was more than fine on that pleasant day I call now to memory.

I entered my lodgings to the smell of a shoulder of mutton simmering away in Mrs. Hudson's kitchen, the sun streaming in the windows behind me. Ah, nothing was wrong whatsoever that day, and how I treasure simpler times such as those as I think back on them now from some years distant.

I entered the parlour upstairs, and walked in on Sherlock Holmes sitting in his favoured chair in apparent consultation with a gentleman of some years, who had his back turned to me as I came upon a scene that was not entirely unusual at Baker Street, where would-be clients came regularly to consult with Holmes on various matters, some departing satisfied by Holmes' counsel without their ever having left the room, others turned away by Holmes himself, but the majority enlisting his aid toward solving whatever puzzling matter had brought them forth to our corner of London.

"Ah, my dear Watson," Holmes called with an uplifted note as I shut the parlour door behind me, "you arrive just in time, for it is a fortuitous hour."

"Glad to hear it," I answered, setting my leather bag on a table just inside the entryway, and placing my walking stick, gift from my family upon my completion of medical school, into the stand just beside it.

The elderly gentleman was well-dressed and somehow sharp about the eye, as I was soon to see when he turned to face me with a polite nod, and Holmes said:

"In point of fact, Watson, you and I are in the presence of royalty here in our humble abode."

"Of royalty?" I quizzed, taking in the visitor's appearance with a more careful eye, for though I had noted he was well-dressed, nothing I espied there indicated royalty, and as I wondered what nation was represented by the figure across from me, Holmes was soon to clarify his remark.

"Royalty is a term that might encompass many degrees,

Watson, for I have long heard of this gentleman, more infamous in his youth than in the years following his reformation. May I introduce you, Doctor John Watson, to Mr. Jack Dawkins, in another age once known across London in tones of awe as the Artful Dodger, pickpocket extraordinaire. In his heyday his skills in that regard, I do not find any shame in confessing, quite exceeded my own in the present."

"Indeed?" It was all I could think to say.

The elderly gentlemen, Mr. Dawkins, rose and extended a hand.

"Dr. Watson, it is a most keen pleasure to make your acquaintance."

"And I yours, Mr. Dawkins," I replied, though it certainly felt peculiar to be speaking so to he whom Holmes described as a one-time master pickpocket.

I noted a strong trace of Cockney in Dawkins' speech, perhaps not to be unexpected, though his words were quite modulated, with propriety in them. He was by no means a tall man, standing but perhaps five foot five, and exceedingly slender, charismatic if not precisely handsome, yet with a medical eye I noted those telltale signs of poor childhood nutrition that lingered among far too many, whatever their station in adult years. On his lapel, I saw, was a small decorative pin topped with a minuscule human hand done in gold.

Seeing me look at this, Dawkins explained:

"A little reminder of my beginnings, as it were, Doctor."

"I see," I said.

"Also," said this man, a wry smile taking over his face, making his pug nose wrinkle, "may I give you back your pocket watch?"

"My...?" I noted with alarm that my watch was indeed missing, and was in fact being held out before me in thin air, dangling by its chain from Dawkins' hand.

I quickly snatched the watch back, ruffled, though Holmes was laughing loudly with clear approval.

"Ah! You see, Watson, I tell you our guest remains a

master!"

"What can a bloke say?" Dawkins tossed at me with a twinkle in his eye, "Some skills a fella never loses."

That my watch had been stolen, however playfully, from off my person in my very own parlour, I did not find quite so amusing as did the other two men, though I supposed no harm had truly been done me, and it had been a demonstration done by way of a prank, so I made myself put it from my mind, however indecent it may have been.

"Watson," said Holmes, taking over matters now, "won't you have a seat, and listen in as Mr. Dawkins relates precisely why it is he has come calling on me today."

So I did just that, and took my place in the brown horsehair chair where I was so often to be found when I was a participant in these interviews. I made myself comfortable, as Holmes said:

"Now, Mr. Dawkins–though I confess I shall always think of you as the Dodger–do continue. You were telling me of your youth, as that relates to the matter at hand?"

"'deed it does, Mr. Holmes," this Mr. Jack Dawkins began, "for I was once, as you know, the most famed and skilled pickpocket of tender years across the whole of London, though back in the '30s this were. Just a wee little thing half the people around me barely noticed, elbow-high on a grown man–which I put to good use, let me tell you. I worked back then under a guv'ner who took me in off the streets, and not probably saved my life in doing, I admit. A father figure, you might say, name of Fagin, a right underworld king in his own right. Had a whole platoon of little pickpockets he'd train up to send out to the streets, and like faithful hounds we'd bring him back whatever all we took, and nothing there was in them times I valued more than a pat on the head from him when I'd done what he considered good work, and turned over some glittery cutter for his evil coffers."

Such a dreadful scheme for child-exploitation! I thought.

"'Dodger,' ol' Fagin would say, 'in all my born days I never seen the like of you, m'boy, and never will no more! Now run along and 'ave a slice o' Nancy's fresh spice cake!' When he'd say words like that, well, weren't nothing I wouldn't have done for that ol' chap. Nothing at all."

Here Dawkins paused and his eyes hardened as he vigorously shook his head.

"All rot, of course, for an evil man was he, knowing half of us were going to wind up with the Old Bill tossing us in the Stir, and he didn't care a whit about me or the lot of us, not in his heart, if he even had one, and not just some cold black stone in its place."

"Yes," Holmes concurred, "Fagin still finds his way into stray remembrances I have encountered in my career, for memory remains of his many years of operating his illicit empire of child-thieves from his lair above Field Lane, in Saffron Hill."

"A dirtier or more fetid den of iniquities one can scarcely imagine," Dawkins agreed, his eye turned inward with memory. "Yet I wanted nothing more than to fit in there."

"What became of this Fagin?" I asked, aghast at the notion of a criminal making use of children for such sordid purposes.

"Got himself hanged, didn't he?" Dawkins said, with a certain satisfaction in his voice. "And well he deserved it, and how."

At that moment I thought he somehow sounded a little like a child again, though how exactly I could not explain, for he was, of course, surely well past sixty.

"Course by then," Dawkins took his narrative up again, "I was well on my way to Australia, and never heard the news of his demise for many a year."

"Oh," I began, "you immigrated to Australia?"

"Of a sorts," Dawkins said lightly and with a self-deprecating chuckle.

"Mr. Dawkins was, in fact," Holmes reported, "transported for life to Australia, the result of criminal activities in his youth."

I raised my eyebrows, wondering if, like his one-time

master, this client was in danger of being hanged for his presence in England, for a transportation for life was no light matter, and it was generally death to return from it.

"It was not easy, I can tell you," Dawkins said by way of explanation, "but I received a pardon and so came back to London again at age four and thirty, some twenty-one years after I was sent away."

"How was that managed?" I inquired, knowing such reversals of fortune were rare in the greatest extreme.

"Through the most excellent good works," Holmes intoned.

"And a select bit of bribery," Dawkins admitted with a twinkle in his eye.

"I believe I shall focus on the 'good works'," I noted drily.

"I thank you, kindly, for that generous description," Dawkins stated, "and it's the truth, Australia changed me. I arrived in New South Wales an angry young boy who'd lost the only thing like a father he'd ever known, I speak of Fagin, of course, friendless, vengeful, sassy, and determined to take up the life of crime where I left off, and doubtless such a path would have led me to the noose I barely escaped in London, being out of second chances, with the ship's captain himself laughing in my face and telling me he'd lay a shilling next to a pound I'd swing down there within a month. But the thing was..."

He halted and for a moment lost himself in thought, though I for one was keen to hear the rest of this tale of moral reclamation.

"In fact when I arrived down there in that wild land, a hungry boy without a home to go to, angels themselves must've been on my shoulder, because I was soon to find a mentor there, of a far better nature than the one I'd tried so hard to please back in London. Met him by chance when I'd been scouting him out as a chump, meaning to dipper his pockets, still as good a fingersmith as ever, and instead found myself invited to sit and take a meal with him, such as it was, beans and toast, for he wasn't far from a poor man himself."

"An extraordinary path to come to in the road of life," I agreed, unsurprised that thoughts of divine intervention might have come into play in his mind.

"I agree," said Dawkins, "and fact was I tried to find the angle behind his kindness, because back then I couldn't imagine doing something for nothing. It was days before I realized that bloke truly was just offering a good turn, something I'd had scant experience with in my hard little life. A Mr. Stanley Arkwright, was his name, and Arky took me off to the gold fields with him, and I admit to my shame I consented to go because it not half sounded like just the spot to commit robberies there on the lawless frontier. Instead I found myself liking the miners, who went out into the stream and panned the gravel all day long under the blazing sun, tearing their hands up, not half freezing their ankles off, knowing every time they dipped the pan they might pull it up again a rich man. I liked them and they took a shine to me, a likely lad–for I'd learned well to be charming–and they'd get me to sing a song around the campfire, or show them a merry dance, or tell tales of my career back in London, and they'd laugh and tell me what a cheerful fella the Dodger was."

He cleared his throat and took a sip of the Ceylon tea which had been brought up before my arrival.

"One day I realized I never wanted to rob from them, no, I wanted to be free out in the wilds under that big blue sky, the heat high enough to like to fry the skin off your back, true, but there was no law out there, and no temptation to do wrong among men who'd taken me in like one of the bunch, just a clean start among blokes all trying for that same thing. So I became like them, though I was just a boy, and panned for gold out in those freezing rivers sun-up to sundown, day in and day out, couldn't even tell you what day of the week it was, cause it didn't matter out there where they all run together, like, with no church to go to, no work to show up for, just the same sort of life day after day."

He looked from Holmes to me, and announced:

"And I loved it."

"So you struck it rich in the gold fields?" I asked.

"Not hardly," Dawkins said, "few do, and that's the hard truth. Maybe one in a thousand. Not one in ten breaks even. Dreams are what it's all about out there, the attraction."

"I see," I said, though I was no closer to enlightenment in that regard.

"Rather I saw an opportunity by catching on to what Arky and the other people settling out in the bush needed, which was someone quick to run errands for them, go to town, bring things back, to carry, to cook, and so I started up with that, and they'd pay me what they had, which wasn't likely to be money, just food and goods I could trade for other items. I lived hard and saved my cutter, and one day bought a mule, ol' Jezebel, half broke down she was, but I loved her despite that, and with her help I doubled my route. Then I bought another, mule, Charlie, then four more. Soon I hired another boy who come along, an orphan, Skinny Jimmy Harvey, he was called, and within two years I opened a little store out of a canvas tent, selling what was needed out there. Two more years and I had a real store in the town that grew up nearby, Barlow Springs, it came to be called, rising up from the ground itself when there hadn't been nothing at all out there before in the wild bush."

"So you were an entrepreneur, then," I said, as Holmes sat silently listening to all of this.

"Yes, indeed, Doctor, I seemed to have the same talent for business I once had for stealing, and made money hand over fist. I invested it right well, too. By the time I was twenty I was well-off indeed, and by twenty-five I was rich by the standards of those parts, even making short-term loans to others and getting back a fair return, better than any bank would pay. I saw Arky buried with a first-rate funeral when he passed in time. Once or twice when folk couldn't pay, blokes would come to me on the sly and offer to do strong-arm work and shake the money out of those as was behind on their repayment, but I'd had enough of that sort of life and told them to be off. If that meant a time or two I never got re-paid, well, that's what it meant, I was done being a criminal. The boys what run with me back in London would never have believed it, nor would I in those times. Instead of calling me Dodger, people started calling me Mr. Dawkins, and the best men in the town would tip their hats in acquaintance with me, nobody down there caring how a fellow got his start or whether he come over free, or transported as a criminal."

"A much more equitable-sounding place than here," I admitted.

"And tell Watson what you did with those riches," pressed Holmes, in tones that fell not far from admiration.

"Well, a man can only spend so much on himself, can't he, whatever else catches his eye, and so I saw there was hardship all about, people just coming in off the ships, families as well as convicts, not to mention orphans sent down under just for being inconvenient, like, and because I seen all this and felt bad about it, I set up a soup kitchen, and had tents put up where folk down on their luck could stay. Eventually I even paid for proper wooden shelters where those in need could bunk til they got on their feet again. Seeing my generosity, other men who'd done right well there on the world's backside, they started giving me money of their own to add to mine for that cause, a benevolent society, we dubbed it, and then one year the royal governor, he sees what all I done, and gives me a commendation what he had read out in front of everybody and all, seeing I got written up in all the papers."

"Marvelous!' I exclaimed, swept up in the account of improbable reformation of a human soul.

"Yeah, well," Dawkins told us, "word spread, you know how that goes, and before I knew it I was a leading citizen, which, between us, I found a greater weight bearing down on these little shoulders of mine than was pleasant to bear. One day I realized despite all the success Australia had brung me, I had a hankering to see the old country I'd left twenty-one years before, so I hired a good solicitor, and saw money was tipped into the right pockets, you might say, and petitioned for a pardon, being so clearly reformed. And to the surprise of some, I was granted one, straight up."

"And you left Australia?" I asked.

"Lock, stock, and barrel, after selling out my stores and house and all my properties. But I didn't leave nobody in the lurch, on account I set up a fund to continue the good works I had put in motion down there. So homeward I sailed, in right better conditions than I had on the trip down, and looked up an old acquaintance from childhood, a Mr. Oliver Twist, who'd done well enough, too, being ward to a proper gentleman up in Pentonville, a Mr. Brownlow had been that fella's name, and I found there were some things I needed to say to Oliver, on account of the fact it always bothered me that I hadn't half-tried to recruit him into the life under Fagin. He accepted my apology straight up, and had me to dinner when I wasn't expecting nothing but maybe a cool sort of forgiveness at best, but to my surprise, we hit it off fine, did Twist and I, and together that very same night we formed a partnership that saw us both do a bit more than all right for ourselves."

"What sort of business was that?" I asked.

"The manufacture of canned goods, a new thing then, that as you know has hit so big ever since. Orders came as fast as we could fill them. Made quite a sound bit of money together, Mr. Twist and I did off our cannery over in Camden, five times what I was taking in down in Australia, though sadly my partner is gone now, never owning what might be called a healthy sort of constitution. Me, though, I spent some of my takings finding other friends I knew back in the day, children who were victims of Fagin, and I helped those out, though precious few remained, most being dead or languishing behind bars in Newgate, or just beyond finding in the twisting lanes of the city. And I spent the money in other ways, feeding the hungry out East in Limehouse and the like, and endowing educational opportunities for a select number of young men."

"You sound an altogether admirable sort of man," I commented, convinced by his words that he was a shining example of how a soul may be reclaimed from even the most depraved of beginnings.

"I do try, Doctor," Dawkins answered, "but of course I had a lot to account for in the first place. My earliest life was not one I am proud of, you, see, despite the shameful tickle it gives me to think back on how good at the craft I was."

"Reported to be the best of your generation," Holmes put in.

"I think that no exaggeration, if I may tempt pride by agreeing. Did you know I once swiped a ring off Mr. Douglas Marshall-Pryce, the famed race horse owner?"

"A fascinating tale, I've no doubt," said Holmes, without a trace of irony or patronizing condescension, his detective's nature being truly interested, I think.

"And what is it that brings you to Baker Street today?" I asked before the telling of this tale should be entertained.

Dawkins took on a frown and looked at the floor, before slowly raising his eyes and with a certain anger in his voice that had not been there before, said:

"A new Fagin has arisen."

"Dear me!" I exclaimed. "A new criminal who uses an army of children to do his bidding? Here in London?" I asked.

And now Holmes shifted his weight forward, his manner quite changed, focused, his interest sparked.

"The same," Dawkins confirmed. "A heartless master who corrupts the innocent and sets them off to worldly and spiritual ruin, caring nothing for their well-being, but I've no doubt pretending deep affection for them all the same. And now this devil is sending out his little minions, to take all the risks of his evil plans, while he basks in their labours, and spreads his cruel influence across a great web, where he lies poised in the centre like a fat and well-fed spider."

"Appalling!"

"Yes," Holmes agreed with my summation, "though I confess I have heard nothing of this individual, I have noted a certain...unease among the urchins of the streets, and my senses have buzzed with a growing awareness that *something* is quite off. It was my intention to eventually make the most discreet of inquiries, though your coming today, Mr. Dawkins, has provided the necessary prodding to make that a priority."

"I am glad to hear it!" Dawkins commented. "For if I could help unseat such a villain now in my antiquity, I would feel I'd done something truly worthy with this second life I have been given."

"There is no villain worse than he who corrupts children," I added.

"Truer words, Doctor, truer words," said Dawkins.

"Then the matter is plain," said Holmes, "I shall send out a specialist, let us say, who shall in due time locate our prey, and soon thereafter tender his report on this matter you have so worthily raised."

"A specialist, sir?" Dawkins inquired.

Holmes flashed a demi-smile and said:

"Oh, yes, I shall summon the Barker, himself, Philly Sargents."

"The 'Barker'..." Dawkins rolled the name around in his mouth before seeming to approve of it.

As this title meant nothing to Dawkins and me, we waited for Holmes' explanation, though ere he said anything, he went to the window, and placed a pot of geraniums prominently there, before coming back to his seat.

"Yes, gentlemen," Holmes began, "sitting high among the ever-shifting ranks of my 'Irregulars' those capable urchins I have long had cause to employ as lookouts and informants, among other purposes in my noble work, has risen one Philly Sargents, age ten, who might otherwise have been destined for a life not unlike that Dawkins lived in his days as the Artful Dodger, but who under my tutelage has found a better path, so that I now regard him as among the more adept of my spies and agents. He has such a talent that in another few years I intend to turn him over to my brother Mycroft, for further training in the foreign office, and should Sargents be willing, as certainly seems likely, eventual work in Her Majesty's service, where I think he shall excel, and be of great service to the nation."

"How fascinating!" Dawkins exclaimed. "See, now there's a better way to bring up a boy what's got talents not unlike those of my own tender years!"

It was but a very few minutes later when two small rather shabby boys came to the door, and were shown upstairs by Mrs. Hudson. Holmes gave them each a slice of glazed tea-cake, and a penny, and bade them spread the word that he wished Philly Sargents, the "Barker" to come see him as soon as he could be found.

"Right you are, Mr. Holmes!" cried one of the lads, the other being momentarily rendered mute after shoving most of the cake into his mouth as soon as it was offered.

The pair were back down the steps on the double, and out the front door, scattering like the wild winds to spread word of Holmes' request.

It was perhaps an hour later, time during which Holmes had shown the utmost delight in listening to Dawkins relate tales of his misspent youth as the Artful Dodger, that a new knock was heard below, and a moment later there stood in our presence the Barker himself, a boy with wise eyes and a calm demeanor, clearly a cut above most of the Irregulars, fine spirited lads though most of them were from what I'd seen of them.

This boy took us all in with eyes I suspected missed little, augmented by the tutelage Holmes had told us he'd given him, sharpening his natural skills and boosting his usefulness, and at last Philly the Barker gave an approximation of a bow, and let it be known that:

"I came straight off, Mr. Holmes, as I gather you have need of my services?"

"Philly!" Holmes cried with contentment. "I do indeed, and no small task it is, though a service that will benefit a great many in its course. But come, my boy, do take a seat and join us, in a bit of tea and cake, while I tell you all."

The boy did so, moving with a cat-like confidence that

seemed far older than his tender years, and Dawkins nodded approvingly at him, before remarking:

"Ah, I catch the *style* in you, lad, indeed I do. Not cut far from the same cloth I once wore, I think."

"I gather you might have once been in 'the trade,' sir?" the Barker questioned back.

"He was the best of the best in his time," Holmes replied, "though his talents were put to the worst uses, shame to say."

"Why is it you are called the Barker?" I piped up to ask, my curiosity getting the best of me.

"On account of the howling it's said I leave behind in my work, when those I act against realize I've done them a bad turn," the boy explained with a vivid seriousness I found quite touching.

"Philly has been indispensable a time or two in my own cases, Watson," Holmes told me. "As he may be today. But I must ask, are you interested in aiding a good cause once again, Philly, and helping me in my work?"

"I'm always up for helping you, Mr. Holmes, and I know you'd never lead me astray," the boy replied, taking a small bite of tea-cake in an almost demure fashion. Another aspect of Holmes' tutelage, I wondered? "Besides," he added, "life's been altogether too dull of late. Boy needs an adventure now and again, doesn't he?"

At this Dawkins laughed heartily and declared:

"I do like this lad, Mr. Holmes! It's an excellent team I note you've gathered. A sort of Fagin in reverse, you are, seeing instead that boys turn to the good."

"I thank you," Holmes said simply. "Now, Philly, if you're on board, here is what I shall require of you..."

So Holmes laid out the scenario, and the Barker scowled at hearing the tidings of a scoundrel using children for low purposes, filling the streets with malice and wrongdoing. He listened carefully as Holmes and Dawkins told of what they knew, and the Barker nodded with determination, prior to declaring:

"I know just how to go about this, never you fear. I'll soon be back here with a report on who and where, for I've got friends of my own out that way and lots of ears to the ground."

A network of his own! I thought, disapproving yet impressed.

"Good, Philly!" Holmes exclaimed. "Then if you're agreeable to this little employment, you can be off to prepare as soon as you've finished your tea."

The boy set about achieving this, with Holmes all-but forcing another slice of cake upon him, though professional that he clearly held himself to be, he also showed every indication of being ready to set off immediately on his task.

As he sat, however, Dawkins compared notes with him on techniques for removing an item from a pocket, "the vanishing act" he dubbed it, and finding himself in the company of a fellow gentleman of the light-fingered trade, the pair traded opinions on the merits of the "high-and-over" method, versus the "straight-around-the rabbit's-hole" procedure, when working in a tight crowd, as well as whether retaining a 'Duke's Man" to make off with the stolen goods handed over to them was worth the added risk.

"Like as not they'll either keep what was properly stole for themselves," Dawkins opined, "or squeal on you in two shakes if they get picked up. Half the time I'd say no thanks when ol' Fagin offered me a Duke's Man to come along on my patrols."

I listened with a dizzy amazement that such subjects existed at all, let alone were being conversed about in my presence, while Holmes listened-in with an aura of avuncular benevolence, contributing his own thought a time or two.

"I once had to pinch a key from a ring of a hundred worn by a guard on a Dutch prison-barge," Holmes revealed, "to see one of my brother's agents smuggled home again from captivity there. To prevent their clanging together, I used the Alexandrian technique, perfected in ancient times in the slums of that famed city. Do either of you know of it?"

"Maybe," the Barker inquired. "Isn't the 'Swedish Wolf' a

variation on that, Mr. Holmes?"

"It is indeed at that, Philly!" Holmes confirmed with a trace of pride.

"Ah, you two do know something of the art, don't you?" Dawkins laughed, and I felt he was truly enjoying himself.

Living with Holmes this past year had brought with it many aspects to life I'd never expected to encounter, but this was near the top of them all.

"I do take a care, though," Philly told Mr. Dawkins, "not to give in to any temptations that might arise to…well, feather my nest a little now and again when the chance to pick a plump purse arises."

"I am glad to hear," said Holmes, "that our little talks upon that subject have borne fruit."

"For if I did such things, you'd chuck me out of the Irregulars, and my future as a spy would go with it, right?" the boy asked.

"I am afraid it would at that," Holmes agreed. "For above all I must be able to rely on the trustworthiness of my associates."

"So you see," Philly told the man who'd once been the Artful Dodger, "it just wouldn't be worth it."

"The straight and narrow is the better path, my boy," Dawkins replied. "Always remember that."

About a half-hour after he'd come to join us, young Philly, the "Barker" was off once more, into the now twilit sky, a supreme confidence in his bearing and even in his stride, though as he departed for the stairs I still felt compelled to cry out:

"Do be careful tonight, lad!"

"It's others who should be careful of me," he replied, with a low brazen grin cast back at me, as the door closed behind him.

"There are always hazards, Watson," Holmes admitted, but I send him out with the confidence that of all those I might have summoned, his is the best nature for work of this kind. A master, I might dub him without fear of contradiction."

"I saw in him many of the same qualities I once bore,"

Dawkins added. "He'll do all right, Doctor, never fear."

I sincerely hoped so, for I was not altogether at peace with the idea of employing one so young to undertake what certainly struck me as an activity rife with peril. Childhood, as I thought it, was supposed to be a chapter of innocence and pleasant enjoyment, or at least my own had largely been, though I knew London was quite a bit different from the countryside of Scotland, where my own beginnings lay. As I lit my pipe and joined the other two gentlemen in a smoke, I admitted that in the wide world much was wrong, indeed, and we could but make the best of things.

As there was little else to be done for the moment, Holmes' client soon took his leave of us, with Holmes taking the unusual extra trouble on his part of seeing him down the stairs and out to the street, where a cab was hailed and goodnights spoken.

Back upstairs, I hazarded to say to my friend:

"Holmes, you certainly seem to show more warmth to this man than toward perhaps any client I have yet seen call upon you."

"As I said, Watson, this man was a master in a specialized variety of legerdemain, a one-time prince among pickpockets, and a clever adversary of the police in his time. Though I may not approve of how he once employed his art, I do respect the virtuosity of it. And on top of all that, we meet him nicely reformed and quite beyond his one-time lawlessness. Knowing me as you do, can you doubt that such expertise might merit my appreciative admiration?"

As I could not argue with that, I did not try, and in any case was shortly settled in for a late dinner of broiled mutton with rosemary and parsnips, which Mrs. Hudson had kept warmed for us.

"So, Holmes," I said when my belly was full and I was relaxed after a pleasantly eventful day, "what are your hopes as to the outcome of the young Barker's foray into locating this villain and his child-thieves?"

"Oh, he shall find them, Watson, he shall indeed locate

this band, though it may take him a day or two, I do not doubt the Barker's determination and resourcefulness."

"And then what?" I inquired.

"And then I move on them and cut the head off the adder in whose coils these unfortunates do find themselves, willingly or otherwise. I'll shut the operation down, send the leader to the police, and leave the pocketbooks of London safer by a measure."

"And children freed from an immorality, of course," I added.

"Until the next arises," Holmes said drearily. "Human nature being an unoriginal thing, Watson, an observer of history sees much which but repeats itself."

And so one did, and so one would.

<><><><><><>

In the morning I went off to my practice, and did not return until mid-afternoon. I asked Holmes if he'd had any word from young Philly, the so-called Barker, and he seemed untroubled when he replied that he had not.

"Though I do await with patient hope," he told me.

I was only at home for a short time that afternoon, as I took my intended, Mary, out that evening for dinner and the theater, and afterward we took a slow and quite peaceful turn through Regent's Park in a hired carriage, where Mary talked in almost dreamy terms about our impending wedding, and the shared life to come.

It was all very happy, and after seeing her home, I returned to Baker Street, where Holmes was seated at his desk in the shadow-filled parlour, lighted by a single lamp, tendrils of his pipe-smoke suspended like fog in the air.

"News?" I pressed.

"Not as yet," he replied tersely.

"Is that cause for concern?" I asked, hanging up my coat

and now turning toward Holmes in full.

"Concern, no, but I confess it was my hopes to have heard something before this."

"How long will you wait before you…"

I paused, for I did not know how to finish the thought. What *could* be done, really?

"Before I send another to seek him out?" Holmes completed for me.

"Does not the risk of dispatching a second child seem an impropriety to you?"

"In truth, Watson, young Philly Sargents has the instincts of one born for espionage, and enjoys my complete confidence. If he has not yet returned to report to me, then I have faith that he has good reason for this, and shall not initiate other plans until a third night has passed."

"You truly have no worries for him?"

"I have already spoken of the risks in such a mission, Watson, risks Philly knew when he set out. Risks he calculated, and was willing to judge acceptable. I must rely on his worthiness, which he has amply demonstrated in past undertakings, the details of which I have never shared with you."

This was true, for Holmes was often gone without explanation for mysterious stretches of days, and I knew there was a great deal about his life and work unknown to me.

"Well," I said to him in bringing the matter to a close, "I hope you do not think me pessimistic if I tell you I am not without my own concerns for the lad."

"Of course, Watson," Holmes said, "I should expect no less."

With that he turned back to the act of writing which had been occupying him before I entered; probably another monograph, I supposed. Thus I went on to my own room and was abed ten minutes later, though I laid awake for some time, thinking of the child Holmes had so casually sent off to locate and infiltrate what may perhaps have been the most dangerous criminal gang in all of London.

Another day passed, and I spent it occupied by my patients and their needs, only to come home and find Holmes gone, so I took my supper alone, and after thanking Mrs. Hudson, sat up a while reading in the parlour, before finally laying aside my tense curiosity and surrendering to the yawns which overtook me, and going to bed late, at nearly eleven.

I awoke in darkness fumbling for my watch, and seeing by the striking of a match that it was a quarter til four, yet it was voices coming from the parlour which had upended my slumber, and with a leaping in my heart I realized one of these belonged to Holmes and young Philly Sargent, the "Barker" himself!

Throwing my robe hurriedly about my person and proceeding out into the parlour, I saw Holmes seated in his favoured chair with the boy, each looking unharmed, across a small table from him, a single taper candle burning between them, sending its light flickering across their faces.

Conscious of Mrs. Hudson sleeping elsewhere in the house, I still let my excitement raise my voice a little when I called over:

"Philly! Good it is to see you, lad!"

This child spy grinned back at me, looking hale and hardy as he replied with discernible pride:

"Sure, Doctor, fine and all, aren't I? Take more than what I run into among that lot to put a dent in the Barker, won't it?"

I took my seat and listened as Holmes' agent, this Wellington among his Irregulars, told of his wandering in the East End, and making inquiries that weren't especially asked with discretion, polling friends about a recruiter he'd heard tell of, who made good use of proper talent.

"I told them I'd like to join up, see, and spread word of this at every chance. Must've told twenty people, if it was one."

Soon enough–and I suppose this would have been early-on in the morning after he'd left Baker Street, Philly was aware he was being watched, and soon after followed, and in an alley he reversed and came up behind his tail, only to let them know that if they were who he thought they were, what he wanted was to see their boss.

"You don't *see* the boss," one of the boys who'd trailed him had said, a tough-looking lad of about eight or nine, little but rat-like and fierce, "the boss sees you."

"Then take me where the boss can see me," I told them, Philly related. "And you know what, Mr. Holmes? They actually did exactly that."

"They took you straight there?" I asked, surprised at the ease with which this infiltration had apparently happened.

"Well, no, not quite, not straight-up, like," Philly corrected my assumption, "but they saw I was quite the prize, an asset, like, for their cause, so they led me to a house off in the Rookery–Bethnal Green, that is, Doctor–where there were some others, boys and girls both, all sharp little things, well-drilled in the game, not a weak sister among them. They gave me a spin to see what I was made of, three leaping on me at once, no warning, all arms flying, and I had to go fist to fist with them, and then once I'd done that, snatch a handkerchief off one of the girls in a way that she never caught me going at it, but I done good, and was let back into another room, where the boss' right-hand girl waited."

"The lieutenant was a girl?" I inquired, as Holmes sat with his fingers steepled, listening.

"Yeah," Philly answered, how about that? Didn't seem to make a difference there what you were, only that you were good at tricks, and loyal."

"And what happened then, Philly?" Holmes finally asked.

"The lot, didn't it? Asked me about an hundred and fifty questions, and said maybe they'd let me join, maybe not, maybe they'd toss me in the drink and be done with me, they'd have to see, but the bossy girl, Theresa Topps, her name, she said I had to stay put there til she said I could go, so I did that too, no arguments, and spent the day dicing and card playing with some of the fellas in the house, losing on purpose, as that's a sure way to make new friends, isn't it?"

The world did love a cheerful loser, I considered.

"I had some boiled potatoes and cabbage for supper, little bits of diced reddish meat in it, best not to ask what kind, so I never, and slept in a pile of burlap bags stuffed with something half soft, about four others sleeping right up by me, half on me, but it wasn't too bad, really. Woke up in the morning and it was more of the same past noon, and I was biding my time, thinking if they were letting me be among them that long, I must've been approved, you see?"

"And were you?" Holmes asked.

"I was at that," Philly said with a grin.

"Well done!" Holmes said with a matching smile. "Now tell me the rest!"

"Long day it was," Philly continued, "but finally I was led down to the cellar and shown a tunnel dug into the wall, covered up behind a shelf, and down into this we went, tight fit with a gang member on either side of me, but manageable, and up we come after a few twists and turns through other tunnels, into some other house."

"How long did you walk?" Holmes asked.

"Ah, glad you asked that," the Barker cried, "for I measured out my steps, and figure on the first distance being sixty-seven feet end to end, before we made a second turn and that was another forty-one steps. But thing was, there other tunnels branching off, too, though where those went, I do not know. Sorry, Mr. Holmes."

"Philly!" Holmes said at once. "Make no apologies to me, my boy, for you have done splendid work!"

"A tunnel network under London!" I cried with a whistle.

"Far from the first," Holmes answered, "though this one is extensive by the sound of it. "Pray go on, Philly."

"Yes, sir. I come up into some other house, and there I got

the surprise of my life, for I was in a cellar, sure, but like no cellar I'd ever seen. It had a chandelier hanging off the ceiling, yeah, burning with a hundred candles, must've been, and rugs on the floor fit for a sultan of Araby, and furniture that looked like it should be in some Duke's castle. And in the middle of it all sitting in a rocking chair, calm as you please, was the leader of the gang no less than in person!"

"What did he look like?" I demanded.

To which Philly grinned at me, and was about to let loose his great revelation, when Holmes beat him to it and said with cool certitude:

"It was not a 'he,' Watson, it was a woman."

"What? A woman?" I cried.

"Right you are as always, Mr. Holmes!" Philly exclaimed, more pleased at Holmes' deduction than angry at his big surprise being undermined. "As old as you please and looking not the faintest bit hard, but like somebody's dear old gran. That was even her name, Granny Midnight, she was called."

Granny Midnight...I tried the name out and found it particularly disturbing to me, like something from a tale about witches out in the fens.

"'Hello there, young Philly Sargents,' she called to me. 'I've been hearing all about you since you came among us, child. You visited us with a wish in your heart to join our little family, did you not, my boy?'

"I did, indeed," I told her, "and I think you'll like the talents I got to offer."

"'Oh, I think Granny shall, Granny shall,' she said to me, 'especially that sharp nose of yours, Philly, for not just any child could have found us here, no. Not even with going around asking half the city, like I have heard was your tactic, child.'"

The narrative unfolded in a long monologue, Philly revealing to us how he was asked to approach this ring-leader who had corrupted the souls of so many children, this Granny Midnight, and at a distance of mere inches she stared hard and long into his eyes, and it was all Philly could do to keep his expression blank, but after a long moment Granny Midnight threw back her head and cackled witch-like, and actually reached out in a sudden movement and pulled Philly's hand to her, and studied it as if reading some story written in its lines, then just as suddenly, she drew the boy against her, and she smelled of apples, he would note, as she hugged him forcefully, and planted a kiss on his lips, dry and hard, then held him a little off from her so that he had no choice but to look into her penetrating eyes as she said:

"If you would be in our family, Philly Sargents, you must kiss me in return. Kiss my old lips, boy, and you are mine and no other's *forever*."

I felt some tingle move through me at the wording there, and demanded:

"Did you do so, Philly?"

"Course I did," he answered, "what else was there to do? I kissed her good right on her old wrinkly lips."

I fought the urge to recoil, but Holmes said:

"Philly, you have achieved all that I could have asked of you. Now tell me what came after."

According to his account, after the kiss, while still holding onto his arm, Granny Midnight withdrew a dagger from some unseen place within the folds of her attire and showed it to Philly and said:

"You see, my grandson, for you are my grandson now that I have made you mine, I could as easily have pressed this blade through your little heart, even as I embraced you, and so I shall without hesitation if ever you betray me. Do you believe me, child?"

"And I did believe her," Philly told us. "I believed her straight up, no backwards march to it."

Death if she learns of his betrayal, I thought. *Dear me, then the sentence was being earned right there in front of us!*

Philly, the Barker, said in closing that after this strange little ceremony, Granny Midnight whistled, and some other children came into her innermost chamber, and ran forward and embraced him crying out a chanted song:

> *"Quiet as a snake that makes no sound,*
> *Hungry as the grave, with its belly round,*
> *Cheat ol' Granny and you shall die,*
> *And in a dark hole you will lie,*
> *No second chances, no time to repent,*
> *Into the furnace your soul be sent,*
> *So when the morning bells toll,*
> *They'll be no mercy for your soul!"*

After he had sung this for us there in the flickering candle light of Baker Street, and the rendition was done, silence swelled for a moment, before with a long breath, Holmes asked:

"And I presume you stayed there this last day, waiting a chance to make your way back to give this report?"

"Yes, because though she saw I was to be useful and was already skilled, Granny Midnight still had some of her hand-picked favourites show me their tricks, limber slips and handoffs and the like, and where to go if ever you needed to make a quick getaway when the Bill was at your heels. I played along, but there wasn't much special to their tricks, Mr. Holmes, just slightly advanced basics, truth be told. You showed me much better stuff."

Holmes chuckled. "Doubtless, Philly, doubtless."

The story was that for the entirety of the day, Philly lingered in the building where he'd first been taken, and was then sent out into the streets at nightfall, to walk a while and get his bearings with the neighborhood he'd soon be working in. According to instructions, he was to reconnoiter the area, undertaking no crimes, just looking about, and so he did for a while, then made a long loop around half the city to throw off any pursuers that happened to be there, watching that he hadn't caught sight of, and finally he made his way back to Baker Street at three-forty in the morning, shortly before I'd first heard him and woken up abed.

"You have, I say again, done splendidly," Holmes told him, as he committed to his vault-like memory the details of the location Philly had passed off to him.

"And what now?" I asked.

"When the sun is up, we summon my client, the one-time Artful Dodger, who has been faithfully waiting for word these past days, and reveal to him all that we have just heard. As for our young friend here, well, the Barker has earned his rest, and I shall not send him again into that squirming adder's nest he has uncovered for us. By mid-day I shall have brought the police into the matter, the buildings, with their tunnel network, shall be stormed, and the career of this Granny Midnight will be brought to an overdue ending."

"A wonderful development for all the good people of London that shall be," I noted.

And so as the morning light arrived, Holmes invited the Barker to table with us, to enjoy Mrs. Hudson's grilled kippers and a lovely pudding, before the boy set off to get some sleep in the territory closer to the dockland that he called home.

Holmes had no sooner said his farewells to Philly Sargents, the Barker, than he dispatched a runner to send a telegram to Mr. Jack Dawkins for him to come to Baker Street and be brought current with the news.

"Why your Barker lad is a marvel!" Dawkins declared, when he was among us at 9.30. "I think highest among all your considerable talents, Mr. Holmes, is the ability to find assets for your cause who outshine all expectations!"

"I do make every attempt to do so," Holmes confirmed.

"How odd it still feels after all these many decades to be making plans to set off into a London police station on the right side of the law," Dawkins laughed. "My younger incarnation as the Artful Dodger would've sooner jumped into the frozen Thames than go into such a location."

I explained that I would not be able to accompany them to the police, for duty pulled me elsewhere, though I should be home again by midafternoon if that was not too late, and both Holmes and the client, Dawkins, seemed glad at the idea of having me with them for the crucial operation.

In fact Holmes remarked with satisfaction:

"By that schedule you should still be in time to travel with us and see the rats flushed from their nests by the baying hounds of the law."

"It's been a rather straightforward sort of case," I said, marveling at the ease with which Holmes' machinations had borne fruit. "The perpetrator of these injustices against the young having been identified almost without effort, and so readily discovered."

Holmes looked thoughtful for an instant, smoking his pipe, thoughts clearly pouring themselves out behind his steady gray eyes, before he finally nodded.

Yet I would soon be eating my words raw, for matters which followed most decidedly did not go according to plan that fateful day....

<><><><><>

It was just as I was refilling the quantity of bandages I kept in my medical bag, in preparation for taking my leave, that from outside Baker Street there arose the voices of several children lifted in a torrent of shouts

"Mr. Holmes! Mr. Holmes!" came the outcry.

Holmes was on his feet in a flash dashing to the window, which he pulled upward and leaned out into the cool morning air.

"Eli! Samuel! Michael!" he called down, obviously knowing the children by name. "Come to the door. I shall let you inside."

Holmes tore through the room, passing both the former Artful Dodger and myself in his flight onto the stairs and down to the first floor. He reached the door before Mrs. Hudson could, and cast it open.

"Come in!" he commanded, and three urchins, barefooted and the worse for wear rushed in.

Not waiting to be brought upstairs, the trio flew into giving their account, and to my ears their mixed voices were little short of chaos, but somehow Holmes seemed to grasp their every syllable, and a look of stark unease came onto his face.

"And you saw the abduction occur?" he demanded, a look of angry concern now taking him over.

The boy called Michael answered:

"We did, Mr. Holmes, they was on the Barker like flies on a dung pile!"

"He didn't have a prayer in a cathedral, he never!" the lad known as Eli added, while the third boy, Samuel, merely nodded his vigorous agreement.

"They've got the Barker, then?" Dawkins asked from his place behind me on the stairs.

Grimly, Holmes intoned:

"Yes, young Philly has been taken by our foe, Granny Midnight."

"Oh, dear me, that poor little mite," Mrs. Hudson said sadly from her place near the kitchen doorway. "Has he even got a prayer then, Mr. Holmes?"

I answered for my friend. "When Sherlock Holmes is in someone's corner, there is always hope."

"How did this happen?" Dawkins asked.

Holmes related the news his three Irregulars had brought him, telling how young Philly, the so-called Barker, had left Baker Street, and no sooner was he a few blocks away, heading home to the part of the East End he called his native ground, than he passed a flower girl seated cross legged on the pavement, a few wilted blossoms in a basket before her, her eyes pasted onto Philly and his movements.

"I knowed there was something off about her!" Eli vowed, interrupting Holmes' re-telling of events. "Almost gave the Barker a shout, I did!"

"And I seen it all happen!" Samuel burst out.

When Philly, who was so tired he was yawing, was no more than a few paces from her, the flower girl stood and began to wave a red scarf above her head, and suddenly, at this obvious signal, an enclosed carriage, driven by a child, pulled from its place on the curb and bore down rapidly on Philly. It halted just short of him, and though all three witnesses agreed he leapt back and was so light on his feet that he nearly made his escape, the doors on the carriage opened and a half dozen children, girls as well as boys, flew out in a tidal wave of grasping hands, some of the young ones laughing, as if this deadly matter were a game to them, while they surrounded Philly and overwhelmed him, piling atop him and binding his limbs with hempen cords, before dragging him into the vehicle and shutting the door right after the flower girl herself ran forward. With a grin of malice at the boys who had been walking near Philly, she, too, leaped inside and was off with the lot, disappearing at a dash down the curving streets of London, sprays of slush from the cobblestones thrown up behind their wheels.

But unwelcome as this account was, a moment later a fourth Irregular, a small boy named Solomon, came to the door, holding some item.

"The flower girl left this behind on the pavement, didn't she?"

In his cupped hands lay a single gleaming red apple, held above palms that were freshly scalded and blistered.

Holmes pulled a handkerchief from his pocket and took hold of the fruit.

"Poisoned," he said at once. "I will have to examine it later, when time allows, to determine exactly what toxin was painted upon the object."

But my thoughts were on the injured child before me, rather than these speculations, and I set down my bag and found an unguent within.

"Let me see your hands," I said to young Solomon.

He obliged, wincing in pain as he held them out.

I wiped at his skin in order to remove whatever caustic

chemical had been painted upon the surface of the apple to cause these burns, then applied a soothing cream, and finally wrapped it all in a section of the bandage I had placed within my bag only moments earlier.

"That should help somewhat with the pain," I told little Solomon, but leave the bandages on for at least a day."

Though time was clearly of the essence, Holmes still set the apple upon a foyer end-table and studied it for a moment. It was as perfect a specimen of round red apple as could be imagined, its colour bright in the slanted morning sunlight, yet it was also glazed with an unseen foulness.

"Whatever did the flower girl mean, leaving a poisoned apple behind like that" Mrs. Hudson asked.

"It was both a message and a warning, Mrs. Hudson," Holmes said quietly. "Granny Midnight is telling me that she knows I have acted against her interests, and cautioning me she is far from defenseless."

After thanking the boys for their aid, and sending them off with a penny each, Holmes began to pace the length of the room, deep in thought, before he said:

"The advantage has flipped to her, for clearly the element of surprise has been lost, and she holds one of my associates hostage."

"Yes, I think her message was plain enough," I said, "for Philly's sake, leave her alone."

"If we did so, wouldn't she still kill the boy for betraying his oath to serve her cause?" Dawkins demanded.

Holmes did not answer at once, but finally said:

"I fear I do not like young Philly's chances, but still I must proceed."

"Then what is the next step?" I pressed him, any thoughts of keeping my appointment that morning now abandoned. "Are we still to go to the police, and storm the place?"

"No, Watson," the detective said at last, "I must, myself, go to her."

"But why?" I asked, seeing no logic there.

"Because with the police involved, it shall become a battle, and casualties will rapidly mount, almost certainly including one I regard as under my protection. But if I go in person, it may stay a contest solely between myself and this underworld queen of child criminals."

Underworld, I thought, how literal the term was in this case, with the Barker's report of this Granny Midnight's network of tunnels.

"Holmes," I spoke up, "I cannot, indeed *will not*, allow you to go into this danger alone."

"Nor will I," said Dawkins, who though elderly drew himself up into an almost soldierly form, his eyes bright with inner determination.

"I thank you, Mr. Dawkins," said Holmes, "but it would be unforgivable of me to endanger a client. And, you, Watson, are to be wed in a matter of days. Knowing this, how can I allow you to come along, when your loss would prove so devastating for Miss Morstan, who plainly has for you an all-abiding love?"

His caution was not meritless, and I did pause to reflect on how a man, once he bonds himself to another through plans of matrimony, could no longer judge his life to be entirely his alone, yet I knew something else, and it was of this that I spoke.

"Holmes," I said, "Mary is a lady of honour, and though I know she should grieve deeply for me were I to meet an untoward fate, I understand just as surely that she would not wish to wed a man who would allow his friend to face a grave danger alone."

"Well said, Dr. Watson," Dawkins told me, with a pat on my upper arm. "And I would not let my comrades face what I would shirk!"

It was then that Mrs. Hudson spoke up, registering an opinion:

"You know you cannot deny these men what they offer out of their high regard for you, Mr. Holmes. T'would be a grave insult."

For an instant I thought that even in the face of these

words Holmes would indeed reject our offers, but instead he nodded and a smile flashed on his face.

"I am grateful for your aid, both of you," he told us, "for it may prove handy before all this is done. If you are to join, then I ask you to leave with me at once. There is an uncertain contest ahead, and would advise you to arm yourselves."

I smiled my appreciation toward Mrs. Hudson, then went hurriedly into my bedroom for the army revolver I retained from my years of service, and when I returned I saw that Holmes was looking on with approval at the pistol Dawkins was showing he carried concealed up his sleeve.

"Respectable I may be nowadays, gents," he said with a wink, "but ol' Fagin told us never to go anyplace without a little protection, and as you see, the habits of my youth die hard."

"You carry that everywhere with you?" I asked.

"Oh, yes," Dawkins replied.

And right then I thought I was seeing the Artful Dodger of old peering back at me, the ghost of a lad who'd been equal parts spirit and shadow, formidable, indeed, but likable above all.

"And now," Holmes intoned, "to success or ruin we go, onward to the subterranean fortress of this Granny Midnight."

The lair described by young Philly the Barker lay across town, far to the east in the river bottoms, near where the crush of the city dwindled amid a landscape of aged, half-ruined houses, which were surrounded by dilapidated warehouses, with gray-wood wharves at their sides. Hardly a deserted district, in fact one destined to grow large in years to come, but still a far cry from the populous heart of the city. It was a place where criminality was the norm, and those who dwelled or worked there tended to mind their own affairs, and as a rule claimed to see little of what went on around them.

It was safest that way.

We traveled by hackney, and the driver was none too happy about heading so far out into this less than inviting area, but Holmes promised to pay him well, allaying some of the man's grumbles, though he perspired profusely as we rolled along, and seemed ill at ease past the divide of the Great North Road. When we left behind the squalid districts filled with overcrowded tenements, and finally came into the boggy slum-lands of the extreme east, barge traffic dotting the water lanes of the Thames at the edge of our vision, he demanded immediate payment, his aspect that of a man who'd been through something of an ordeal upon the nerves.

It was a sensation I could well share.

"I've lost fares in taking you three so far," he grumbled, an untidy and less than gracious man with a shaven head, but full whiskers spread about his cheeks. "Not to mention the risk, me up here thinking the whole time we was about to be set upon by bandits at any minute!"

He mopped his pate with a graying cloth and held out a leathery worker's-hand for the fee.

"I shall pay you fare and a half for the trip here," Holmes told him, handing over the money, "and double fare home again, if you wait here for us to emerge. I do not know how long this may be, but bid you, if we are not back out again in an hour, do make haste away from this unwholesome place, and report our disappearance to the landlady of the Baker Street address where you picked us up. She will see you compensated in full, though I caution you, do not seek to cheat her!"

"If I have to fly off, I won't be bringin' nobody back here again, guv'nor," the man said, though I noticed he was holding the horse in place, apparently considering the offer of waiting for our return, as requested.

He thought a moment more, and perhaps seeing a chance to tighten the screws on desperate men, added:

"Make it triple, or no deal. I shan't wait."

Holmes looked back at him sternly, and his voice rougher

now, he said:

"Double is what I offered, and double is what you shall get for faithful service."

"Well then, if you're going to take that tone with me," cried the driver, "it's a good day I'll bid you, and devil help you all back into the city proper through these thief-ridden parts!"

But Holmes was not done. "Furthermore," he added, "alongside paying you double-fare, as promised, should you wait the full hour for us, I will forget that you are, in fact, driving stolen hack."

The effect these words had on the unkempt driver was electrical.

"How the bleedin' seven hells did you—"

"Because he's Sherlock Holmes, that's how!" Dawkins spoke up.

"It is quite elementary, sir," explained Holmes with a hard smile. "That horse is familiar enough with this hackney cab, but she doesn't know you, nor are you entirely versed in its operation, having, I think, never driven one before this day, nor I suspect, have you ridden in many, either, in your life of low-dissipation."

The man turned and gaped, duly struck mute by these words.

"Come, you cannot fool me," Holmes declared, "Your crime was so clumsily-done that I have been aware since back on Coppersmith Lane that you stole this conveyance this morning as opportunity presented, hoping to make some quick coins, and then abandon the hackney and horse, or perhaps if you're more well-connected than you look, sell both for quick profit."

"I never done...!"

"I will overlook all of this, provided you do as I say and wait the hour, and then return the horse and hack back to where you took them. Give in to any notions of running off on us, however, and I shall track you down myself, and turn you over to the police for a year's hard labour, so do not think to make a run for it the second we vanish inside."

The man was cowed, and said meekly:

"All right, guv'nor, all right then. It'll be as you say. One hour and then if I spy neither hide nor hair of the lot of you, back to Baker Street I go to tell the lady you didn't come out again."

"Precisely," Holmes agreed. "She will know what to do, for I have left her an envelope with instructions, to be opened if we do not return. Now," he turned back to us, "as the matter of our return transportation has been seen to, this is the house we must enter."

He pointed out a two-story brick structure, probably a century or more old, and in just slightly better condition than many of the places around it. I saw that on the dusty ground before it were the footprints of a number of children.

Heaven help us, I thought.

From a comfortable distance it was all well and good to contemplate the mission ahead, but to now stand before the place, stooped and age-worn as it was, and brooding in its menace, I felt my heart begin to pound, and my senses heighten, for I doubted not that a struggle lay before us, likely an ambush involving dozens of children, maddened by their fanatical loyalty to the mistress they served, this old Granny Midnight.

"I don't like the feel of this place, Holmes," I said, voicing my inner thoughts.

"It doesn't have a proper soul, does it?" Dawkins agreed. "Reminds me of a place I knew in my days as the Dodger, said to be the site where a particularly vicious cut-throat name of Monks would dump his victims. After that there was always this tense cloud of menace around the place."

He shuddered, as if the memory were particularly terrible for him, and added:

"I feel the same dread here."

"We must be steady," Holmes instructed, "for we half defeat ourselves if we approach with other than a courageous spirit. Also, do be mindful, for I expect traps have been laid in wait for us."

It steadied my nerves to see him advance so fearlessly

upon the heels of these words, and after he had examined it carefully for a moment, to open the door to this run-down place.

"Unlocked," he noted, with a tiny, un-mirthful chuckle.

This news was somehow more menacing than had there been a bar in place upon the door, for it reminded me our entry was both expected and desired by those within, and when Holmes stepped inside there was only quiet, yet I wondered how many unseen eyes were even then trained upon us.

"Is anyone here at all?" Dawkins demanded.

"That remains to be seen," said Holmes, though one thing I know…. we are certainly expected."

Chilling thought, I considered.

Not a man to let a friend go where I would fear to follow, I went next, with elderly Mr. Dawkins to my rear. I glanced back to see his eyes were sharply peeled, and ever in motion traveling around us, seeking out some sign of the danger I knew he surely felt as strongly as did I.

"Have you ever noticed, Doctor," he whispered, "that fools and heroes are often cut from the same cloth?"

I could not argue there.

Holmes likewise was peering about the large room at the front of the structure, and for a moment held up his hand, halting us, as he listened long before saying:

"There will be nothing above ground to concern us, though I note signs that, as the Barker reported, a large number of children have made it their habit to live here, and sleep on a pile of stuffed burlap sacks, there, to the far corner. Note how the dust along that wall betrays the long-presence of makeshift mattresses, recently cleared away. There has been a retreat from here only in the last hours."

I did not find the news encouraging, but rather felt it removed the last lingering shred of hope that our coming had not been anticipated by our adversary and her minions. In all my career I do not know that I ever felt the grip of dread as keenly as I did at that moment, heading toward a tunnel where a deadly enemy surely lay in wait. Thus I withdrew my revolver, though wondered at its usefulness, for surely I could never fire upon a child.

Holmes led us next to a kitchen that showed signs of recent use. Someone, I thought, had been feeding the children here, for the stove had burnt porridge spilled out upon its top.

At the far end of the room lay a trap door built into the floorboards, the entrance to the cellar at last.

Holmes was cautious in opening this, though once he had it wide, it showed no more obvious menace than had the front room. *So they wish to draw us down there, do they?* I noted uneasily.

Quietly, Holmes said:

"If the Barker is to be brought out again, I fear it is there that one must go."

Looking toward us, he next whispered:

"You have come far with me, gentlemen, and mindful am I of the dedication you have shown, but you need not take this final journey beside me, for I would not ask any man to face the dangers that lie below. If you wish to wait in the hack, I'll hold your courage none the lower in my esteem, for the debt of honour which brings us here is mine to bear, not yours."

"You know a soldier never lets his comrade face danger alone," I reminded him.

"And the Dodger ain't one to fail his friends," Dawkins said with a nod to each of us.

"Then let it be noted," Holmes said, "that rarely has any man faced danger in better company."

Down ladder-like stairs we descended, into a large cellar which, like the upstairs, showed signs of recent occupation, even to my untrained eye. There were chairs thereabout, and thinly-stuffed cushions, a set of dice sat on a small table, and a number of cards were stacked nearby. I lifted one of the cards and found it to be plain and cheap, the sort available in almost any store. Surely there were few useful clues even for Holmes to discern here.

It took Holmes but a moment to find the entrance to

the hidden tunnel the Barker had mentioned, and this too he examined cautiously before lighting three candles and passing two back, then stepping into the darkness of this space excavated through the raw earth. It was barely high enough for me to walk upright, more easily done by Dawkins, but Holmes, with his great height, ducked a bit at the shoulders, and holding out his candle, advanced slowly.

There was an utter and absolute silence there, and a motionless darkness around us in each direction, and I kept peering back, thinking if an attack came, it would be from that quarter, yet nothing appeared, and in time we reached the first of two intersecting passages, likewise dug deep beneath the other structures in the district.

"I questioned the Barker most carefully," Holmes whispered, "and he reported it was the left-hand passage down which he was taken. It is there that we will go."

The left-hand path, I reflected, *was ever said to be the most luckless direction in old Scottish folk tales.*

As we moved deeper into this space, I noted a slight flickering of the candles, the flames waving toward our faces, and from behind me, Jack Dawkins rather authoritatively said:

"There'll be a large room ahead, for you see the current in the air."

He had barely uttered this, than I saw Holmes freeze still, and draw sharply back, then chuckle as he handed me his candle, and ordered:

"Watson, do hold this for me, but make sure to give me a little light."

At first I had no conception of the reason for this pause in our journey, but then I saw dangling from space in the darkness, exactly the height of a grown man's eyes, the thinnest string imaginable, into which was woven knots holding a number of fish hooks, and the glistening-shards of razors.

After first examining the trap, Holmes removed it with a deftness that saw the task finished in a trice, yet I was not prepared to hear him laugh.

"Ah, gentlemen, that was no effort to cause true injury, no, it was...well, it was what it was, and it says much concerning what lies ahead."

"Holmes?" I asked.

"Be encouraged, Watson, let me say that much, if not more."

Encouraged? I wondered. *How so?*

I recalled the apple left by the flower girl, coated in some poison that had burned the hand of the boy who'd retrieved it, and I asked:

"Are the hooks and the blade perhaps coated in some poison, Holmes?"

"Who is to say at this time?" he answered. "Though were I to hazard a guess, I would say, no, for I think that was less a trap, than a message."

"A warning?" Dawkins spoke up.

Holmes waited a moment before answering.

"More a salutation," he said cryptically, then took back his candle from me, and started forward once more. "I believe she is telling us that she expects us to come this far."

So intent was I on our surroundings, this tunnel that lay so closely around us, that after a moment I realized I had not for some minutes been thinking of Philly, Holmes' Irregular, whose capture had brought us here. I ardently hoped we would find the boy alive, though in my heart I feared otherwise, remembering as I did the oath of fealty he had been required to take, sealed with a kiss on Granny Midnight's lips, and the promised penalty for treason against her: death.

This may be grim, I thought. *And all for nothing.*

After another minute's walk the tunnel ceased, not at a doorway but simply at an opening, and into this Holmes stepped, bringing us into the same ornate chamber the Barker had described as the scene of his fateful meeting with Granny Midnight. It was something of a shocking sight after the bleakness of the earthen tunnels, for its walls were stone-lined, and its roof capped by a dangling chandelier, though unlighted at the moment. The trappings of a certain opulence were all about, and in the middle of it all, a white wooden rocking chair, turned away from us, sat unprepossessing for a throne, but a throne all the same, I did not doubt, the seat of this reigning queen of a pickpocket empire.

Then, as my eyes adjusted, I cried–

"Holmes!"

–though which of the two startling sights more inspired my outcry I could not have said, for across the room, on a couch which bore lavish quilts draped across it, lay the Barker, Philly Sargents, who was, I saw to my greatest relief, clearly breathing, though in some condition of unconsciousness, yet also spread out upon the far side of the rocking chair, which had been turned away from the entrance, lay a heap of clothing, and a long white and gray wig.

Seeing it himself an instant after me, from my rear, Dawkins said:

"The remains of Granny Midnight."

Dramatically stated, but in a fashion accurate enough, I saw, as I rushed past this heap of materials toward Philly, against whose throat I thrust my fingers, seeking a pulse, and finding it slow and strong, as with one asleep.

"Drugged but not harmed from what I can observe," I announced to Holmes, who had stopped by my elbow and was gazing down at his associate with concern in his eyes.

"Then that much is well," he said.

"I think we should carry him between us, and hurriedly go," I spoke up.

Dawkins, though glad to hear of the boy's condition, stepped back now to the tunnel entrance, as if sharing my worry that all of this had been far too easy, and that we might now be followed into the room by foes.

It was not for me to count him wrong there.

"I think we are going to have to convey him out with us," I said, as I moved the child into a sitting position on the sofa, and began to rub his wrists in an effort to hasten his return to consciousness.

"I'll leave him to your masterful care, Watson," Holmes told me, "and most exceedingly glad am I to find my young Barker alive against my expectations to the contrary, but for a moment I have other matters to see to here."

Dawkins and I shared a look of uneasiness, each of us wanting to get back outside, for every alarm of danger our instincts had granted us were crying out in the loudest manner.

Holmes, though, walked back to the rocking chair, and using a stick of kindling wood he retrieved from the floor, poked through the heap of attire that had been left behind.

"It defies my every expectation," he commented, as he looked over the pile most carefully.

As I sat beside Philly on the couch, propping the boy up, Dawkins and I watched as Holmes first lifted up the long gray-white wig, which he regarded before setting it aside, then did the same to the black dress that also sat there, its sleeves and skirt long and old fashioned, as an aged woman might wear, hearkening back to the days of her youth. Next he lifted false teeth, and even a set of false fingernails, such as were sometime sworn in theatrical productions.

"Behold," Holmes intoned, "that which constitutes the so-called Granny Midnight, a woman of might, but not substance."

"She...she doesn't even exist in the proper sense!" Dawkins exclaimed.

"No," Holmes agreed, "our villainess, leader of a band of child robbers, is but a construct, brought into being in order to conceal she whose play-acting brings her into creation."

It was starting news, this revelation, and my mind turned over to come at what it meant.

Dawkins was faster, an identity out in the real world, then, and this...this was her disguise."

"Her rôle," I added.

"Beyond all doubt," Holmes agreed with us. "And she has plainly left it behind her for me to find, that I might know something of the truth, just as she left the obvious and careless trap in the tunnel hallway, also as a message."

"What message?" I demanded.

After a dramatic pause and a long moment spent peering through the costume, which he carefully placed in its entirety into a sack, he said:

"Our foe seeks a truce."

Saying this, Holmes paced off the distance in the room from one corner to the next, and finally came to a halt before a section of wall, where he knelt to examine the stones more closely.

"What have we here?" he wondered aloud, as he worked a moment at a space between un-mortared stones, before pulling wide a door fitted into the natural stones there, and I confess what he revealed made a gasp depart from my lungs, and the client released his own signal of surprise, for Holmes had revealed a room, in which lay a great heap of every imaginable loot which a child pickpocket might conceivably plunder from his victims, from watches and tortoise-shell combs, to purses, pocketbooks, and cufflinks. Even coins and a number of printed banknotes lay openly scattered throughout.

And at this heap of valuable goods, I simply stared, for a moment all else forgotten.

Finally it was Dawkins who broke the silence, saying as if awed:

"That makes no sense whatsoever."

"Does it not?" Holmes pressed, not looking toward him.

"That's a right treasure room," Dawkins marveled, "like a vault."

"That is how I make it," I agreed.

"But that isn't how the great game goes at all," Dawkins insisted. "No, not by half! Why wasn't the loot fenced instead of just left all heaped in there, doing nobody a lick of good? What's the sense in stealing all this off the streets of London, if it isn't turned into cutter through the back-alleys of the hot markets? It's just so much junk now, laying down here in the dark."

Holmes listened as he stared at all that lay piled before

him, surely several thousand pounds worth of goods purloined from hundreds of victims.

"It's...quite a mystery," I said.

Holmes remained kneeling just outside the room, until finally he reversed whatever process he had initiated in opening that secret place, sending the stone door shut once again. Then he rose and breathed out deeply before saying:

"Come, gentlemen, it is past time for us to depart. Our hour is nearly up, and it would not do for the driver to strand us here while rushing back to worry Mrs. Hudson without cause."

Seeing that Philly Sargents, the Barker, had as yet failed to re-gain anything like full consciousness, Holmes asked me:

"Watson, can you bear him alone, half-draped across you, or shall I take his feet?"

"I think I can manage," I said, as the Barker had begun to be able to stagger forward on his own power, though with supreme grogginess that showed the boy still knew nothing of his whereabouts, or who was with him.

And so we made our way back down the tunnels and into the cellar, before returning to the world outside, bright to the eyes after our subterranean sojourn. I for one was most pleased to see the hack still remained, though its driver looked like nervousness itself. Only then did I wonder how he was to have counted down an hour, when he seemed to lack a watch. For just a moment–the fleeing of tension from me–this seemed almost irresistibly humourous, but I forced down the laughter that threatened to rise in me, and carefully laid Philly in the hackney, before we three crowded in around him as the driver, clearly relieved to be getting away from this perilous neighbourhood, turned the horse back toward the heart of London.

"I made that fifty-one minutes by the count in my head," he called. "I was ready by half to set off again."

"It is fortunate for you that you did not," Holmes told him, with enough menace in his words for no further annotation to be required. "And I still hold you to the command I issued ere I went inside, you must return this hackney coach to where you found it. What you do after that is your own affair, though I shall pay you, as arranged."

The driver grunted, probably glad for the money, but not looking forward to the risks associated with putting the stolen property back again.

"I do not see," I soon voiced, "how we entered into that place unopposed, and made our way back out again, none the worse for wear, and with Philly alive and in tow."

"Personally, I was expecting I'd seen the last of the sun in this old life of mine," Dawkins agreed. "Yet here we sit, right as rain from Heaven. Can you explain that, Mr. Holmes?"

"Being a witness and a participant, you have the same facts as I, Mr. Dawkins," Holmes answered cordially, if not the least forthcoming. "I bid you chew on them a while, and tell me what you come up with."

As we made our way on our return journey, Dawkins did indeed sit silently a few moments, but seemed too supremely troubled by what had been found inside the wall to let the matter rest any further, and soon asked Holmes more about that utterly bizarre discovery.

"I tell you, that is the part I can't figure out, Mr. Holmes, for more than the disguise–which I grasp to a point–that room full of loot defeats all logic!"

"All logic save one," said Holmes mysteriously.

"And what is that?" Dawkins demanded, and I confess I leaned closer to hear.

"The facts thus far seem to suggest that this is not a criminal enterprise undertaken for reasons you might suspect, but rather, it is someone's game."

"Game?" Dawkins said, dazzled, as if this reply was one he least expected.

"Quite," said Holmes. "We seem to have someone's perverse and self-satisfying amusement wrapped around very serious wrongdoing."

"But then this Granny Midnight, whoever she is, is having her bit of fun at the expense of children!" Dawkins thundered.

"That's still sheer villainy!"

"On that scenario, Mr. Dawkins," Holmes said nebulously, and with a singular tone, "I again bid you invest yourself in reflection upon the facts we possess, for several I find ultimately *revealing*."

And after that peculiar remark, neither I nor the former Artful Dodger could entice Holmes to say anything else for the duration of our journey.

<><><><><>

Safe again at Baker Street, Holmes invited Mr. Jack Dawkins to dine with both myself and a now fully awake and markedly hungry Philly Sargents, but informed us all that while he would be on-hand, he would not be among us at the table.

"My work here," he explained, "is not only far from done, but only just beginning."

While we waited for Mrs. Hudson's late luncheon, I sat Philly down and had a look into his eyes, before listening to his heart and breathing, and testing his reflexes.

As he claimed to feel fine again, I felt no scruples about questioning him on what he remembered about his abduction. He claimed he was aware only of some liquid being poured down his throat in the enclosed carriage after the hands of many giggling children had grabbed him from the street while he stared toward the leering flower girl, who had been grinning so pointedly at him. All this was followed by a sleep so deep he was untroubled by dreams, and knew nothing else until he came awake in our company this afternoon.

"I guess it's lucky I am," he added. "Luckiest bloke in the city."

"Lucky you are to have friends who care about you," said Dawkins. "That is not something to be taken for granted, my boy, for not every child has that resource."

Philly also ate well at lunch, falling onto his food so

hungrily that I found both Dawkins and myself looking on in amusement as he put away most of a tray intended to feed four.

"Always a delight to see a growing boy eat!" Mrs. Hudson said with a chuckle, as she came to clear away the dishes.

It was only then that Holmes, who had been off at his chemistry laboratory with the items he had brought back from the lair, put aside his work and approach us.

"I ask you, Mr. Dawkins, for a favour," he began.

"Yes?" Dawkins replied. "Anything, of course."

"I thank you, and would ask that for a time, until I have brought this adventure through to a more informative conclusion, Philly here might stay as your guest, at your home."

"Oh, certainly, certainly," Dawkins said quickly enough. "It would be no bother, and quite an honour to play host to a successor to my own one-time craft–though a practitioner toward better goals than were my own."

And so that was settled, and a very few minutes later, Philly departed with Dawkins, off to the older man's not insubstantial house in Portman Square, a place befitting a cannery baron, as the one-time thief had long since become.

This achieved, I found Holmes returned at once to his own work, and I had no opportunity to engage him in further conversation, or learn of any new insights he had achieved into the matter. Thus I went out for a bit, and returned just after four, to find not one but two delivery boys in bright red livery departing from Baker Street at a dead run, coins gleaming in their clenched fists.

Inside I came upon Holmes seated in his favoured chair, a cat-like grin upon a face I could instantly tell was lit from within by the glow of satisfaction.

"There you are, Watson," he began, "on-time as always."

"I am?" I asked.

"Perfectly," he replied, "for I am about to take a most satisfying carriage ride, and would be much obliged were you to take it with me."

A grin not unlike his own took over my face, as I said:

"I am, as ever, at your service!"

<><><><><><>

As we were conveyed from thoroughly respectable Baker Street toward the opulent houses of Mayfair, I asked Holmes:

"Am I correct in sensing you are onto something? Something significant?"

"That would be an understatement, Watson," he replied, "for in truth, I have solved the case."

"Solved the case?" I cried.

"Yes," he avowed, "does that news surprise you?"

"Well, I retained every faith that you should make it so, but I suppose I expected more time to pass, with more research, perhaps some experimentation in your laboratory."

"Oh, that indeed went on," said Holmes, "though rapidly, while you dined and while you were away."

"And what have you learned?"

"Everything."

"Then perhaps I should ask you to explain it to me from the beginning, if you'd be so kind?"

"My pleasure, my dear Watson! I noted in the subterranean chamber that within the wig itself, which I had no doubt had been deliberately left behind for us, lay an indispensable clue."

"Which was?"

"A single brown hair, long, therefore from a female head."

"And one hair was a great clue?" I asked.

"Oh, quite so," he told me, "one of the cornerstones of my deduction."

"But, Holmes," I said, "there must be scores of thousands of brown-haired woman in London, yet from that alone you tell me you have identified our Granny Midnight?"

"From that alone? You mistake me, Watson, it was but one piece of a very solid puzzle. Think, you yourself have identified that there are a tremendous number of women residing in this city who are endowed with brown hair."

"Yes," I agreed.

"And what are we to make from my discovery of the hidden area within the inner chamber, that contained what looked to my eye to be the entirety of what has been taken by the platoon of child thieves, acting in Granny Midnight's name?"

I thought a moment, then said:

"That...she did not want the loot?"

"That she did not *need* it. What does that suggest?"

"A woman of means," I said.

"My thought as well," he said lightly, as the horse continued to trot on under the driver's direction. "And that does narrow our potential pool considerably, wouldn't you say?"

"Well, by perhaps four-fifths of its number," I agreed, "which is still a vast selection to sift through."

"Ah, but neither was the hair afflicted as yet with traces of frost, showing me the woman in question was young in years."

"All right, the pool narrows still farther," I concurred. "So your interest falls upon a wealthy, or well-to-do brown hair young woman. Let us say less than middle age?"

"Very good so far," he said with a twinkle in his gray eyes. "It might interest you to know that as I said, I carried out certain tests upon that single hair, and discovered traces of a perfume upon them. It was one of Parisian manufacture, *Parfum des Odalisque*."

"Oh, that one is pricey!" I remarked, for I did know of it.

"And available at but a half-dozen boutiques in London."

"The net tightens!" I stated.

"I can further assume that to be able to undertake the rôle of Granny Midnight, our lady must have a certain freedom of movement in her possession, therefore I focused upon the ideas that she was either the wife of a military man given to frequent absences from home, or a young woman of independent means."

"Ah..." I released the word admiringly. "The search narrows still further."

"From starting off with a hypothetical hundred-thousand women," he said, "by mid-afternoon I had brought my search down to a pool of twenty-two."

"No longer a vast sampling," I agreed, growing more excited. "Pray, go on."

"In making inquiries through certain channels of mine within the trade industry, I was able to take that group of twenty-two, and reduce it to six, as sixteen who purchased the *parfum* did not fit our description in one fashion or other. Either they lacked the freedom required to fit my profile, or there was some other disqualification."

I recalled seeing runners departing as I came home, and uttered:

"Fascinating."

"Which left me six chances to pinpoint my suspect, which I did through...unorthodox means, let us say, which an honest man such as yourself is best off not knowing."

Surely not some form of burglary! I thought.

"And not seven minutes before I discerned your sure and steady step coming into Baker Street, I knew my woman by name."

"Who is she, Holmes?" I demanded, too overcome with impatient excitement to wait."

Just as I launched my question, the hansom stopped in front of a house of considerable opulence, a mansion by any standard, and Holmes said to me:

"Lady Danyse Havilland, daughter of the late Sir Miles Havilland, maternal granddaughter of the French Comte Claude de Cossé."

The lady's name meant nothing to me, but it rang beautifully in my ears, and as I gazed out at the house before us, I wondered why anyone able to dwell amid such palatial surroundings, would turn to petty crime.

"Come, Watson," Holmes said, as he handed the fare over to the driver, and prepared to step down onto the well-scrubbed, sand-coloured cobbles below us, "it is just possible we are expected."

That idea sobered me, and focused my thoughts.

Up the walk we went, Holmes in the lead, looking quite dapper in his broad confidence, I behind, curious and slightly on-guard, and no sooner had a polite knock been given at the door, than his summons was attended-to by a portly and blank-faced butler, the very model of every propriety.

"Yes, sir?" the servant asked.

"Mr. Sherlock Holmes, and Dr. John H. Watson, to see your mistress," Holmes told him curtly, though without malice in his tone.

"Yes, sir," commented the butler. "And is her ladyship expecting you?"

"Ah," Holmes laughed, "that is the question which has preoccupied me this last hour."

Looking at him with puzzlement, the butler bowed and escorted us into a withdrawing room off the main entryway, and proceeded elsewhere to inform his employer of our coming.

"Holmes," I asked, "shouldn't we be somewhat at the ready? Is this not likely a scenario potentially fraught with peril? To corner a villainous in her own lair is surely...."

He gave me a pleasant stare and smiled before saying:

"Why, Watson, surely you are not frightened by a lady?"

And there I did not know what to say in reply.

A moment later and the woman in question was among us. Her eyes betrayed nothing, nor did her expression of supreme neutrality. I judged her to be just under thirty, her hair of a dull and not unattractive brown, her build rather ordinary, her height neither tall nor petite, her attire that of a wealthy woman of means, "carelessly rich" as the Americans might term such a state.

She stopped a little distance from us and said:

"Yes, gentlemen. What matter brings you to my home?"

Holmes gazed longer at her than propriety normally allowed, and a smile, almost like a twitch, waved across his lips, there and gone in the blink of an eye.

"Lady Danyse," he began, "you can, of course, continue to play the innocent for as long as you desire, but as you see I visit you here without the police, alone and in a show of good faith, displaying no deception on my part, so come, is it too much to ask that you give me honesty in return, to match the courtesy you showed earlier in emptying out the tunnels below Granny Midnight's hideout?"

The lady stood motionless, and in her eyes I saw her mind rushing through scenarios and responses, and in the midst of her deliberation, Holmes pulled something from his pocket, and extended it his hand, and though at first I could not see what was within his hold, it had a decisive effect upon the woman, for she showed a distinct reaction of surprise, and then all hesitation left her eyes. Whatever course she had chosen had certainly been decided upon in that single instant.

"Won't you be seated," she said then, "both of you. Should I offer you refreshments? Tea, or something stronger? The cellars here are quite accommodating."

"I leave that to your ladyship," Holmes replied, "though for me I require nothing save candor, and a few welcome explanations."

It was only then that I saw the item he had held out to her, though I did not understand the strong reaction Lady Danyse had had to it, for it was but a teacup from Baker Street filled with kitchen matches, yet she stepped forward and took this from him, and enclosed her grip around the cup, as if it were both a treasure and a source of pain to her.

"How did you learn of it?" she asked, nodding down at the cup.

"I can uncover truly startling things when I set my mind onto a problem," Holmes replied.

"I think the answer is not such a mystery," she challenged. "When you learned of my father, you learned of this tale, and now use it against me."

"I confess the former part of your statement is true, if not the latter, yet not everyone would have understood, as I did, the effect that tragic tale had upon you."

"Well, then therein lies your genius," she said ruefully, but not with anger.

"What do the matches signify?" I finally asked, though whether of my friend or the woman behind the sinister criminal enterprise I was not sure.

When Holmes did not give me an answer, Lady Danyse stated:

"My orphaned half-sister, the natural child of my father, the baronet Sir Miles Havilland, an unkind man, whom I mourn not, was unacknowledged by our father and left to fend for herself on the streets, while he lived in luxury."

With deep pain in her eyes, she finished:

"Her name was Sarah, and she froze to death on a street corner in Westminster selling matches from a cup one winter night. She was but seven."

I felt the blow of this revelation, though I was still unsure how such an event, tragic though it was, fit into things.

"And when I learned of this," the lady said, "only many years later, after my father was dead, and having no sons, had left his fortune to me, I resolved to aid street children, by whatever means I could."

This puzzled me, though Holmes seemed well aware of it, and nodded.

"I do not understand," I pressed, "you did not aid children caught up in poverty, you exploited them, turning them into criminals."

"Watson," Holmes spoke up amid my tones of outrage, "there is a bit more to the tale than you have so far been privileged to know."

"I thank you, Mr. Holmes," Lady Danyse said. "In fact, Doctor, I operate several shelters for children across the East End, and kitchens where the poor may be fed. I would like to think in the two years of my efforts, I have prevented at least one little girl from meeting her end on a cold sidewalk."

"Yet you have recruited from those ranks, and sent them

out to steal!" I charged.

"I confess, I have done so," she said, staring hard at us both as she did. "And doubtless shall now face the taste of justice for my deeds, am I correct, Mr. Holmes?"

"That is not a certainty, your Ladyship," my friend replied. "For if I thought you as villainous as 'Granny Midnight' the character you have impersonated well enough to fool the discerning eyes of children, I would have had the police here already. But I think there is more to the story of your motivations, and would very much like to hear it."

The woman chuckled.

"Ah, would you now? Then I suppose it is in my own interests as well as that of your boundless curiosity that I provide you with my story."

"It is," Holmes said, with only the faintest hint of reptilian menace under his friendly outer tone.

"When I came into my father's money, I found myself among the wealthiest women of independent means in the city. Suitors, why, they came calling from far and wide. Titled men, captains of industry from the North, holders of vast Irish estates, American tycoons...and I wanted none of them, so I sent them away, and soon barred my door against the lot. No, I cherish my freedom too greatly, so I shall likely never wed. I felt the secret tragedy too keenly, the knowledge that my father, a cruel man, though at times indulgent with me, had another child he left to the mercies of the world, my own blood sister, only for her to meet so horrid an end, while I lived like a princess. He found out about her death, I assure you, yet felt not at all remorseful, or responsible. By contrast, the news, though many years in the past by the time I learned of it, left me determined to save as many children as I could from similar fates."

"So the soup kitchens," said Holmes.

"So those," she agreed. "More than twenty do I fund. But to my surprise I realized not every child would go to these places where help was on-hand. Some were simply too abused by the hard lives into which they'd been born. They are like wild things,

Mr. Holmes, Doctor Watson, frightened of all, their eyes fear-filled, knowing only the rules of the street: steal, eat, fight or be beaten. They were beyond all normal means of helping."

"So..." I felt the pieces fall into place, though what they seemed to signify amazed me. "So you found a means to reach out to these children, too?"

"I did, or rather Granny Midnight did, and so was born in one night of careful thought and creation, my alter-ego. I had her lair constructed, secretly and quietly, then reached out to them, the most feral of children. Where they would not trust church or law or philanthropy, they were surprisingly quick to throw their loyalty, even their love, to a leader who seemed to be one of them grown old. A woman, they thought, born as they were, one who had passed through the fire of their difficult lives, and risen despite it. I threw in the superstitions as well, the sing-song warnings of the fate of those who betrayed her, the oath of loyalty sealed by a kiss on the lips."

"To what end?" I demanded. "You still marshaled what I'm told is the most disciplined cadre of child thieves seen in London in many decades."

"Since the time of the infamous Fagin," Holmes added.

"To what end?" the lady asked. "In the most immediate sense, I kept them alive! I opened the doors to the houses I bought there. I kept them fed. I kept them safe and warm, especially in wintertime, when so many die unheralded on the streets, while the good people of the west end go on about their merry lives. People like you, Doctor. I looked out for them. If some I could wean with time off the dangerous game of crime they all played, so much the better. That was my ultimate hope for them all. Some incidentally, I did reform, but few, gentlemen, so few, for the habits of survival run deep among those who are born unloved and unwanted."

"And so in order to save them, to provide them with shelter and safety, you allowed them to break the law," I pressed.

"But not for my own ends," Lady Danyse stated. "I made not one shilling off it all."

"So I have seen," Holmes agreed. "For I found your hidden chamber."

For an instant the lady showed surprise, then said at a mumble:

"Of course you did."

She then gathered her thoughts and continued:

"I had rules. No violence. No one would be hurt by their partaking in what they called the Game. Since many had previously used violence as a tool in their work, striking out with stones, the use of jackknives to slash the skin of victims, that edict alone did some good. I may even have saved the lives of potential victims by this time. And they needed a parental figure, one that dear Granny Midnight, who loved them all, gave. You may think to sit in judgment on me, gentlemen, oh, yes, but it was I, not you, who saw the plight of children beyond reach, beyond notice, beyond the soft touch of any who would care for them, and I stepped forward to help them all."

I felt myself devoid of reply to that. Here was right and wrong writ out in equal measures, crime, yet charity, the practice of wrongdoing, yet the shielding of lost children from the elements, and the dangers which abounded.

"Yet you drugged Philly Sargents, the boy we retrieved from your lair," I reminded her.

"Unharmed, no worse than dosed with a sleeping draught," she said. "I had to find out who he was, and for whom he worked, for I had to protect my small ones, and the world I'd made for them. But when my little eyes near Baker Street told me of what opponent I faced, all I could think to do was relocate the children to another safe house I maintained, and leave your Philly and the disguise itself behind, in my hopes that if you were not stymied by all this, as I hoped you might be, then you might see it as the offer of truce I meant it to be."

"That was as I guessed," Holmes told her.

"Well," the lady finally asked after a moment's pause in the strange conversation, "you wanted candor from me, and you have had it, Mr. Sherlock Holmes. What say you now? What is to be my fate, for I see it is held in your hands alone."

Holmes stayed in thought for a moment before he said:

"The collected loot you have stored away, must be given to me alone. I will see it turned over to the police, who stand the best chance to see it returned to those from whom it was taken."

Lady Danyse nodded at this, voicing no opposition.

"And Granny Midnight?" she asked. "And when you answer, take note that should she vanish tomorrow from the lives of those little ones, half, I judge, should lie dead for one reason or other by year's end. One cannot leave out a saucer of milk for a starving fox each night, then the take it away, and think the creature shall live."

"There may be a way for your other self to go on," Holmes told her. "I have, as you may have guessed, a vast and far-reaching network within the city. If Granny Midnight, were to turn the children away from the picking of pockets and the climbing into open house-windows to burgle, and instead, under my guidance, re-train them to become lookouts who serve my purposes, then that could be the final cog in the wheel of reclamation."

The woman considered this.

"You would come to the underground warren, and help me train them to this end?"

"I would," Holmes said firmly, "under a different name, and in some appropriate disguise fanciful and impressive to the eyes of children. Together we might turn many around and set them productively onto a path that need not end in ruin, while sparing you the life-sentence you would invariably incur should it be the police, instead of I, who one day happen upon your operation."

Granny Midnight was to continue, I considered. Of all endings this was one I would never have expected.

"I have little choice but to agree," Lady Danyse said, "though given the generosity of the offer you make the children, it is one to which I gladly consent."

"We have a bargain then?" Holmes asked.

"We do," she answered him, "and children to save."

<><><><><>

"I have my secrets," Holmes said to Mr. Jack Dawkins, the one-time Artful Dodger, some two hours later, as we took whisky with the man in his own vast house. "So I cannot say more, save that I repeat what I had said a moment ago, Granny Midnight's days of sending urchins out to rob the unwary are quite permanently at an end."

Dawkins sipped the whisky in his glass, nodding as he considered this promise before at last saying:

"Then I emerge from this matter, which I brought to your doorstep, a happy man, for I know only too well the ruin a cold-hearted crime boss can bring to the spirits of the young. Perhaps one in fifty will escape such a quagmire, I being among those so lucky."

"I and a great many in London are indebted to you, sir," Holmes said, "for calling this criminal enterprise to my attention. Now its days of doing harm are quite ended."

Across from us on a sofa sat young Philly Sargents, the Barker of Holmes' soon-to-be reinforced Irregulars. He looked none the worse for wear from his ordeal and sat drinking a club soda with us.

I asked him:

"How are you feeling, my boy?"

"Right as summer rain, Doc," he replied. "Hard to keep me down for long."

"I have sent a letter of inquiry across town, to White Hall, and my brother Mycroft," Holmes revealed to the Barker, "and it may be you shall soon be set on the path to a new career in Her Majesty's service."

An expression of pure delight took over Philly's narrow face, and I felt good for him, and hoped his future was a bright one, whatever the dangers such service entailed.

From his seat, Dawkins piped up:

"As my old friend and partner Mr. Oliver Twist used to say, 'Sudden shifts and changes are no bad preparation for life.'"

I laughed at that, for it was very true.

Holmes and I took our leave soon after, gladdened by the news that Dawkins had extended an offer to Philly to stay under his roof as long as he liked, pending a summons from White Hall.

I reflected as we stepped into the hansom to take us home on that starry night some two weeks before my wedding, that there was no denying it had been an odd case, one I would not have guessed the ending to if I'd tried all day. Nonetheless, our little adventure with the former Artful Dodger had been no bad affair, and much good seemed destined to arise from it.

"To Baker Street and sleep now, Holmes?" I asked as the hansom jolted to a start beneath us.

"To Baker Street," my friend echoed, pipe in hand, "and on to the next case, whatever it shall prove to be!"

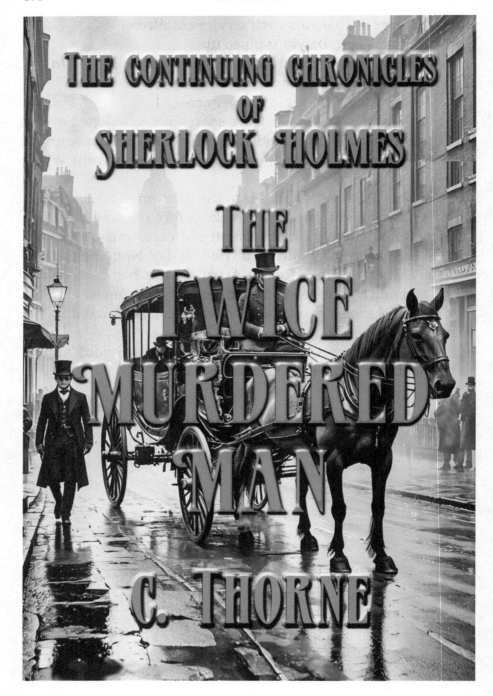

THE CONTINUING CHRONICLES OF SHERLOCK HOLMES

THE TWICE MURDERED MAN

C. THORNE

THE TWICE MURDERED MAN

I t was an odd case, as I remember only too well. It was within a month of my first marriage and I'd been back from my honeymoon for less than a week, that particular working day complete, when a young boy ran up to me on the pavement off Marylebone Circus, and said:

"Aren't you Dr. Watson, Mr. 'olmes' friend?"

I recognized at once that this must have been one of the Baker Streets Irregulars whom Holmes held in such affection, and they in return had elevated him to the highest regard.

"I am at that," I replied, leaning low to be nearer the lad's height, and offered him a smile that he at once returned to me from his scruffy young face. Though I did not know him by name or think I had ever met him, I recognized the traits Holmes prized in his young associates, as well as signs of the training he gave them.

"Yeah, well," the boy said, "Mr. 'olmes mentioned if we was to run into you today—and with so many of us spread across London, it was a near-on certainty we would—we was to mention he is expecting a client today 'round 2.45, and if you're available, he'd 'ave you be with 'im."

"Like old times," I said with a nod, though indeed, those 'old times' referred back but barely two months into the past.

"Yeah, that's the thinking, ain't it, Doc?" the boy said merrily. "Despite his steadfastly carrying on, like, we can all tell he misses you plenty!"

Grateful for the invitation and the news, I reached into my pocket and presented the boy with a ha'penny, which inspired him to tug his forelock before bounding away on his heels an instant later, off to whatever it was that occupied boys his age in the city.

I calculated that I had several hours before I was due home, and there was still time to reach Baker Street before 2.45 —barely enough but it was feasible—so I reversed course from the general direction in which I'd been heading, and went on toward my former home.

In a quarter of an hour I was back at the familiar building where I'd lived until the happy morning of my marriage, and a knock at the door brought Mrs. Hudson, who greeted me with a smile and asked if I'd like her to send up some tea and sandwiches.

"That would be most welcome, Mrs. Hudson," I replied, "though something light, if you please, my wife will have dinner for us in a few hours."

After making polite inquiries after my wife's health and my own, she went off to see to her self-appointed task, and I showed myself upstairs.

I discovered Sherlock Holmes, beyond all doubt the world's foremost detective, leaning low over a test tube kept at a low boil over a gas flame, and for a moment was not certain he noticed my arrival, but just as it had been on the tip of my tongue to call over to him, he spoke out:

"Watson, what shade do you make this compound? Indigo or violet?"

I walked across the parlour to the corner where his strikingly advanced laboratory lay spread out across several square yards, and peered at the well-agitated liquid in question.

"Does someone's fate depend upon my perception?" I inquired.

"Incidentally, it does," he answered with a steady seriousness.

At this news I looked more closely, and decided:

"Of the two choices, I'd lean toward indigo."

"Well," Holmes said, straightening himself up and shutting down the flame, "that is good news, then, to Laird Alton Gilesby, a Scottish peer, currently engaged in the preparation of an utterly prideful lawsuit with the Spanish *maestro* Jesus Enrique Fonseca de Guzmán y Pérez, over a libelous letter the Spaniard claims not to have authored, and which Laird Alton insists he did."

"What is the libelous accusation" I asked.

"Cowardice on behalf of the Laird's father in the Peninsular campaign under Wellington."

"Dear me," I noted, "such talk could sting a family's pride."

"More than that," he demurred, "for in a family with a proud martial tradition such as that held by Gilesby clan, who, as the Laird boasts, have fought in every war of note for some four centuries, the matter could be ruinous to their reputation as soldiers of the first order. In fact, if the letter were shown to be genuine, it is his proposal that he travel to Madrid to challenge the *maestro* to a duel to the death, with sabers."

"Good Heavens! So, thankfully for all, these results indicate, then, that the *maestro* did not in fact send the letter?" I guessed.

"Indeed my good Watson, the results prove both men

have been defrauded by an as-yet unidentified third-party intent upon setting them bloodily upon one another. With this knowledge, the bellicose Scotsman can make his peace with the hot-natured Spaniard, a good development, as his lairdship is seventy-three, and the *maestro* seventy-two, though should one or the other of these contentious gentlemen care to hire me to act further on his behalf, I can set their attentions on whatever roguish troublemaker has concocted this viciously slanderous facsimile of a letter."

"I see," I said, as I watched Holmes write his findings out on a sheet of paper, which he folded into an envelope, and set on the door-side table, for its inclusion in the mid-afternoon post.

"Now," he said, as, hearing her rising footsteps on the stairs, Holmes opened the door for Mrs. Hudson and removed the tea-tray from her hands, "I would say, my dear Watson, that we have just enough time to partake of this excellent refreshment before my client arrives."

I took my seat and had a thirst-quenching sip of the excellent Himalayan tea my former landlady had brought up, before asking:

"So who is this client to whom you have alerted me, and asked I be present to see?"

"A lady," Holmes replied, handing me a small plate on which a pair of watercress and cream cheese sandwiches lay. "A Mrs. Martin Andrews, of Olive Wood Square, Tyburnia."

I nodded, knowing Tyburnia was a prosperous part of town, home to mostly young and growing families whose heads of household were doing well in various trades. If it was not the loftiest address in London, it was certainly far from the worst.

"Her note, sent last night, tells me little," Holmes said, "though when a woman comes alone to pay a professional call upon me, I can somewhat narrow the eventualities down over those which might compel a man to come to Baker Street."

"How so?"

"A woman's worries, Watson, tend to be domestic, and more personal, less of the outer world than of the universe of the household....which, incidentally, is the more important hemisphere of life. There have been exceptions, of course, but as a rule I think a case brought to my door by a woman will concern her family in some manner."

"Ah," I noted. "So nothing else was gleaned?"

"On the contrary, I could see much in her writing. I saw she was educated, both at home among governesses of a high quality, and at least briefly at a domestic finishing school for ladies of the prosperous middle class. I dub her a reader, and see in her prose that she is upset but containing her emotions. I judge she is an intelligent woman, and that it is possible she has suffered some injury to the right hand in her youth, which still pains her, and plays a rôle in the stiff, downward strokes I perceived as visible on the letter F, when she forms it. I noted her as a reader, because the long-time practice of holding the lower portion of a book between thumb and forefinger has had a stretching effect upon the musculature, and exacerbated the effects of this old injury, as is apparent in her handwriting."

"Like a straining injury to the *thenar* muscles?"

"Yes, very probably, most likely resulting from a fall down stairs as a girl."

Ah, staircases, I thought, the most hazardous part of any home, which had sent a score of injured patients to me in my career.

"And what is the nature of the indisposition which brings her to Baker Street?" I asked him.

He shrugged and began to pack his pipe before answering:

"There I reach the limit of my deductions, but as the time for enlightenment has nearly arrived, our mutual agnosticism on the matter is imminently to be dispelled."

It was at 2.44 by the clock above the mantel that the bell outside 221B Baker Street rang, and a moment later—exactly at 2.45, I noted with some amazement—Mrs. Hudson showed the caller in among us.

"Mrs. Martin Andrews," Mrs. Hudson announced, before taking the tea tray down with her again, and leaving Holmes and me to carry out the consultation in private.

"Mrs. Andrews," Holmes said, rising and bowing mildly to the lady, who, I saw at once, to my distress, was dressed in the black of widow's weeds.

"You are in mourning, Madam," I noted.

Allowing Holmes to lead her to the comfortable chair he reserved for clients, Mrs. Andrews said with a control over herself that almost concealed the slight wince in her eyes at my words:

"For my husband, Martin."

"Ah, I see," said Holmes.

"My condolences," I offered, "and I'm certain those of Mr. Holmes as well."

"I thank you," she replied.

She was a woman still in the grasp of youth's last lingering touch, before the oncoming of middle age; her hair was dark, her eyes of a hazel note, and her height of medium stature, trim but not overly thin. She had in her voice overt traces of the education Holmes had forecast she'd once received, and I could well believe her to be the prodigious reader he said we would find her to be. There was a dignity to her poise, though I could discern that sadness had a deep hold on her. I found that, somehow, I admired her.

"Please," Holmes began, coming straight to the matter, "when you are ready, do tell me that which you wish me to know concerning the loss of your husband, for I assume this factors into why you have come to me today?"

"It does," the lady replied. "For you see, some five days ago, my husband…"

Her pause filled the air, its silence louder than a sound. She swallowed and finished:

"My husband was the victim of murder."

"I am so terribly sorry," I told her.

Holmes, sitting quietly and leaning slightly forward, his attentions focused, likewise gave a grunt of sympathy and said:

"There are few deeper tragedies which may befall a

household. I perceive you have two children, a boy of still-young years, and a girl, younger still, I make it? I hope they are bearing up as well as you, Mrs. Andrews."

"I do have two children," she confirmed, puzzled that he should somehow know this, "a daughter, Adelaide, who is three, and a son, Martin Junior, who is six, and they are brave souls who are making me proud each day with their fortitude and practical acceptance of a thing so utterly terrible that it surpasses any other event which has ever been visited upon their lives, or my own."

"I can imagine," I noted quietly.

"In what manner was your husband's life taken?" Holmes asked with some tactful reticence in his tone.

"He was stabbed," Mrs. Andrews answered. "Stabbed twice through the heart."

Ghastly! I thought.

"Were there other wounds upon him, beyond the fatal pair?" Holmes asked her, and though I did not doubt the necessity of the question, I pitied the lady its directness.

"There were no other marks upon his person except the strikes to his chest," she answered.

At this Holmes squinted and nodded almost imperceptivity, and asked:

"And where did the fatal crime take place?"

"In Helmark Square, not far from our home, as he was setting off upon a business trip that had been planned for some time. It was to have been one of five days' duration, and to have taken him to Birmingham, to meet with clients."

"What was his line of business?" Holmes inquired.

"He owned interests in several companies, only very small minority shares, but it allowed him to earn a sound income and support us well. Though he was to be en route to Birmingham, he had returned only the Monday before from a trip to the Morgan-Gilliam Iron Works in Macclesfield, just outside Manchester, which he visits...which he *visited*...several times yearly."

"Tell me, if you are able," Holmes said with some gentleness to his verbal probing, "of the crime. Where there witnesses?"

"There were no witnesses to the assault itself," she answered, "which the police have decided was most likely an attempted robbery gone horridly wrong. Martin walked into an alleyway to make a shortcut to Victoria Station, for the 8.59 train, and re-emerged into the same street which he'd just left behind, clutching his chest, which was exceedingly bloodstained."

As a knife wound to the heart was likely to make it, I thought.

"Though the alley had been deserted of witnesses, so far as we know, for none have come forward, many others were nearby on the street itself and witnessed him stagger forth a little distance, before falling, loosing hold on his suitcase only at the last instant, to spill face-forward on the ground, and…"

Here she swallowed hard and said quickly, as if glad to have her mouth freed of the words.

"—laid in a widening pool of his own blood, while several passers-by rushed to aid him, and send up a call for the police. However, before he could be turned over onto his back, he was already dead."

A dreadful event, and horrid it was for a widow to have to tell of it, I thought. Holmes, however, immediately asked:

"Did he say anything in his final instants?"

"It has been reported that he did not."

"The suitcase," he asked, "was it returned to you?"

A germane question, I supposed.

"It was," she answered. "After the police opened it and looked through its contents."

"And their findings?"

"It was unquestionably that of my husband, for it contained letters addressed to him, and his effects, including clothing he had packed that very morning, sufficient for his time away. Beyond that there were only mundane notes on the business he sought to transact in Birmingham. From what I could see, nothing was taken from inside, nor was the lock on the case violated. He retained the money he'd set off with, so the killer took his life to no purpose, even the fulfillment of those ill-desired gains which had motivated him to violence."

"I see," said Holmes. "And on what basis did the police arrive at the conclusion that your husband was the unfortunate victim of an attempted robbery turned tragic?"

"I do not know," she confessed, "save that it was decided it was the explanation that best fit the facts of so sudden an attack in an alleyway."

"Helmark Square is not an area which tends to be prone to violent street crime," Holmes declared. "Nor does your husband fit the profile for one who might draw special attention to himself, if his business is as you have said."

"His investments," she provided, "were all in companies that were quite ordinary, none set about revolutionary discoveries or in possession of special government contracts. Iron works and shipping companies and a large printing concern being the focus of most of his professional interests. I had thought Martin the most straightforward of men."

"You *had* thought?" I asked, catching the phrasing of the statement.

Here she nodded.

"There is much more I have to tell you, gentlemen, for much has come to light about my husband in these last days."

Somehow I had expected as much, given her presence at Baker Street.

"Please," Holmes invited," share all. Being a doctor, my friend understands confidences, and I assure you, your secrets shall not leave this room without your permission."

Mrs. Andrews nodded, and began the second portion of her narrative.

"You can imagine the shock of that initial morning, the hard knock at the door, my servant ashen-faced when she arrived to notify me the police were asking to see me, and then the dreadful news they brought into our lives. It was all I could do to grip the arms of my chair that day and force myself not to cry out in bleakest anguish, but I did not, for I did not want my children, upstairs, to hear."

"You are a strong woman," I told her, with admiration.

"Who were these policemen?" Holmes asked.

"The constables I know not, but I was delivered the news by an Inspector Jacobson, of Scotland Yard, who oversaw the investigation."

"I know Jacobson," Holmes commented, "and find him in general to be a cut above the average London policeman, for what that is worth. I do thank you, please go on."

"As it was Inspector Jacobson's wish to spare me what was next required, he asked if I had any male relatives of adult age who knew Martin, and could go to the morgue, to make the legal identification, though of course the police were fully satisfied as to my husband's identity, and felt certain that he was the murdered man. I mentioned my brother, Mr. Terrance Cartwright, who lived but a mile away, and was a frequent guest in our home, he being a bachelor some six years my junior, and he was fond of Martin and Martin him, almost like brothers themselves. The police went to Terrance's house and informed him of the dreadful news, and in my stead, sparing me, my brother went with them, and returned pale and worn, and seeing me at the door waiting for him to come up the walkway upon his return, I needed no more confirmation than the grim nod he gave, and my last hope that it was all some dreadful misunderstanding faded. Then, I admit, I somewhat broke down, and lay weeping on my own foyer floor."

"Not beyond understanding," I told her. "The shock of such a day would have rendered many others far more wounded."

She nodded in acknowledgement of my words, and said:

"Terrance told me Martin's face was placid, as if somehow at the end he'd felt no pain when he passed from life. He stayed with the children and me that night, and went the next morning to see the undertakers who handled the funeral."

"And who was this?" asked Holmes.

"A Brite and Sons, off South Hastings Street."

I knew them, and I felt sure Holmes, with his encyclopedic grasp of London, did as well.

"The funeral was the day after that, so two days after his death."

She halted and added:

"I should tell you, there was only the most minimal service, only family, no friends, and no clergy present, for we are skeptics, Martin and I, not individuals who subscribe to the notion of a higher power which created the universe or who governs it now."

She added:

"For where, one must ask, is any sign of its goodness?"

Atheists, I thought, that rare but noteworthy number who counted perhaps one in a hundred of my countrymen among them. While many men approached the subject of religion with varying degrees of ardor or equanimity, it was no common thing for one to be willing to state an outright disbelief in the Creator. I registered neither disapproval nor shock at the news, nor it seemed did Holmes, who was listening without expression.

"Thus after a few moments, when we were gathered around Martin in his casket, which was open, and I saw for the first time that it was undeniably him—that is an important fact as you shall soon hear—the lid was shut and sealed and he was cremated."

"Cremated?" I questioned. "I thought that practice illegal."

"It is permissible with a warrant issued by a magistrate, Watson," Holmes answered.

"And my brother and the undertaker, a quite progressive man, Mr. Brite the Younger, obtained this after making petition to the court. It was granted, though with less than open approval, and the magistrate, a Mr. Justice Hutton, lectured for several minutes on the questionability of the practice in light of the Day of Resurrection, before shaking his head and signing the warrant."

I did not feel what I would exactly term horror at the idea of burning a loved-one's body, for I had witnessed the practice in India, when one of our *sepoys* was killed in the line of duty, and several of us went to pay our respects, but somehow for it to be imposed upon an Englishman, even with his wishes for such posthumous treatment having been expressed in life, seemed offensive in a manner I could not quite grasp. I also was left wondering if there were not, just by some chance, something suspicious there, for cremation certainly rendered a body beyond examination.

Holmes, for his part, nodded and said:

"And I gather some events came soon after which were unexpected and perhaps out of the ordinary?"

"Yes," she answered. "We returned home from the service and found to our utter shock, that in our brief absence, our abode had fallen victim to burglary."

"I say!" I exclaimed.

Holmes seemed to snap forward at this news and said:

"Describe what was taken."

"Some of my jewelry from upstairs, the household silver, but much else had been upturned and rifled through. It was quite upsetting."

"Indeed so," I commiserated. "To have to face that violation on such a day as your husband's funeral...."

"Tell me," said Holmes, "you have mentioned your late husband having a study. In what condition was that room to be found?"

"It was the most assaulted of all within the house."

Holmes stared unblinking into a space beyond the woman's head, and then slowly nodded, as if at his own unspoken thought, then inquired:

"What was taken from that particular room?"

"I confess I do not know, for I have rarely been inside, but I can testify that every drawer in the desk and within the bureau behind the desk was upended, the contents strewn across the floor."

As if the scene of a hurried search, I thought.

"The police were notified?" Holmes inquired.

"At once, and first two constables and then Inspector Jacobson, himself, came onto the scene."

"And what opinion did they render?"

"They were ever-so sympathetic that my home and family should have been subjected to such an assault at so delicate and difficult a time."

"Did they speak of their suspicions in the matter?" I asked.

"Inspector Jacobson looked through each room carefully, and finally with something like embarrassment that such a fate should befall us at our unhappy hour, told me there had been a rash of housebreakings in the district throughout the summer, the work of a particular gang the police were diligently pursuing, and he thought these thugs, somehow learning of our being away at Martin's funeral, used the opportunity to enter and remove what they could. He said it was but a matter of time before Scotland Yard closed their net around them, and promised to make sure the magistrate knew of their callousness toward a grieving widow and her offspring."

"I suppose there was little else he could do," I commented.

Holmes was quiet a moment, then asked:

"Your husband's study. I should like you to turn your thoughts back there for a moment. Tell me, without my question being too specifically posed, was there anything whatsoever about it that at that time struck you as odd, or which stands out to you now in memory?"

Mrs. Andrews honoured his question with a moment's deep thought, and finally I saw her head begin to nod.

"Aside from the overall savagery of the rifling through that space, even the paintings were pulled from the walls, and I did note that the globe which sat upon his desktop, a beautiful specimen of the art, had been shattered from above, and it felt so deep a violation, that one of them had taken a hammer to that object which Martin had so treasured, as if out of hatred for his fellow man."

"Or out of the belief that something was hidden within," Holmes told her. "There is significance there."

"But what should my husband possibly be concealing?" Mrs. Andrews asked. "We are comfortable in our life, or were... but he was certainly not a wealthy man. We possessed no noteworthy jewels or the like which could be hidden in such an artifact as a hollow globe."

"Perhaps the burglars did not know this," I put in, "and were of suspicions and hopeful minds, acting quickly and leaving as few stones as possible unturned."

Holmes appeared to wish to ask more about the topic he'd just raised, but I saw a divergence of thought come over him, and instead he said:

"Please, if you'd be so kind as to continue your account. Tell me of events after this incursion.

Mrs. Andrews said:

"I invested myself in soothing my children for their loss and for the distinct upset of having their home intruded into by low ruffians. Being there to soothe them and dry their brave tears became my occupation, though at night I lay awake and felt the most intense horror that someone walking the streets of London at that very hour had taken it upon himself to assail Martin, who was the wittiest and most generous of men, as my brother or any of several family friends could attest. It seemed the most utter wrong I had ever confronted, almost maddening, so that a few times I... If you will permit me to risk indulging my candor, I put my face into a pillow and gritted my teeth and keened in anguished outrage."

I let my eyes go to the floor rather than look toward her after so heartfelt a confession, and felt a great deal of pity for this much-tormented woman.

She halted, however, and said:

"And then, two mornings later, on the fourth day after my husband's departure and death, yesterday, in other words, an incident happened, the first of two momentous events that have come on the heels of my husband's slaying, and which, perhaps, have even surpassed in their utter magnitude the abomination of his murder."

Here her words halted, and her voice fell away, even as her body trembled as if from a single penetrating wave of emotion.

"How can that be?" I asked. "Surely there is nothing to rival, let alone surpass, the killing of one's spouse."

"All I can say, Doctor," she told me, "is that each of these two events, of which I shall tell has and left me in a state of bewildered grief and hurt, so that I know little anymore of what is reality itself."

That a woman could fall victim to torments surpassing even the murder of her husband left my mind a blank, and I leaned forward to hear what she said next, joining Holmes in his intense pose.

"It was the next afternoon," she said, "moments after my brother, Terrance, had taken the children out to the park, one small mercy that they were away then, that a woman came to my door. I did not wish to receive anyone, and told my maid so, when she answered the knock, but the maid returned and said, with a strange look upon her face, that she believed it best I meet this visitor, so, trusting her judgment, for she is a devoted and level-headed woman, our Sylvia, I rose from my place on the sofa, where I had sat slumped and grieving since the children had left, and went into the drawing room, where this woman waited."

"Tell me of her," Holmes intruded into the narrative to ask.

"She was about my age, taller, though, brown-haired, clearly of a middle-class standing…and like me, she wore the black of mourning. In fact she kept herself veiled the entire time."

"But you could see her face and features through this veil?" Holmes asked.

"Oh, yes, it was somewhat diaphanous, not opaque, but she never removed it, and below this I saw her eyes were swollen, as if from ardent weeping, so I think its purpose was two-fold, extreme propriety, and also to shield others from her state of despair."

"Another widow," I commented, thinking my thought aloud.

"Yes," said Mrs. Andrews, "that is true. I identified myself and asked her what she wanted. In the accent of the north, Newcastle, I guessed then, and was soon to find I was correct there, this woman stared probingly at me, a look verging on anger, but controlled, with much curiosity also within her. She produced a newspaper from Newcastle, the *Herald*, and I saw it was bent to an inner page where the headline spoke of a murder. She lifted it out to me and pointed to a name, and I saw to my shock it was the obituary of my own husband, for it seemed the circumstances of his slaying had been sensational enough for the press in other parts of the nation to pick up the story, and run it as filler in the inner pages, past grander headlines.

"'Mr. Martin Andrews was your husband,'" she demanded of me.

"He was," I replied.

"'And he has been murdered, as this article says?' she asked me.

"I confirmed that he had, and wondered why this stranger to my doorstep was ripping so at my wounds, but what she said next came as such a shock that for an instant it drove away all grief, for she said to me:

"'He was my husband, too.'"

"Oh, my!" I burst out. "Was she lying?"

"She produced a license of marriage," Mrs. Andrews stated, "dated to fifteen months after the time of my own union, bearing her name, Helena, nee Rice, and a date for her wedding to Mr. Martin Andrews, age twenty-five, who shared the same date of birth as my own husband, and whose signature I recognized, though I also saw the signature was slightly different, as if..."

"As if your husband were attempting, perhaps, to conceal his usual penmanship?" Holmes added.

"That was my thought," Mrs. Andrews confirmed. "From

within my utter and all-encompassing shock, I asked her if she'd like to be seated, which she did, and then she proceeded to show me photographs of…of what was undeniably my own husband with a young boy, their child, in scenes of the domestic life he enjoyed there. It was something that froze my feelings and filled me with absolute betrayal. My husband, a bigamist!"

I should have thought I could feel no deeper pity for her than I had to that point, yet here was an offense against her that pushed my feelings to even greater depths. This poor woman…

"Your husband was often away?" Holmes asked. "You have mentioned his business trips several times per year to the north, but how frequent were these?"

"My own thoughts traveled similarly," Mrs. Andrews admitted, "and this part did puzzle me, for though Martin journeyed to other places on a fairly regular schedule, he was away no more than perhaps a total of two months out of every year, and these dates were scattered about irregularly."

"I see," Holmes said quietly. "Please go on."

"I found I felt a good deal of sympathy for this woman, who had traveled half the length of the country to bring this news to me, and we were soon speaking in tones of commiseration to one another, and I saw she was anything but an unkind soul, this Helena Andrews, so that I felt an anger rise in me that Martin had betrayed her trust, as he had my own. I asked about their son, a boy of four, Tyler, his name, and was told of him, and I felt a greater anguish still that he, as with my own children, would now be raised devoid his father. Oh…it was all a dreadful horrifying mess, and I felt such anger toward Martin for what he had done to us all, and for just a little while, I forgot even the unalterable fact of his murder."

"And this other Mrs. Andrews," Holmes asked. "What became of her?"

"She stayed only another hour, for she had a train to catch home to Newcastle, but before she parted, she gave me her address there, and I dare say that as she squeezed my hand in parting, I know there was a bond between us, though a harsh one, based in betrayal and cruelty from the man we both had loved, and trusted."

I offered the lady words of sympathy for her plight, among the worst misfortune to befall a woman I'd ever heard, hollow and to little deep effect I knew my condolences to be.

"Only to you today have I made this revelation," she added. "I have told no one of this news. Not my brother, not my children, not even my own diary, which I have kept since I was a girl of nine."

She grabbed her right hand then with her left, and began to massage at her fingers, and I noted that one of them was slightly twisted, as if it had once been broken, and badly set: an old complaint, I judged. Holmes had been correct in picking up this detail from her handwriting.

"We thank you, then, for the trust you place in us," I said.

"So there I was," she continued after this revelation, "still dressed in black, as you see me today, though I had begun to wonder why, for did such a creature as a bigamist deserve to have those he had betrayed grieving for him? Still, the house itself remained set into the mode of mourning, even the maid, Sylvia, loyally wearing a dark dress. In a show of support, a black band was to be found about my brother Terrance's arm, and my son Martin Junior's, as well. Our little girl I judged simply too young to understand too much of the customs of death and remembrance, so was spared the duties of mourning. When my brother and children returned, we ate a small supper, Terrance went home, and the night came in due stead, that terrible time when I was left alone once again with my thoughts, my torments, my unanswered questions."

There was then a measured pause and finally Holmes said:

"You mentioned another incident, so great that it, too, exceeded even the impact of the murder. Would you tell me of it?"

"Yes," she answered. "Yes, indeed."

She drew a long breath, and then she said them, words I could scarce believe I was hearing, even as I did so, for Mrs.

Andrews said:

"On the fifth morning after his death, today, in other words, my husband, Martin, came home."

"What?" I exclaimed. "He *came home*?"

She did not drop her eyes from my face, but nodded and said:

"I was at my front window, gazing out at the world, as I had often found myself doing in those interceding days, when I felt my every fiber clench in confusion and astonished disbelief, for stepping from the street and coming up the walk as he had so many countless times before, was Martin, carrying the same suitcase with which he'd departed, the same suitcase I knew lay in the study, where I'd set it after the police had brought it by."

"But this is unbelievable!" I cried.

"Yet I insist it came to pass," Mrs. Andrews stated.

"Indeed," Holmes said, his eyes intense and focused with so grim a depth that I could not tell how he was truly receiving this claim.

"I have already told you I am a doubter on the subject of the most high, and have been since I reached anything like the personal age of rational thought, so needless to say I bear no convictions on the subject of ghosts, and never quite entertained the idea of one, even as an apparent phantom came walking toward me, his eyes locked innocently on my own, a merry whistled tune passing his lips, and straight to the door he strode, no sign on his features of there being anything amiss, or different from any of a thousand other times he had come home in this manner, bearing little gifts from his travels to give us all."

"How did you meet this event?" Holmes asked her.

"I stood rooted to the floor for a moment, before falling back to the parlour which sits left of the foyer at the fore of our home. From the doorway, he having stepped just inside, Martin looked at me in a peculiar manner and chuckled as if he suspected some jovial cause for my dramatic response to the sight of him, and asked:

'Why, Viola, whatever is the matter with you today? You

look like the cat that has swallowed the canary.'

"At that a sound burst from my lungs, one I cannot begin to describe or define, but it was a primordial noise, from deep in the instinct chambers of the brain, for all that was too much, and I think for just an instant I saw my surroundings swirl, as if I were about to fall into a faint. Martin moved forward in a rush and took hold of my arm, and I felt his hand was quite normal, warm and firm and even from so small a touch I felt the transmission of the love I knew he still, despite his transgressions, surely bore me, as he sat me onto the sofa and asked if I was well, and were the children and Terrance."

"And what did you say?" I asked, not knowing what to think at that moment.

"I told him we were all well, but without even quite thinking of what I was saying, I burst out, 'Martin, it is you who are not well, for you have died, and we have had your funeral!'"

"And his reaction?" Holmes inquired.

"Momentary puzzlement, confusion, as if I were teasing him, or overcome by some illness or emotion. He said:

'My funeral?'

"I should have couched my words, I know, but I said: 'Yes, husband, we have been to your funeral. Your ashes were scattered in the park, as we spoke of. I saw you. You were dead in your casket, a murdered man, struck down at knifepoint the very day you departed from us for business!'"

"Dear me," I breathed.

"And what did he think of this news?" asked Holmes, his directness containing little of diplomacy but much of dire curiosity.

"I tell you at first his face was blank, uncomprehending, struck by the sheer impossibility of what I was telling him, then..."

"Yes?" Holmes demanded.

"Then a change came over him, a most remarkable thing to see, a complete transformation, part terror, and part its twin, horror, a seeming understanding of something of such terrible magnitude that it appeared to crumple him, causing him to fall forward, partly into me, though he caught the edge of the sofa in his hand and steadied himself. Without another word, but with his eyes locked on my own in a condition of all-possessing comprehension of some horrendous truth to which I was left ignorant, he rose and backed from me a few steps, then fled out the door he'd just entered, and from the sofa I watched as he departed, nearly running, out into the street and past the few others milling about there, until I lost sight of him around the corner."

"I have never heard the like of such an account," I told the woman, as I sat utterly still in my astonishment, wondering if I just been given first-hand details of one of the most convincing encounters with a ghost I was ever to receive.

Holmes rose and walked across the room, where he stood with his hands behind his back, head bowed in thought, before, after a number of seconds returning and demanding of the woman:

"Did anyone else witness this event?"

"The phenomenon was confined to my eyes alone," she said.

"So no other witnesses at all?" Holmes pressed.

"Mr. Holmes," she said, "I believe I see where you are going with your questions, and though I do understand them and concede the nature of what I have just told you demands they be made, it is no less difficult to sit here and perceive the unspoken explanation you hold in your voice, that a woman, driven past her senses by too much tragedy, experienced an episode of hallucination."

"I confess the idea seems the most likely explanation," Holmes granted her.

"Yes," she said, "I admit that is true, and so I have saved the final revelation until now."

Holmes leaned closer to her and I held my breath in anticipation, wondering what was possibly to be added to this incredible tale.

"The body of my husband was to be found off Alfred Street, some blocks distant, later this morning, just before nine, roughly an hour after I had seen him. Once again, he had been stabbed through the heart, in the presence of no witnesses, and left lying on the street, just beyond an alleyway. The only difference in the two crimes being that this time the suitcase he bore had been opened, and the contents were scattered on the ground."

"His body was found?" Holmes pressed, his face aghast with the magnitude of this information.

"And lies now in the morgue off Twick Street," she said. "I was informed by the police but two hours before I came to you. If I have seemed calm in my telling of these past days, it is only because I have no more shock and grief to display, and only seek to know how such a thing is possible, for my husband's death five days ago was duly attested to by the coroner, he was prepared for his service by the undertaker, Mr. Brite, and we all saw him in his coffin, and looked on even as he was conveyed to the furnace for cremation. Yet he came home, he spoke to me and touched me, only to flee, and have the fatal crime repeat itself, resulting once more in his murder."

I heard noises in the street beyond but no sound within 221B Baker Street followed these words until Holmes finally rose and found a sheet of paper and a pen, and setting these on the table before the woman said:

"I wish to see the body of the man you say was your husband, and to do so, I require you to authorize my visit. To that effect, would you please write out a little note, granting me permission to do the same?"

Mrs. Andrews slid the paper across the little table, and wrote out the requested words, and Holmes took the note back, before folding it and placing it in his pocket.

"I thank you," he said. "You have brought a tremendously singular matter to me, madam, and there is much for me to consider, though I will go at once to the morgue, and start from there. Are you able to see yourself home?"

"Yes," she replied, and I felt she was a resourceful and capable woman, not the least for the manner with which she had borne so many tragedies and unfortunate occurrences.

"Then I shall call upon you there as soon as my business elsewhere has been concluded," Holmes told her. "There is more I will discuss with you, and with your permission should like to undertake a small search of your home."

"Of course," she answered.

"Rest assured," said Holmes, "I am acting to come to the heart of this baffling case, and shall report all my findings to you."

With that, he turned away and veritably dashed across the room, preparing items he intended to take with him to the morgue, and as was so often my rôle, I undertook the demands of polite propriety, and led Mrs. Andrews downstairs, and summoned a cab, which I saw her into, and bid her be steadfast, and promised Holmes and I should call upon her soon.

Back upstairs, I came before Holmes and said:

"Is it the other wife, do you think, who has done this? The one in Newcastle? Women have killed for less than the news their husband has another family elsewhere. She could have been fabricating the fact she had only learned of this information from the newspaper accounts of the murder."

I did not ask what I had also considered, however unlikely, that my friend's own client could have somehow been the killer.

"Many things are possible at this time, Watson," Holmes answered me, "though I think your scenario sidesteps the most interesting and germane fact of the matter."

"How a man could come back from the dead, as it were?"

"That is not how I should have put it, but, yes, if you like. The answer is of course that a man cannot, death is final, which suggests most clearly and immediately, a second probability."

I had only to think for a moment before I said:

"That there was not one man who died, but two. Two men have fallen victim to murder." I then put a name to the idea. "Twins."

"Indeed," he answered, "though this places us no nearer to the solid ground of fact, for aside from the peculiarity of these men inexplicably keeping from their wives all knowledge of their brother's existence, I have never heard of twins sharing the same name, have you?"

"I have not. I cannot imagine any parents undertaking such a practice, which might even be illegal, I have no idea."

"Which brings me back to a profound and singular mystery, why would apparent identical twins share the same identity, and why were each slain?"

"And," I added, "slain in the same manner."

As we descended the stairs to proceed on from Holmes' lodgings to the Twick Street morgue, Holmes carrying his client's note, he said to me:

"I direct your thoughts, Watson, to the reaction of the London-based Mr. Andrews, to his wife's news of his apparent death. Was his reaction what you would judge to be normal?"

I answered at once:

"Decidedly abnormal. A man might perhaps suspect some lurid jest was being made, and react with shock, but I think he should then feel a great stirring of curiosity, and seek to learn the facts of the scenario, in order to remedy the misunderstanding."

"Instead," said Holmes, "it seems this man responded with what I might dub a certain comprehension, as if it touched upon a pre-existing fear, and he fled away in an instant, ultimately to his own death. From the first I drew several possible conclusions based on my client's account of his behavior."

"Which were?"

"That the late Mr. Martin Andrews of London died in full possession of knowledge as to who his Newcastle doppelganger was, and likely why he died. He felt both horror and a terrible comprehension, likely linked to an understanding that he, himself, was in grave danger. Perhaps there was some nobility in his fleeing as he did, seeking to draw the peril from his home, or it is just as probable he was thinking only of himself, or even that he was making away for a pre-arranged place of safety."

"Safety from whom? From what?"

"There I cannot as yet say," he replied. "Though I draw your mind back to the break-in of the Andrews' family home, in London, certainly unlikely to be a coincidence, and the fact the perpetrator or perpetrators focused so heavily on Andrews' personal study."

"They were looking for something!" I cried.

"Almost certainly."

"And did they find it?"

"Again, it is too early to say, though I intend to visit the scene as soon as my stop at the morgue is completed."

"So," I stated in summary, "we have two men, likely twins, living half the nation apart, each sharing the same name, the same identity, as if they were one man, a ruse perpetuated with such acuity that not even the wives suspected a thing. We have one man slain in London, far from his home in Newcastle, on the same day the other left his family for a supposed trip of some five days' duration to Birmingham. The London-based brother then returned home, unaware of the first murder and his own presumptive death, and realized with horror that the brother he had kept secret from his spouse had been violently struck down and misidentified as him, inspiring him to flee, only to himself fall in a strikingly similar manner moments later, also a few blocks from the Andrews home."

"I find nothing to quarrel with in your encapsulation of the probable chain of events," Holmes told me.

"May I safety conjecture that the proximity of the first murdered Mr. Martin Andrews, of Newcastle, to the home of the second Mr. Martin Andrews, of London, husband of your client, indicates they were to have met with one another, and taken the trip to Birmingham, or wherever it was they were actually going, together?"

"A definite possibility, Watson, but not a certainty."

"If so, to what end?"

"An important point. One I suspect might bring great

clarity to the matter, therefore something I must learn."

"Two murdered men," I said with finality, "each stabbed in the same vicinity, each sharing not just identical features but a common name, secret lives, mysterious trips far from home, a burglary, and two ruined families.... But what does it all mean?"

"That," Holmes said with a certain joy in the contemplation, "is for the moment a mystery most profound."

<><><><><><>

The morgue at Twick Street was a building I had entered before on three occasions, two of them professional—deceased patients, both elderly—and once in Holmes' company, concerning a *demimonde* who had acted as his informant, and who had been pulled from the Thames, though ultimately it was determined her death had been as a result of a drunken fall, not retribution for acting on Holmes' behalf.

However, my familiarity with the place left it no more welcome as a location in which to spend the latter-part of my afternoon, for I hated death and had invested my career fighting against it, and here on display was the proof that in the end mine was destined to be a losing battle. It was a low-slung brick structure from the middle-years of the century, business-like and with little pretention in the minds of its creators to play at it being anything other than the site of the necessary but quite grim function it served.

Holmes inquired at the front desk, where a short, thick-waisted man with the dull look of a pug-dog sat at a desk, and soon examined the note he presented from Mrs. Andrews.

"You are acting on this woman's behalf?" the man asked. "The wife of the deceased? Are you, then, making the official identification?"

"I believe that may have already been made," Holmes answered, "by an Inspector Jacobson of Scotland Yard. No, rather I am here in a professional capacity, with this doctor," he gestured to me, "to make an examination of the body."

The man frowned, as if not quite sure where this request and its circumstances fit in among the multitude of regulations which kept such a place functioning, and I believe he was about to cite there being a lack of proper paperwork in our possession, but whatever his reply was to have been, it was rendered moot by the opening of a door to the side of the outer office area in which we stood, and the emergence of none other than Inspector Jacobson, himself, of whom Holmes had just spoken.

"Sherlock Holmes!" the Scotland Yard Inspector called out in surprise when he spied my friend on-hand.

"Ah, Inspector Jacobson!" Holmes replied, full of bonhomie despite the location in which we all stood. "It is little short of providential to encounter you at this time."

Jacobson came to stand beside us and asked:

"Pray, why is that? In fact I have had you in my thoughts as well, for you wouldn't believe the case that's landed on me, Mr. Holmes. You simply wouldn't."

"Is it by any chance a twice-murdered man?" Holmes asked.

The expression on the Inspector's pale, oblong face was all-but priceless, but as Holmes soon brought him up to date on the facts as they appeared to be, Jacobson took on a look of relief, and nodded.

"That is the one," he agreed, "and a troubling situation it is, for by all appearances the same man, possessing the same name, has been struck dead hereabouts in a five-day stretch. But come back and see for yourself."

As Holmes and I were led to the door, I turned and gave a nod of thanks to the man behind the desk, courtesy and a certain diplomacy being my reasoning there, for it was not unlikely my professional path might cross his again, and then I followed the other two men down a long hallway painted a murky and unpleasant shade of green, which was so frequently in those times to be found in government hospitals and the like. As was often my lot, I seemed forgotten as the other two carried on a conversation, Jacobson giving the detective details of the crime that had not been within Holmes' client's hemisphere of knowledge, including the fact that the first dead man's hand had been gripped so tightly to his suitcase that it had required two men on staff there at the morgue to wrench it free again.

"And yet when I opened the case," Jacobson confided, "there wasn't anything noteworthy within, any more than there'd been this present time I investigated the apparent murder of the selfsame Mr. Martin Andrews."

"The suitcase remains on-hand here, for me to look over?" Holmes asked.

"Yes, in the room with him. But I can save you some trouble and say it held nothing more than the clothing he'd taken with him on his supposed five-day trip, and some paperwork that looks ordinary enough, which concerns companies I cabled up to verify existed, which they do. Also...."

Here even Jacobson paused, for the revelation was not a pleasant one.

"And also some gifts the man had bought to bring home to his wife and children. Perfume, and a spiral-top for the boy, a small Norman-style doll for the little girl."

"How horrid that he never got to deliver them," I spoke up.

Jacobson nodded his agreement, less hard-hearted than many policemen, and added:

"Aside from being so deucedly strange, this entire case has nothing but sadness at its heart. Two grieving families, as you tell me, two dead men, each posing as the same person, and now each slain, leaving others behind....? It's madness on top of mystery."

"So you, too, had begun to seize upon the idea that there were two men?" Holmes inquired.

"Well, of course," Jacobson said with a wrinkle of his brow. "What other notion could there be?"

"Men have set off down stranger streets before," answered Holmes, "and sown the seeds of implausible explanations. I am glad to find you so level headed, Inspector."

With a light and unmirthful laugh, Jacobson said:

"Of one fact I can assure you from my eighteen years on the force, Mr. Holmes, and that is that once dead, men do not come back to life."

He cleared his head of this thought and then said:

"I shall shortly have the police in Newcastle on the case at their end, too," he promised, "looking into the affairs of that particular Mr. Andrews, though both murders occurred down here in our jurisdiction."

"As we reached the door to a room prominently marked with the number 3, Holmes paused to ask:

"Now that I have acquainted you with these greater facts, may I ask if you have formed any theories of explanation for the entirety of this matter?"

"I admit it dazzles me," Jacobson told him, "but let me try. Brothers, long lost, each unaware of the other, brought up by different families, perhaps after an early-life adoption separated them, and in some coincidence that proves truth is stranger than fiction, each are given the same Christian names…?"

He sighed heavily and said:

"I confess, Mr. Holmes, I am so far defeated by the unlikeliness of anything I can come up with to cover the presumed facts."

Holmes smiled and said:

"Then let us learn more. Inside room 3, if you please."

Within the aforementioned space was the same typical mortuary chamber one might find anywhere in the nation, presenting an economy of size, and displaying the necessary tools of its function, a drain on the floor, and a table made of cast iron, upon which, nude and devoid even the drape of a sheet, lay the body of a man of early middle age, bloodlessly pale, and even to the eye clearly stiff with rigor mortis.

Holmes approached these remains without hesitation or reaction, his observational skills forming the whole of his thoughts, I felt sure.

Though the body bore the marks of the resident

pathologist's investigation, which had been undertaken upon it, the chest still plainly showed the twin wounds which had extinguished life from within, and it was upon these that Holmes focused his gaze, while I stood slightly back, with Inspector Jacobson, his face utterly expressionless, as his professional status demanded, standing beside me.

"Not a facet of my work I like," he noted to me.

It did not take long for Holmes to conclude his visual inspection of the corpse of Mr. Martin Andrews, of London, and aside from his leaning close-in to study the death-wounds, and then his looking into the exposed chest cavity to inspect the heart itself, he touched the form only once, taking hold of the right hand and lower arm, before peering critically at it.

"No defensive wounds?" he called.

"None," Jacobson answered.

"So the attack was as swift as it appears to have been proficient."

"Proficient is a word that came to my mind as well," Jacobson answered. "Not the work of a street thug, I gathered, but of someone who knew where to stab, and did so without hesitation, which adds one more wrinkle of the unknown to the matter."

Holmes next removed the paraphernalia I knew to be concerned with fingerprinting, and applied the residue of a finely-powdered cork ash to the fingertips of the body, which he then carefully pulled away onto strips of a thin gelatin-like film of his own devising. These he slid into several glass vials, which he pocketed.

He then straightened, and after a mere two minutes before the body, I would judge, walked away from it as if it were of no further interest to him. He came to stop before the Inspector and me, and despite the presence of a sign on the wall which prohibited smoking, lit his pipe.

"As I did not see it, I cannot speak of the first body," he noted, "the one quite understandably assumed to be Mr. Martin Andrews of London, but which we can now safely say was Mr.

Martin Andrews of Newcastle, and as no exhumation is possible, given the fact of its cremation, I never shall be in a position to offer comment there. Incidentally, cremation is the apparent future of these remains, I presume?"

"I am going to protest that," Jacobson told us, "at least until the case is more at-hand. Never know when the body might reveal more."

"I think it has told us all it can," Holmes said shortly. "As to this man, I can tell you his death was not the result of street crime, but was, as you have rightly noted, the work of a skilled assassin, and master of the blade."

"Chilling news," I said.

"But not entirely unknown," Inspector Jacobson confirmed, "for there has been all manner of crime in London, including that carried out by professionals."

"I would also draw your attention to the wounds themselves, Inspector," said Holmes. "Did you or the pathologist note anything irregular about them?"

Here Jacobson looked mildly chagrined, and said:

"I confess I noted nothing revealing about them beyond the infliction of violence entering so precisely into the heart, and the strikes penetrating so cleanly therein."

"Yes," agreed Holmes, "well said. With such wounds death would have come within seconds."

"At least he did not suffer long," I said hollowly.

"But to add to this knowledge," Holmes stated, "I would tell you, the blade was unusual. Tellingly, and perhaps significantly, so."

"In what way?" Jacobson demanded.

"It bore a diamond shape, to add to its lethality. The fore of the blade was wider than the rear, making its design one of thrusting rather than slashing. It would have required more force to drive it home than a thinner and more traditional blade, but the resulting damage would have been tremendously greater."

He paused and added:

"Its wielder had every intention of killing his target."

"And did so," I said, almost before I realized I had made this unnecessary annotation.

Jacobson stepped back and turned to look toward the body, not flinching before the sight of death, and I marked him as one dedicated to his profession, however often Holmes may have denigrated the members of the force. He said:

"Then the case grows more murky and complex, not less. Instead of two men so luckless as to have fallen victim to stray street crime—which, just to be clear, I always found unlikely— we now have twin brothers, who shared a name and hid the existence of the other, being murdered by what looks to have been a cold-blooded assassin."

"Entirely correct," Holmes told him.

The inspector tossed up his hands and said tiredly:

"This is going to be a right proper beast to solve."

Holmes smiled as he exhaled his pipe smoke, and said arrogantly but with truthfulness:

"Then it is fortunate you also have me likewise actively seeking the solution."

We concluded our visit to the morgue with Holmes taking samples of fingerprints from the handle of the suitcase, and likewise setting these into glass vials, which, I noted, he placed into a pocket opposite the samples taken directly from the body itself.

Inspector Jacobson then voiced a question that had occurred to me as well, when he inquired:

"Out of curiosity, Mr. Holmes, for we of the Yard are not taught this supposed science of fingerprint analysis, would the prints of identical twins be precisely the same?"

"They would not," Holmes answered, "as I have myself ascertained from experimentations to determine exactly that. The fingerprints of twin brothers would be each as distinct from the other as those of any two strangers who crossed paths on the streets of London."

"Then it seems that would usefully aid us," I noted.

'I don't see how, since the body of the first victim has been," Jacobson wrinkled his face in distaste, "ceremonially burned beyond human form."

"Watson is correct, this fact might as yet prove useful," Holmes said simply. "And now, Inspector, I thank you most gratefully for your courtesy and time here today, and vow I shall keep you apprised of any developments in my investigation."

"That is all I might fairly ask," Jacobson replied with a tip of his hat, as we made our parting.

To emerge from a morgue is never a bad development, and I noted the air outside had not seemed quite so fresh ere I'd gone within this house of death, nor the sun so bright and cleansing.

Glad to be out amid the bustle of life, I followed Holmes to where a hansom cab waited, and climbed in beside him as he gave instructions that we be taken to the Andrews house in Olive Wood Square, in Tyburnia. There was no need to direct the cabbie there, for like all his kind, he possessed what was dubbed The Knowledge, that great inner resource that amounted to an absolute mastery of the map of London, and its every street, lane, alleyway, and avenue. It was a proficiency also shared by my friend Sherlock Holmes, though this fact made such a feat no less impressive.

The shadows were lengthening when we drew back up before the Andrews house, and I knew I should soon have to take my leave of my friend and return to my own home and wife, but was glad time permitted me to be present for at least this meeting.

Holmes and I were shown inside by the housemaid, Sylvia, a plain but bright-eyed woman of silent bearing and obvious diligence, who then went to bring down her mistress who was resting upstairs, according to the report she gave.

Among us a moment later, Mrs. Andrews demanded at

once:

"Pray, have you news, gentlemen? It is what I crave most amid the cloud of confusion which rules life in these stressful times."

"I can bring a little more knowledge to you concerning certain matters," Holmes answered, "and can tell you of my plans for the morrow, which involve a trip north to Newcastle, where I think more facts, still, do lie."

"I thank you," she said.

"To begin with, I am glad to inform you, at least, that whatever else may prove true regarding the manner in which he conducted his life, your husband was no bigamist."

Her mouth fell open and a sound like a deep sigh of relief fell from it, as she pressed both hands to her heart and leaned slightly forward, as if exhaling a great weight from herself.

"But how could that be?" she demanded, as if not daring to accept the welcome news Holmes bore. "I saw the license of marriage, as well as photographs the woman from Newcastle possessed of Martin, and noted her child's unmistakable resemblance to my husband."

She listened with steady focus as Holmes informed her of his deductions regarding the existence of twins, each for reasons yet unknown claiming the same name, and keeping their identities hidden from the families of the other, yet each man, at least, clearly being aware of his brother's presence.

"It was why Martin reacted as he did this morning," the woman said, grasping this much in an instant. "He realized his brother had been killed. Oh, Mr. Holmes, was the assailant after *my* husband then, and not the other man?"

"There I cannot speak," Holmes confessed. "It may be as you say, or it may be the killer sought both men, and had some intonation they were to meet and travel together, though why, if so, your husband went on alone, cannot be understood as of yet."

"Then there is much more here than can be grasped without further facts," Mrs. Andrews said quite rightly.

"Exactly so," Holmes agreed.

Mrs. Andrews rose and strode across the room to the far window, the same window through which just hours before she'd seen the approach of a husband presumed to be dead, and looked out for a moment, only to turn back in considerable agitation, and cry:

"Oh, Mr. Holmes, you have helped me in fulfillment of my every hope, but…but the fact remains, I fear I lack the means to pay for your involvement from this point forward, especially in light of the uncertainties that lie ahead for my children and myself."

"Money is no consideration in this matter," Holmes told her. "Indeed I thank you for bringing this case to me, for it is one I find contains a depth that stimulates my innermost desires to pierce through to the heart of such a mystery. I will see this through for you, Mrs. Andrews, never fear, and shall soon tell you why your husband and his brother conducted themselves as they did, and who it was that moved against them in so fatal a capacity."

A tremendous relief poured into Mrs. Martin Andrews, easing away the tense pose that had taken hold of her, and setting in its place an expression of most profound relief which displayed itself upon her face. But with decorum she said simply:

"Then for that promise you have my most bounteous thanks, sir. I am surely indebted to you, as are my children."

With the widow's permission, Holmes collected samples of fingerprints from a number of objects in the late Mr. Andrews' study, including his desktop pen set, the cigar cutter that rested in his drawer, and a mass-produced ceremonial medallion which commemorated the fiftieth anniversary of the Battle of Waterloo.

"Shiny objects frequently yield the best results," he offered us.

As for me, I stood beside Mrs. Andrews and watched my friend at his work, then let my eyes take in the room itself. It was of good size though not overly large, and several paintings hung decoratively upon the walls, including a small one, which depicted a stone cottage in some rural setting.

Holmes then answered a few further questions Mrs. Andrews brought to him, before he and I took our leave together.

As the cab pulled away, transporting Holmes to Baker Street and I to my own abode further across the city, Holmes said to me:

"Now a secondary but peripheral question arises, Watson, that being whether alongside the prints of my client's husband, the London Mr. Andrews, I might discover an unidentified set among the somewhat personal items I have dusted."

"What would that show?" I asked. "That the intruders themselves touched them?"

"My thoughts, Watson, ran into more untoward matters. If such prints were to be found, and if I confirmed those same fingerprints to be common in the house in Newcastle which, with the as yet un-met grieving northern widow's leave, I intend to visit on the morrow, it would open many more questions, and might even hint at a certain depravity which it is best to hope has not been the case."

"Depravity?" I inquired. "Oh!" I then exclaimed. "Dear me, do you refer to the possibility that these brothers lived interchangeable lives to the degree of switching off between households in Newcastle and London, and the families there?"

"Including the very wives there, yes, Watson, an immoral possibility, one I sincerely hope for the edification of both my client and the more distant widow is not founded in practice."

I ruminated upon the repulsive idea of this deception of two trusting women, and felt myself joining with Holmes in hoping the two Mrs. Martin Andrews, however deceived in other ways they may have been, could at least lay claim to faithful husbands.

My contemplation of the ramifications of this scenario was interrupted when Holmes stated:

"Watson, I have long found you in possession of certain valuable insights foreign to my grasp."

"I thank you, Holmes," I replied, touched by this

unexpected compliment.

"Yes," he said, "I place a hardy value on your sense of understanding certain matters which elude me."

I felt quite flattered to hear of my friend retaining such regard for me, or did until he clarified:

"I value your understanding, as I find you utterly representative of the common man which surrounds me."

Oh, I thought, deflating somewhat, *he thinks me common, of course...*

"Which is why I ask you now for your opinion on a matter I suspect may be central to a deeper grasp of this case."

"And what is that?" I inquired, not allowing my feathers to be ruffled.

"Why would any man choose to live in Newcastle?"

"And *that* question is central to this case?" I demanded.

"Oh, yes," he said, without explanation.

I sighed and said:

"Newcastle is a charming city, Holmes, ancient and modern at once, and quite a fine place to dwell, especially if the hypothetical man in question is raising a family."

He listened and for a moment I thought he was to fail to afford me any response, but at last he nodded, and seemed content to let the matter end there.

"You are not going to tell me why you should ask me such an oddly general question in the midst of a murder investigation, Holmes?"

"I should think the question self-contained, as I for one cannot comprehend why a man who in theory might chose all of the nation for his home excepting London itself, may fasten upon Newcastle. My conclusion is he should not, therefore I think there is more to this connection with the city of Newcastle than mere chance."

"So you are attempting to find what is in Newcastle that plays a part in all this?"

"Precisely."

"And have you any insights?"

"None."

"I say," I answered to that, and feeling somewhat flummoxed by my friend's peculiarities, let the topic pass.

Within half an hour I was at my own door, and felt the familiar glow of gratitude that such a happy home was mine, shared with my Mary, whom I loved so dearly, and at table with her shortly thereafter, I recounted to her those details of the case as were fit to tell a woman, only to be surprised by her display of insight when she asked me a question I realized only then I , myself should have laid before Holmes ere we parted for the night:

"Why, my dearest, John," she asked, "did the wife from Newcastle, with her claims of bigamy, not grasp that her husband could not have been the same man as the London wife's, if he was with her as often as the facts seemed to suggest?"

The question rested heavily atop me for the remainder of the evening, and was the last thought on my mind that night as I lay abed, resisting sleep in my perplexity.

<><><><><>

As the next day was Saturday, and I had no patients to see, I was able to hurry over to Baker Street just after breakfasting with Mary, and found Holmes standing before the great window that overlooked the busy city beyond.

"What news today, Holmes?" I asked at once after the most rudimentary of greetings. "What did the fingerprints show?"

"A capital question to begin with, Watson!" my friend said, showing me his spirits were high. I wondered if he'd enjoyed a productive evening that perhaps had set him closer to the solution of the case of slain twins who shared a name.

"So you have learned something?" I asked, encouraged.

"I have determined that the man we visited in the morgue

was indeed the husband of my client, and that he was primary occupant of the study he used for matters of business. No other prints of significance were to be found therein."

"So the 'distasteful matter' we were forced to consider yesterday was unfounded," I said, feeling relief.

"It would seem so. Each man, I think, was master of his own household, and kept to it in proper fashion. In fact, save for the still-unanswered conundrum of the two sharing a name, and the telling manner of their deaths, I have come across no evidence to suggest this pair were in any way odd."

"Oh, I think it is clear enough they were that," I laughed.

"Hmmph," Holmes exclaimed.

"So you are still left with two otherwise normal twins, each with a family and business, each sharing a name, each shielding the other family from knowledge of their existence, and each meeting the same violent death within days, in very nearly the same area. I find it all mystifying."

"It does rather defeat the mundane mind, I expect," said Holmes, "but it might interest you to know I believe a theory I have formed in the night explains all, though still as yet faces a wall of the unknown, for much remains undiscovered this morning."

He pulled himself from the window with a sudden movement that I knew signified nothing so much as that his natural reservoir of energy had found an outlet.

"Watson, as you are a married man, I know your time is not always your own, but I still dare hope you might take a trip with me today, up to Newcastle."

"That has been arranged with Mary," I told him, "who is quite agreeable to the matter, and thoroughly interested in hearing how things turn out."

"Ah, then you shared with my former client, the one-time Miss Morstan, details of the case?"

"I did," I admitted, "for I figured with so many now knowing the details she shared with us, there was no further need to keep her confidence. Was I not to have done so?"

Holmes shrugged and said:

"It is no matter, what is done is done, and as you say, many now know of the matter."

Though he did not criticize my candor with my wife, I received the impression he would rather I had not spoken of the mystery, and from then onward in the future I was always decidedly circumspect when it came to conversing about the cases it was my privilege to be part of.

Within the hour we were on a northbound train, headed at a rapid clip toward Newcastle's Central Station, as grand an edifice as any one might find in London, though in the capital we had several such stations, not merely the one.

I found the northern city to lie under skies chocked with industrial smoke, nearly as thick as one expected to find in Manchester, though if I looked beyond this, there was an undeniable charm to the place, spreading as it did from a central region of clock towers and prosperous shoppes occupying the lowest floors of quaint Tudor buildings, before radiating out into the newer sections which had sprung up with the coming of industry in the earlier days of the century, leading to great rings of dwellings built by '50s to house both the factory workers, and the middle-class families of those men who oversaw them.

We hailed a hansom, driven by a cheerful local who spoke freely and with an easiness I felt was less evident in London, and I soon found myself liking him, and asked a number of questions about the city which he seemed to take pride in answering, telling me:

"Ours may not be the largest town in the realm, Doctor, but I can't think I'd be happier living anyplace else, and I reckon you'd find that sentiment echoed by nine out of ten men you'd care to ask hereabouts, as Newcastle upon Tyne is probably the biggest village in the world, disguised as a city. Everyone is friendly, and everyone is glad to be here in this little slice of Heaven on Earth."

Yes, it was the most exuberant summation of a city I'd ever heard given by a resident, and somehow his loyalty and love of his native town added charm to it in my regard, and perhaps excused some of the flaws I might otherwise have found.

One thing Newcastle was not was sprawling, and it was barely a quarter-hour after stepping into the taxi that we were out again, before a brown brick row house of tasteful appearance and generous size, amid a like number stretching across the entire block.

The residence of the late Mr. Martin Andrews of Newcastle, the first twin to die.

My knock at the door brought a black-clad housemaid to answer, a woman of dour aspect and lips set in a pucker, as if she felt somehow affronted that anyone might call on her mistress in her time of sorrow. Nevertheless Holmes' curt and somehow commanding request to see Mrs. Andrews yielded the desired result, and rather than protest her mistress' indisposition, we were admitted into a drawing room, where thick maroon drapes had been left closed, but which the maid drew open before setting off to carry out Holmes' request.

The light revealed a room of sober tastes and little of the auspicious, the single painting that stood on the walls was one which showed a plain cottage set in a country landscape, with distant hills behind it.

"This is clearly a home in mourning," I commented quietly.

"There can be no doubt there," the detective agreed. "Whatever confusion there may be in this case, we are in the house of a woman who loved her husband, and I think we shall find this state of grief to be no mere window dressing, but a show of genuine despair.

And so we did, for into the room came a woman of early middle years, wearing the simplest of black dresses, which matched shoes of like color, her hair drawn back by a dark ribbon. Her pale face was almost expressionless, her eyes lifeless and reflecting no emotion I could see. Ah, I perceived, we truly had intruded into another's tragedy.

Holmes, I noted, stared at her with an expression of what

seemed perplexed fascination, and I felt an awkwardness to see him regard a grieving widow in so strange a manner.

"The police have told me I might expect you," she said. "You are the detective gentleman from London, and his physician companion?"

"We are, Madam," Holmes replied, giving her a tiny bow. "I thank you for receiving us, and vow we shall do our best not to keep you long."

"For that I thank you," the lady said. "Please do take a seat."

We did so and Holmes asked at once:

"How often was your husband away, Mrs. Andrews?"

"Martin was gone about three days per fortnight."

More often than the London brother, I thought.

"And his explanation for his absences?"

"Business. He had investments in several firms scattered across the nation, and was often required to go to meetings concerning these."

"He made a good income from his work," Holmes noted, not making it a question. "Did he ever mention the names of these companies?"

The woman blinked and said:

"Martin regarded business as his hemisphere within our marriage, just as the domestic side was my own, and it was improper of me to inquire into his affairs. We believed in a clear division of duties."

"I see," Holmes answered. "And in the matter of religion, what were his views?"

"He was always a doubter in the existence of God. I, myself was brought up in the Church, and it was to the distress of my parents that I wed one who held such views, but Martin never hid his feelings, and I entered into our union fully aware of them."

"And did you share his sentiments regarding the Almighty?" Holmes asked.

"I confess, when on occasion we would enter into discussion on the subject, my husband could raise certain

THE TWICE MURDERED MAN

questions I could not answer concerning the presence of suffering and injustice in a world evidently overseen by a beneficent creator, but I retain my faith in Him, and do attend church. Martin had no objections to this practice, but forbade me to take our son along for spiritual instruction."

"I thank you for entertaining the question. When did you learn of the death of your husband, Mrs. Andrews?"

"From the police a few hours ago."

Here I froze, and though I managed to abort the expression of shock I'd been about to express at her answer, I suddenly realized several other things, including why Holmes had stared at her in so peculiar a fashion, for the woman I saw before me, seemingly beyond any doubt the rightful widow of the late Mr. Martin Andrews, of Newcastle, in no way fit the description the client had given of her own visitor: the woman claiming to be this selfsame widow! This woman standing before us had auburn hair, while the other was spoken of as having brown hair. That woman had been taller than the client, this one was diminutive, a good three inches shorter. And while this woman dressed in black, she affected no mourning veil, to cover her face, as had the supposed Mrs. Andrews, who had visited London, a most telling addition to the wardrobe, I now grasped. Who *was* it then, who had come to see Holmes' client in her own parlour, bringing a cruel claim of bigamy? And to what purpose had the lie been uttered?

"I am most terribly sorry for your loss, and the harsh news you received," Holmes told the woman.

"We..." she fought with tears, "we shall not even able to hold a proper funeral service for him, as I am told he was rendered to ashes, like a heathen of old."

"Surely, though, this had been his wish?" I pressed.

"We never spoke of the matter, so I do not know," she told me. "We had every reason to think Martin had decades of life yet to come. Who does not?"

"Madam," said Holmes, "as you are so severely tried by this most difficult of life's visitations, I will keep you but a moment more."

She nodded, and pressed a handkerchief to her eye.

"Though you have spoken of his business affairs lying beyond your knowledge, I ask, do you know where it was that he so frequently traveled?"

"I have told you, he kept those matters from me, for—"

"Yes, I know," Holmes said with a gentle tone, "but surely in all the years, you must have gained some insight into where it was he went most often?"

The lady's face became troubled, and at this I could tell Holmes had hit upon something that had been problematic to her in the past, for certainly she was aware that most husbands, however dogmatic they may have been on the subject of the division of jurisdictions between spouses, were not so secretive on this subject.

Finally, she said:

"Bristol. I know he frequently went there, for over the years there were indications, such as a train ticket left undiscarded, or a newspaper cast into the tinder box, or even once or twice in the homecoming gifts he brought back for me and our little boy. I knew that though he may have gone elsewhere, Bristol was a not uncommon point of visitation for Martin about his travels."

"And Birmingham?" Holmes asked.

"He went there as well." She answered. "Nearly as often."

At this news my heart leapt, for it had likewise been to Birmingham that the London Mr. Andrews, husband of Holmes' client, had been traveling. It may even have been likely the brothers were to have met in London and traveled on together, with the London gentlemen thinking his brother's absence simply owing to him having taken a different train, or perhaps bypassed the trip altogether.

And of course I may also have been wrong about all of this, for I knew I was no Sherlock Holmes, yet these large and unwieldy puzzle pieces seemed to come together far too conveniently to simply set them aside.

I was further led to believe I was not wrong about the significance of all of this when Holmes rose and said to the widow:

"Madam, you have been most accommodating to take a moment to speak with my friend and me during this tragic chapter in your life, and we shall trouble you no further, but take our leave, with our condolences extended."

"And our heartfelt wishes that better days will soon dawn," I added, recalling an old Scottish sentiment for such times.

Out in the street, I could not wait, but burst forth:

"Holmes, you saw it, I am certain, even before I did, likely at first glance, but that poor woman, who is genuine in her grief, is not the person who called upon Mrs. Andrews in London, claiming to be the Newcastle brother's widow!"

"Indeed she is not," Holmes agreed, as we walked down the way. "This woman is the widow, the other...."

Here he straightened ever so slightly, and instructed me:

"Do not look behind you, Watson, but continue on."

"What is it?" I demanded, though complied with his instructions.

"We are being followed, as I suspected we would be."

"Followed?" I repeated. I then noted that he held a small round mirror almost entirely concealed in his hand, and was tilting it in such a way as to give him a near-perfect view of the sidewalk to our rear.

"In another thirty paces we shall come to a side street. I need you to turn with me there, and then to pause, and crouch, and be ready to spring."

"There is danger?" I pressed him, but he made no reply, merely continued on, glancing in clandestine and well-concealed fashion at the mirror in his left hand.

We came upon the side street, and made our turn, Holmes doing so casually, but I with a certain sharpness I rued as soon as I had made it, but I confess a nervous energy was upon me, as it often was before a confrontation I knew was soon to arrive.

We stood just beyond the building that marked the corner, concealed from the sight of anyone coming from the street upon which we'd just been walking, our poses coiled, ready to launch a suddenness of movement, but seconds ticked by and nothing happened, and no one made the turn toward us. Finally Holmes straightened and stepped back onto the street, I straight behind him, and there, perhaps twenty feet back, I saw the figure that was certainly the stalker Holmes had spoken of, for there stood a thin man of moderate though not notably sub-average size, clad in black, his skin slightly olive, his eyes all but radiating some force that was impossible not to make note of, and I saw he was laughing even as he shook his head *no.*

"None of that, Mr. Holmes," the man said, and his accent was strange to my ears, not quite of any one place I could identify.

Holmes sprang at him and a chase was on, his fleetness launched after the smaller, thinner man's utter swiftness, like a hound chasing a light, dexterous deer. I was well behind, as was usual in such scenarios, but not so far back as to be out of the action altogether, and by sheer determination alone drew up nearly onto Holmes' heels, even as I spied the man ahead of us suddenly turn and with a sweep of his arm cast a handful of small metal objects onto the pavement, where they bounced and rolled and came to rest with a single lethally-sharp point jutting upward.

At once Holmes extended his arm, halting me, crying:

"Stop, Watson! Look out!"

I knew at a glance that a quantity of caltrops had been thrown onto the ground, small weapons, each somewhat like those jacks with which children played, only larger, and with spikes instead of muted edges.

Holmes started off again, carefully avoiding the dangerous path, but I knew at once the time the other man's gambit had cost us would prove telling, and so it did, for even as we again drew within sight of him in his flight, I spied him bear down toward a footbridge above the Watersford Canal, that ran through Newcastle's' centre, and up and out he sprang, nimble as a mountain goat, to land on the opposite side, even as the little footbridge lifted into the air. There Holmes paused, and I saw the man vanish into the crowd on the far side, though I noted something I took to be a failing of my eyes, namely that after a very few seconds I had lost track of our opponent altogether, not only the sight of him, but any trace at all, even of his movement, or his clothing.

I turned to remark on this to Holmes, but he was gone, already heading back to the sidewalk where the caltrops had been scattered, trotting forward and calling out to by-standers:

"No! Do not touch them, for they may be coated in a lethal poison!"

At his words the several curious passers-by who had likewise stopped flinched back, especially one portly man who had been about to stoop and retrieve a caltrop for himself.

Holmes removed a thick cloth from his pocket, and gathered up the eight weapons, and dropped them into a sack which had been rolled to smallness in the same pocket.

"I will need to test these," he said to me. "Though at some distant time, well removed from this case."

"Holmes, who was that?" I asked, once we were again walking toward Newcastle Central Station."

"That, Watson," he replied, "was none other than the infamous and legendary Milanese assassin known as *Il Mutaforma*—the Shapeshifter. A man as skilled in his own profession as I am in mine. A being of utter lethality and expertise in every facet of his deadly trade. He takes on only a very few and highly select commissions, and for his work he is paid exorbitant fees. No one truly knows his identity, and the methods of reaching out to him are shrouded in a secrecy so profound as to contain a trace of the arcane, even within his own lifetime."

"How do you know this?" I asked.

"Watson, I suspected it almost at once when in the morgue yesterday I noted the fatal wounds incurred by Mr.

Andrews were inflicted by a diamond-shaped blade, which is one of the hallmarks of assassinations carried out by this Milanese master. I made inquiries and learned of rumours on the continent that *Il Mutaforma* is operating in England, on a special, and secretive contract."

"But what on earth could have been so special about these two men, the Andrews brothers, to merit their murders by such a master among assassins?"

"I have theories, but theories only, so I will not speak of them, for in truth I am still largely denied sufficient knowledge to answer that question."

Pausing, he said:

"You do of course realize that it was none other than *Il Mutaforma,* the Shapeshifter, who paid the call upon Mrs. Andrews in London, posing as the northern widow, and delivering the false tidings of bigamy?"

"That was him?" I exclaimed incredulously, shocked.

"Oh, yes, I have no doubt, for you need only consider that he is named "the Shapeshifter" to come to some understanding of why he is so legendary among members of his profession, for by all accounts he is an absolute master of disguise, perhaps even exceeding my own skills in that regard, for given my build I could never pose as a woman, but he is of a height, with slender construction, and of delicate features and almost an androgynous appearance, so as to be able to transform himself into....nearly anyone. It is his talent, and a deadly one."

"So was the client in danger when she let this killer come into her home?"

"In all her life, I think she had never been closer to death."

"Then why was she spared?"

"Because our foe is a professional to the utmost degree, killing without hesitation when necessary, but regarding, I think, such acts outside his profession as beneath him. Rather like an artist who would disdain the painting of a canvas for which he knows he would not be paid."

"But why did he visit her at all?"

"He came to closely examine Mrs. Andrews' reactions and ascertain what she knew concerning whatever matters lie at the heart of all of this. Had she betrayed a hint, however slight, that she may have been aware of any knowledge whatsoever that either would have aided the assassin, or which I alternately propose may have needed to be kept quiet, he would have struck her down without hesitation. As it was, he saw she was truly innocent of all understanding, and so she was safe."

"But why tell her about bigamy when no such thing existed?"

"There I can but conjecture, though I think it likely he was attempting to anger her, and thereby strip away any loyalty she may have retained toward her husband, and leave her open to revealing what she knew, out of spiteful anger, or for revenge."

"I see," I said, and mostly did, though this was a great weighty knot of facts to set down all at once, and I reflected on it as we stepped aboard the London-bound train, our time in Newcastle itself barely occupying eighty minutes from arrival to return.

<><><><><>

While on the train, seeing the same countryside we'd glimpsed on our trip up that morning, Holmes and I said little concerning the case, though he did speak at length about a chemistry experiment he proposed to undertake at some point in the near future.

"If ever I find an afternoon when crime leaves me to my own devices," he stated wistfully.

The matter concerned his conviction that somewhere within every man and woman there lay a sort of chemical that was unique to each and every one of us.

"As singular as a fingerprint," was how he put it.

"I have no proof that such an identifier is resident in every person, Watson, but it is a theory I have formulated based on certain indicators, for just as no two of us are alike in a great many particulars, so I do believe within us all lies some chemical originality, a code, if you will, unchanging, errantly present within the blood or the tissues. It is as if nature has stamped a name inside our beings, and nothing can change or eradicate that name."

"And from this identifier, each person could be marked as a unique individual," I said, grasping at once the applications this would have for his work, "and through this alone you could single out each person."

"Correct, my dear Watson," he said, "from a single drop of blood, let us say, I could identify he from whom it was shed, out of the billion and a half persons currently resident upon the Earth, and should I one day have the time to pursue the discovery of this marker, I think the profound contribution I might therein make to science may surpass even my contributions in the war against the forces of crime.

It was a grand notion, I thought, and one probably rooted in solid fact, though as Holmes dropped the subject of there being some singular, detectible code within us all, I said no more, myself, and the topic faded like smoke on the wind.

<><><><><>

As I had informed my wife that I was to be away the entire morning, I returned to Baker Street, intent on taking some luncheon there, and then seeing how the afternoon might unfold before I returned home that evening, but in fact Mrs. Hudson appeared upon our arrival, bearing the news that a constable had come with a letter from Inspector Jacobson, himself, addressed to Holmes.

My friend took the letter at once, forgetting, as was often his way, to thank Mrs. Hudson for her trouble in bringing it to him, inspiring her to meet my eyes with a little amused shake of her head.

I watched as my friend's eyes raced across the page, and then I noted a light seemed to glow from somewhere deep within his gaze.

"Yes," he said, "it most certainly proves to be as I suspected."

"What is it, Holmes?" I asked.

He did not answer at once, but halted in thought a little longer before rushing upstairs and calling back to me as I followed:

"Last night I had word sent to Jacobson at Scotland Yard to make inquiries as to any men of a certain name who had gone missing in the last week. He has found one in Bristol, and there can be no coincidence there."

"And what is the name?" I pressed him.

"Mr. Martin Andrews," he replied.

"Why, that is the name of the twin brothers!"

He halted just inside the door and turned back to me.

"The *triplet* brothers, Watson."

Three brothers all bearing the same name, Martin Andrews, each living spread far out across the country, in London, Newcastle, and now Bristol? Two murdered, a third missing under what I certainly saw as the most suspiciously telling of circumstances?

I cried out grimly:

"Then this third brother has likewise been murdered?"

Holmes hesitated before announcing:

"I think not, or perhaps I should say I believe not as of *yet*, for the wife and two daughters of this Andrews brother are missing as well, which is out of the pattern with our suspected killer, the Shapeshifter, who takes meticulous care to remove only his target whenever possible, as a show of his lethal artistry. Furthermore, fully half of this Andrews' money was withdrawn from the bank hours before he disappeared, as reported to the police by a bank clerk."

"Then there is still hope for him?"

"Perhaps, Watson, but we must hurry!"

And so, in an almost comical fashion, I found myself back out the door next to Holmes, the merest note of explanation scrawled and left with Mrs. Hudson to convey to my wife, ere we headed for Victoria Station, en route to the magnificent edifice that was Bristol's Temple Meads Station, almost a cathedral to the invention of the railroad, a palace-like colossus that veritably awed the heart of any who looked upon it.

Back across the nation we sped, westward this time instead of northward, as the heavy late-afternoon sun fell around us, Holmes lost in the machinations of his mind, I somewhat out of sorts, for I knew my wife had not calculated on my being away for the evening as well, though trusting that she knew of the kinetic life my friend led, and the place I was privileged to have within it.

We reached Bristol before sunset, and within twenty minutes more were at a house not entirely unlike those with which we'd had recent familiarity in London and Newcastle, it being the home of a prosperous gentleman of middle-class standing.

The place was empty, for absent their employer and the wages he paid them, the servants had departed, and Holmes showed little hesitation in deftly and unobtrusively picking the lock to the servant's entrance in an alleyway around side, and making his way within, I less confidently behind him, glancing nervously back over my shoulder.

The residence had the oppressive and vaguely eerie silence shared by those abandoned places that once knew the noises of daily life, and the sound of our feet on the stairs as we headed upward seemed loud indeed in the vast echoing chambers around us.

"What are you seeking, Holmes?" I demanded.

"The fulcrum to this entire matter, Watson, for I think it is to be found here."

He came to a closed door before what I guessed was the study belonging to the gentlemen of the house, this third and last-surviving Mr. Martin Andrews, and pressed his ear to it for a moment, before carefully stepping inside with a cat-like caution that almost left me wondering whether he expected someone to be waiting within.

The room was caught in the mixture of shadows and faint light that accompanied most evenings, and heavy drapes had been pulled nearly shut, adding to the effect of gloom, leaving only a small space of lace curtains to illuminate within, though for Holmes this seemed enough, for he moved slowly through the room, looking closely at several of the features, until he came to a cabinet which sat behind a fine mahogany desk.

"As I suspected, Watson," he said almost as if distracted and speaking his thoughts aloud, "someone has been in here since the family left."

This news sent a chill through me, but still I said:

"The police, surely."

"Yes, the police, but beyond that, someone has searched this room with care, but has attempted to conceal all sign that he has done so."

"The assassin," I breathed, my heart speeding up a pace.

"Almost certainly," Holmes agreed. "Have a care, Watson, to stand where you are, and touch nothing, for it is not impossible that our adversary has left traps behind, counting on our coming here."

I needed no further warning, and stayed rooted to the middle portion of the floor, where I stood in the open space between desk and doorway. From there I took in the room, with its walls almost cluttered with bric-a-brac and several paintings, including one of an early-century battleship, and another of a stone cottage amid a rural scene, but mainly I looked on as Holmes opened the cabinet with utmost caution, peering closely at each drawer and outward-swinging door before he opened it. He made a rapid search of all the compartments, and every shelf, each drawer and file within, scanning and discarding what he found.

"How can we be sure the Shapeshifter did not already take what you seek?" I asked.

"Because he was on our trail in Newcastle today," he told me. "Had he found what he desired, there should have been no need to stalk us from London to that northern town, as I saw he did. Having already burgled the home in London, as I strongly suspect he did the residence of the second Mr. Andrews in Newcastle, though undetected and unreported that time, and come up empty-handed, he followed us to see if we emerged with the item, or items in our possession, which we did not."

"Holmes," I asked, a certain unease filling me as the question entered my mind, "how do we know he has not followed us here?"

Holmes stopped and gazed back at me.

"Watson, I am certain of that fact."

I felt a deeper fear then, a sort of sense of peril close-by, and though I can say with some pride that this trepidation did not cause me to falter in my loyalty to my friend, I would also be lying if I claimed it was a calm man who stood waiting for him in that darkened study.

A moment later, Holmes declared with a snort:

"There is nothing in the files here."

I felt both relief—to perhaps be leaving this place we had entered illegally, and to our peril—and disappointment, for it meant our departure would come at the heels of failure, but then Holmes added:

"Unless there is a place of concealment *underneath* the cabinet..."

He ran his hands under the cabinet and across its carved decorations of swirled leaves and tiny flowers, until he pressed at the center of a budding daisy, and even I heard the resultant click from where I stood ten feet distant.

"Ah," Holmes said with relish, "this will be it, Watson!"

He pulled out a small sliding drawer which I saw was carefully fashioned into the lowest portion of the cabinet, near its leg, and a long thin tray slid loose, revealing a small stack of papers within. I watched him take these and sit back upon the floor and begin to quickly read.

"There will be time for their study later," he said after a few seconds, as he placed the papers into an envelope he'd brought in with him, and put this into his coat. "Let us take these with us, Watson, and make our leave."

It seemed an excellent idea, and I was about to tell him so, when from just outside the doorway a voice spoke. It was a calm, careful voice, relaxed and somehow even relaxing, lullingly high for a man's voice, slightly low for a woman's, but until I turned around to see who was speaking, I could not have said which sex it was, though in my heart I already suspected.

In the doorway stood the same figure we'd chased for a block in Newcastle, the Milanese assassin, *Il Mutaforma*— the Shapeshifter—and I felt the hairs on my arms rise amid gooseflesh.

"That will do, Mr. Holmes," the assassin said, almost at a whisper, and I saw in his right hand he held a throwing knife carefully poised, with another at the ready in his left: silent tools of murder. "As it shall for you as well, Doctor Watson, who will take several steps back now, and keep your hands carefully at your side. Any sudden movement will result in your immediate death."

His accent was Italian, though his English was excellent, and for some reason, to this day I know not why, while I stepped back as he directed, I told him so, to which he laughed quietly and replied:

"I thank you, I have studied long to make my words as I wish them to be. Listen, if you please to a little demonstration."

He then proceeded to speak a number of lines from Lord Byron's *Don Juan*, though each in a different accent, one the perfect English of the upper classes, another in swaying Cockney, still others in a Yorkshire dialect, or the West Country, or the Midlands, and lastly in the nasal tones of an American.

"Or perhaps you'd rather I say it in other languages as well?" he asked me with amusement.

I felt he was like a serpent who somehow knows the scales within its coils sparkled with beauty as he then spoke rapidly in

French, and Italian, and German, and what I think were several other tongues as well, Polish, Spanish, and Russian.

"As you see, I can be all men or any man, or any woman as well. I am a being of absolute fluidity and infinite forms. I am the best in my profession not merely for my lethal arts, but for the fact I can, quite literally, be anything I desire to be."

The longer I looked upon this person, the surer I felt this was not merely an empty boast, for arrogant he may have been, and clearly he enjoyed an audience and its adulation—however briefly he let it be expressed—but the individual I saw in front of me had the most androgynous appearance I had ever beheld, and from second to second, depending on the play of the scant light, I realized I could have been looking at a woman or a man, one twenty years in age, or one twice that. It was uncanny.

"Now," he said at last, once my retreat had reached the mantel to my rear, "I will instruct you, Mr. Holmes, on what you are to do next. I bid you, be sensible, as your friend has been, and do not deviate in any way from my commands, or I shall certainly send these knives through each of your hearts, deadly enough in itself, but as you might guess, each blade is also augmented by a quick-acting toxin, which is not the least bit survivable."

"I will comply," Holmes said simply, from where he remained still seated on the floor.

"That is excellent," the assassin said, and I heard he had switched back to what I assumed was his truest voice, a steady speech, his English perfect, but his accent slightly of another land. "If you are the opponent I believe you to be, Mr. Holmes," he went on, "you will know that I could easily have killed you many times since you first entered into your investigation of what is, I assure you, a highly private matter, into which you and so many others have become haplessly entangled, but I find much in you that I respect, for you are in your own fashion, like me, the best among all those in your profession. Thus, if you cooperate here today, I will find no reason to take your life, or that of the good doctor. Is this understood?"

"It is," Holmes said, though whether resentfully or carelessly, I could not tell, for I only knew he sat completely immobile before the intruder.

"Now," the Shapeshifter said, "you will slowly raise the folder of papers you have found within the cabinet, and place it onto the desktop."

This Holmes did, and moving with the fluidity of the wind itself, *Il Mutaforma* stepped forward and took the papers into his left hand, the throwing knife in his right never wavering, and his eyes never leaving Holmes.

"Now," he said, and I think I heard a certain relief even in so soft-spoken and carefully modulated a tone as the killer maintained, "this is what will transpire. Mr. Holmes, I know your nature, and am fully aware that this matter between you and I will not end here, nor will your desire to pierce the mystery wilt under any sense of caution you might peripherally feel. Therefore, I am aware that it would be wisest for me to end things now, and yet…"

He smiled.

"And yet I shall not."

I felt some tension begin to lift in me, until I saw what the killer did next.

From his pocket he removed a strange looking device, metal and gleaming, part foot trap, I thought, part mousetrap—it was all I knew to think of its appearance—and from it I saw a number of small blades protruded.

"I must, of course, be permitted my departure," he said slowly as he placed the dangerous-looking weapon on the desktop, and gave something inside it a twist, like winding a pocket watch, yet held his finger to what I thought must have been some sort of trigger. "Once I remove my finger, a coiled spring within will begin to unwind. This will take but a few seconds, sufficient for me to exit, but insufficient for you to pursue before the tightly-wound springs within uncoil and propel a score of razor-sharp blades through the air in all directions, each capable of slicing deeply into a man. In the path of this weapon, you would be sliced to ribbons, and neither of you would survive. My advice is you will not try to follow me, but rather the very instant I remove my finger and dash from this room, you fall to the floor and stay low, preferably behind some heavy furniture. By the time the blades fly, I will be away and I care not if you try to pursue then, for my appearance will be entirely different."

"You are the shapeshifter, after all," Holmes said, almost admiringly.

"*Il Mutaforma*," the man agreed with a small smile.

"Are you ready, Mr. Holmes? I ask you especially, Dr. Watson, and advise you crouch behind that chair to your left."

I did so, or at least was moving to do so, when the Italian raised his finger from the device, and a distinct click was heard, and with a motion like the leaping of a deer, he sprang from the room and out the door, which he pulled shut behind him.

"Watson, down!" Holmes cried, he himself flying face-down against the rug, and an instant later there was the noise like a small shattering of metal as twenty blades, each as long as a finger, flew through the air at tremendous velocity, hurled outward by the springing of the coils within the device, then the sound of the blades striking all about us, burying themselves into the plaster of the walls, into the bookcase, into a painting, and—I still shudder to reflect on how close it was—deeply into the chair which was before my own face, the blade in its keenness penetrating fully an inch into the wood.

"A magnificent spring-trap!" Holmes exclaimed, as he leapt to his feet.

I rose as well, though more cautiously than was his example, and so high was my blood, stirred by the excitement, that I announced:

"That is all you can think to say of that trap which nearly killed us?"

He looked strangely at me, then walked over to peer at where one of the blades had embedded itself into the woodwork on the cabinet above him, almost precisely where he had stood moments ago. He said:

"Ah, I am sorry, Watson, I know your reaction is surely different from my own, it is just that I have on occasion read of such devices, but had never acquired one before this."

So he declared as he placed the machine into a sack he produced from inside his Ulster.

"It is truly a work of art, and my admiration for he who crafted it, whoever that person might be, is near-total."

A moment later he composed himself, however, and said:

"Now...I would say that went rather to plan."

"To plan?" I repeated. "Holmes, he took us by surprise and cornered us, and nearly took our lives to boot!"

"Yes," Holmes agreed, "it must seem so to you, but I assure you, Watson, we emerge precisely as I intended we should, and our chivalrous foe is sent off quite on the wrong trail."

To clarify his point, with a theatrical turn of his hand he pulled a folder of papers from inside his coat virtually identical to that I'd seen the assassin carrying when he departed.

"Sleight of hand, and a switch of one thing for another," Holmes said with a smile I could only describe as sly. "Surely, Watson, you do not believe I would be caught so unaware?"

"Well, er..."

"No, my good man, I took it as a matter of course that *Il Mutaforma* was trailing us and would wait to see if I had success in locating the papers he desired, and upon hearing that I had, he entered, just as I counted he would, and departed thinking he had them in tow."

"But that was rather a great risk, Holmes," I declared, still quite shaken by our brush with danger.

"A calculated one, based on the fact that, as he said, he could have killed us before this."

"And had he made the attempt when you turned over what he believed were the papers he sought?"

Holmes made a small expression of dismissal.

"Unlikely, though even then I was ready. Behold, Watson, my backup plan."

With that he extended his right arm, and I saw that carefully fitted up his sleeve was a strap, which secured a derringer in place, and the means to fire this weapon rested under his thumb, neatly concealed in his clothing.

"I dare say my shot would have been faster than his throw, and in a fair contest, I liked my chances. Also, I never forgot, Watson, that you were with me, and are hardly what I should rank a defenseless man."

This last comment made me feel slightly better about myself, as did his explanation concerning the situation that had just unfolded around me, so that I calmly considered everything in the space of a few breaths.

"Now, Watson, let us depart while the advantage is still our own."

"What if he learns his papers are false?" I asked as we made our way back down the servants' stairway and to the alley door. "And for that matter, what on earth *are* those papers, Holmes that someone should be willing to kill two men and carry on so much additional mayhem to obtain them?"

At that moment it was the one question I most wanted answered, for I had seen but a little of them, and knew only that they were quite old in appearance, and bore a peculiarly neat form of handwriting I associated with manuscripts from another age.

But I was not to be entirely satisfied in my ambition to know more, for Holmes told me:

"Watson, I regret to say I can as yet tell you little more, for I know not, myself. I only cling to the knowledge that there is some significance to them, and some grave import for them to be pursued by such rigorous means. *Il Mutaforma* does not work cheaply, I can tell you, and takes on a very few and highly select number of assignments, so whomever has retained his services is a party of both means, and a certain importance."

"And power," I added.

"Precisely."

He guided me swiftly away and finally to a small library

off Plum Street, where amid several people still on-site at the late hour on a Saturday evening, we sat down at a corner table, while Holmes opened the file into which he'd placed the papers, and began to meticulously look them over.

To my eyes I saw only an impressive and obviously quite antique series of loose pages, not illuminated but composed in a precise and ordered hand, the neat rows of block letters spelling out words in a language I did not recognize.

'Is that Latin, Holmes?" I asked.

"It is known as 'Occitan,'" he told me, as his eyes covered the page side to side and row to row. "It is derived from the most ancient forms of Latin, keeping purer to its primeval mother tongue than any of the romance languages, or even the Latin of the Caesars. I recognize it, though I cannot read it. Few in the world can, for it has been dead since the 15th century."

"Someone, it seems to me must be able to read it, or they'd not be willing to go to such lengths to have this brought to them."

"I do believe these papers, Watson," Holmes said, straightening now and replacing the papers into the folder, in preparation for departing, "are not the object, but rather the finger which points to the object."

"It is a map in words?" I guessed.

"Essentially, if I understand it correctly. Certain words leap out at me in my cursory examination, namely one which repeats several times: *thessoaurus*."

"Meaning thesaurus?" I asked. "A book like a dictionary?"

"In this instance I think it refers to an older meaning of the term. *Treasure*."

Now all came clearer to me. "Someone seeks a hidden treasure!"

"So it seems, though 'treasure' is a subjective term, and can have many natures. To a man dying in the desert, a drink of water may be a treasure. To a child, a rattle might mean more than all the Queen's gold in the Tower of London. This tells the location of something its writer considered a treasure, and someone believes this treasure is a most valuable thing indeed."

"Why," I asked, "didn't the three brothers then acquire the treasure for themselves? And why did they all have the same name, and keep their identities secret from the families of their other brothers?"

"I think I may know those answers," Holmes maddened me by saying, "but it is only the same theory I have held since near the beginning of my investigation. This discovery strengths it, but as there are still holes of considerable size in my knowledge, I will decline to answer as of yet."

"Then where are we to go now?" I asked, as we stepped out of the library just before its closing time, the skies more night now than day, my senses still wanting to be on alert lest *Il Mutaforma*, return for us, having discovered Holmes' deception.

"Now, Watson, we return to London, for I think if there is a key to the final act of this matter, it may lie in the study of my client's late husband, for surely there among his remaining papers there may be something to point at the direction toward which I need next to proceed. You have a wife to go home to, and I have a client to visit. On the morrow, there shall be more to tell."

It was an unsatisfactory answer, unwelcome and annoying, though I knew certain matters could not be hurried, and in truth I was tired after our travels, and I missed Mary, from whom I had been apart this entire day.

Thus I said little as we made our way back to the ornate station, which looked like some majestic palace of the Tudor age, and felt myself relax as the sun set out over the wide expanse of Bristol Channel.

We were moments away from boarding our conveyance, when beside me on a bench Holmes abruptly stood and cried:

"Watson, I am an absolute and utter imbecile, who has missed the forest for the trees! Of course! I see it clearly now!"

Startled at the suddenness of this unexpected exclamation, I quizzed:

"What is it?"

But instead of answering, he raced to the ticket seller, and demanded:

"Is there a train tonight for anywhere near the Cotswolds?"

The man checked his schedule and declared:

"Luck is in your corner, sir, for a train to Cirencester leaving in twelve minutes."

Without another word, Holmes all-but slammed the fare down on the counter and grabbed the pair of tickets held out to him, before racing full-tilt toward the platform in question.

When we were aboard the rather deserted train and had found our compartment, I demanded to know what was behind the sudden change of plans to take us north once again, in this earliest portion of the night.

"I was correct in what I told you earlier, Watson, the key to the next and surely final stage in this mystery was to be found in the study in London!"

"Then how did you uncover it without going there?"

"It was to be found also in Newcastle, and Bristol, each equally, for I overlooked something, Watson, overlooked it entirely, but as I sat unoccupied on the bench in the station, walking back through each man's study in my mind, able to see them with absolute clarity after a life of training, it came to me, and I espied it most clearly!"

Perceiving me staring at him with an impatient eagerness, Holmes cried:

"Did you not note anything in common in each of the three studies, Watson? Anything at all?"

I thought but could think of no common link.

"Do not despair at your lack of perception, my dear fellow, for the detail nearly eluded me as well, but if one wishes to conceal an object, it is sometimes wisest to place it in the open, where it is most easily ignored, and least suspected. So it was that the key was to be found on the wall, Watson, hidden in plain sight the whole time."

"What was it?" I called, all but tormented by my desire to

know.

"In each house sat the same painting, so small as to be unobtrusive, so dull and unworthy as to invite the eye to pass it by, yet in each instance it was the same image, a small stone cottage sitting just east of what I identity as Shenborrow Hill, in the Cotswolds, beside a small brook. It is, I see now, not some long-ago artist's fanciful invention, but a reminder to each brother of where to retreat if confronted by imminent and overwhelming danger. It was a wordless map to a meeting place, passing itself off as a poorly-done bit of decorative art of the sort that might as easily be pitched in the rubbish as hung on a wall. It was masterfully clever and insidiously meek all at once!"

"I understand!" I cried. "Yes, I see the slyness there. Can you locate this place?"

"Of course, though it may take a short time to pinpoint it directly, as it lies two miles or more outside the city proper."

"No hacks to rent at this hour,' I said, "we'll have to hoof it ourselves."

But at that moment Holmes was too filled with the thrill of pursuit and the elation of his deduction to care if the distance were a pair of miles, or a score of them, for now the game was afoot....

<><><><><><>

The train ride was not a lengthy one, and we had barely settled in and set ourselves poised for the journey when the announcement came from the aisle that we were drawing near the village we had sought, which sat a short distance beyond Cirencester, and its miniscule depot: barely a platform and a small tin roof set above a space for one or two people to stand sheltered and wait. However, just past that sat a sizable train yard filled with engines under repair, or idle for the moment.

Down Holmes leapt, and I right behind him, as he set off at a brisk pace, easily a four mile per hour walk, his stick swinging at his side.

"Come, Watson, though it is the middle of the night, we cannot wait for the dawn, not when a family is in such peril."

I followed closely, but was unable to resist the urge to gaze back, seeking to verify that we alone had exited the train, and that the shadows did not conceal the Milanese cut-throat who had so often stalked our path in this matter. Seeing nothing, even as the train steadily pulled away, I breathed more easily, and kept pace with Holmes as best I was able.

"Have we truly thrown him off?" I asked. "*Il Mutaforma*?"

"If we have," he answered, "it is through sheer good fortune, for he is a formidable opponent by any man's measure, who stalks his prey with the relentless fortitude of a jaguar."

"Where are we to go with the family in order to elude him?" I demanded as we covered the distant out to the cottage at a remarkably steady pace.

"Into London, where I know of places to conceal them, even from so wily and far-sighted a foe as the Shapeshifter. If we can see them clear of this setting, I can assure their survival while I pierce to the heart of this puzzling matter."

Another five minutes saw a stone cottage come into view across the dark landscape, and my heart lifted to recognize that Holmes had been correct, it was assuredly the same structure from the paintings we had encountered in each of the three studies.

Another instant and Holmes had raced ahead of me, to the door, upon which he rapped loudly with his walking stick, calling:

"Mr. Andrews! My name is Sherlock Holmes, and I am a detective from London, set upon this case by the widow of your brother in the city. You and your family are in gravest peril, and I alone can transport you to a place of safety."

"Do open, sir!" I added, desperation and urgency activating my voice, though my fear was that the assassin had already come and set upon his grim business, and no one was left inside to hear our entreaties.

Thus one can imagine my relief when I heard a voice from

within the cottage call out:

"Is it Sherlock Holmes, you say?"

"The same," the detective replied. "I caution you, there is no time to delay, so do admit my friend and me with all haste!"

The door opened a crack before it widened all the way, and before me I saw the perfect doppelganger of a man I'd seen lying on a mortuary table in London, and in photographs in three houses. It was, for all the distractions which confronted us, an uncanny moment.

"Come inside, quickly," Andrews called, stepping back, though peering with concern bordering on terror out into the night behind us.

"You are no longer safe here," Holmes told him, "for the man who has struck down your brothers is surely on his way here to do the same to you, and perhaps to all your family, should he deem that cold-blooded action necessary."

From behind the man, in the dark, a woman gasped, and in the light from a curtained window I saw her eyes were wide with terror. Likewise two young girls, perhaps ten and nine, clutched at their mother, and I realized unlike their cousins in Newcastle and London, and the aunts there, this family understood only too well the horror of their situation.

"Is there a back door to this cottage?" Holmes demanded.

"This way," Andrews said, pointing and stepping toward it.

"Then each of you, quickly, dress yourselves for travel, using not a second that can be spared, and grab what you can, then meet Watson and me outside. Quickly now!"

Holmes pushed past the family and went out the door, where he crouched and scanned the surroundings. I was relieved to see that the yard was fairly open, no trees in close, and few places for a murderer to conceal himself, though I worried that a skilled marksman could lie in ambush far beyond, and hit his mark without even Holmes detecting him in the night.

A half-minute transpired, and the four emerged from the house, with Holmes leading them forward into the darkness of the valley, and I coming last, hoping to function as a rear guard, for I remembered from my years as a soldier, that this was the direction most at risk when passing through hostile terrain.

Holmes led the way for a quarter of an hour, until he found a small thicket at the edge of some farmer's sheep paddock, near a substantial hedgerow that doubtless dated back centuries, then instructed us all to sit quietly and make no sound. He then doubled back, scouting the direction from which we'd come, using such stealth that within seconds I had lost sight of him entirely.

"Has 'the enemy' come?" the younger of the girls asked her father in a small frightened voice. "Has he found us at last?"

"He will not reach us, Maribelle," Andrews told the child, his voice determined but somewhat high with his own tremulousness. "And now we have a great and formidable friend to aid us in Mr. Sherlock Holmes."

"Be still," I cautioned, "and listen..."

I said this not only because it had been Holmes' instruction, but because from somewhere nearby in the shadowy terrain, I had heard a sound like a man moving with deliberate slowness: stalking, I thought at once as a flinty chill ran through me.

I drew a deep breath, and found a small tree branch on the ground below me, around which I wrapped my fingers, and tightened my grip. A pathetic club, but any weapon was surely better than lacking one altogether.

The family now heard the noise as well, and the girls clutched harder to their mother, with the older of the two sinking her small head against the woman's side, terror nearly overcoming her. Beside me Andrews' face was locked in profound horror as this scenario he had doubtless dreaded across these many days unspooled around us in the dark, for the sound was undeniably the footfalls of a man, drawing close.

My heart rushing, my senses drawn keenly to a single point, the fear-energy high in me, I clenched the makeshift club in my hand, and waited for whatever would come next...only to feel the most indescribable relief as from some twenty feet off I spied it was Holmes drawing close to us, his clothing dark against the night, and the relief that came over me was such that I wanted to shout out to him in joy.

"Oh, Holmes," I said softly, "we are all relieved it is you."

He drew to within ten feet, his Ulster trailing behind him as he came, and then my joy curdled, as I saw the face across from us, just beyond the thicket's rise, and felt my soul turn to ice, for though the attire and even the stride were a match for Holmes', the face below the deerstalker cap was none other than that of *Il Mutaforma*: the Shapeshifter.

"A rather convincing disguise, wouldn't you say, Dr. Watson?" the master assassin called with a tiny laugh that had within it a terribly predatory glee. In his right hand he now raised a revolver and pointed it just beyond my shoulder, at Mr. Martin Andrews, of Bristol, the third of the brothers, and the last surviving triplet.

"Do not move, Doctor," the killer said with a voice so soft it was like hearing a violin played in the hands of a *maestro*, "or in this darkness I may miss my mark and claim you instead."

Perhaps it tells of something noble within my character, I shall let you judge this for yourself, but instead of heeding his instruction, with a lunge I hurled myself sideways, throwing my body against Andrews, so that the two of us not only fell flat to the ground, but lay now above and in front of the woman and the little girls, shielding them.

"Crawl out the back, through the brush, maybe the branches can protect us!" I cried, but the woman was either too filled with fright to move, or was unable to do so with the children clutching her, so that *Il Mutaforma* had but to step forward a few paces to have us once more in his sights.

"It is a pity, Doctor Watson," he said with what sounded like honest regret, "for I think I must now shoot you all, tangled together as you are, though you must concede I did *try* to be kind here tonight and spare the innocent."

I heard him cock his revolver and saw the barrel catch

the gleam of distant starlight, and anticipated the shot I knew would crack through my ribs, bringing my life to a cease.

Mary.... I thought, her image filling my mind as I drew what I anticipated would be my last breath.

Yet it was not one shot that came, but a pair, the first a hundredth of a second before the other, and I heard the assassin cry out in pain as his own shot went wild, flying through the air and shattering low-hanging branches just above our heads.

"Holmes!" I cried, the relief I felt at even this extra instant of life overcoming me, for I knew the first shot must surely have been fired from somewhere in the dark, at the hands of my friend.

But I saw just as quickly that this had been no killing strike, for *Il Mutaforma* whipped around and dropped to a low pose, and fired back several times, rapidly, towards where Holmes' report had come. He cursed in Italian—

"Maledetto diavolo Inglese, quanto odio quest'uomo!"

—and then rapidly raced off toward the shadows that lay under the trees along the hedgerow.

"Stay here!" I instructed the family, then hurried out of the thicket at a low crawl, seeking Holmes. Had he been hit by the return fire? Was the Italian about to fall on all of us from behind?

I cried out to my friend, and then saw him coming nearer, his body likewise low to the ground.

"Watson, stay down!" he called, and I did so, just as another shot cracked out from somewhere behind me, and whizzed past my ear with its horrid music.

I fell flat and laid still as Holmes crawled to me.

"Are you injured?" I demanded.

"His shots went wild," he answered, "for he was firing blindly, and I was well concealed."

"Thank Heaven for that," I replied, "though he has us cornered! It is surely too perilous to pursue him when his location in unknown, and he may fire on us with the advantage of surprise."

"Yes," Holmes agreed, "but pursue him I shall, for look at

the ground, Watson."

I did so and saw something I had missed. Where the Shapeshifter had been standing lay a small spray of blood, black and fluid in the darkness.

"You hit him!" I cried.

"In the arm, I make it," Holmes told me. "He is not incapacitated but he is wounded, and losing vitality. It is not his plan to take his stand here tonight and fight us to the death, he will be making his retreat even now, and I may yet have him!"

The savageness of Holmes' declaration matched the ferocity with which he sprang from where he'd been lying on the earth, and with which he raced forward, up the hill.

I was worried about the family in the thicket, but more concerned still with my friend, who was in pursuit of an armed and exceedingly dangerous criminal. Thus I set off after him, though I confess a part of me expected at any moment to feel the sting of lead.

Yet none came, and instead Holmes paused several times for the merest of seconds to indicate blood upon the ground.

"He will be losing vigour by now," I testified, knowing as a doctor that the loss of more than a pint of blood would leave almost any man in no condition to carry on such a flight.

We rounded a hilltop and saw the little village down below, and—I gave a shout of exultation—we spied the fleeing assassin, his wounded arm clutched to his chest.

"After him!" Holmes called.

Down the hill we went and into a small train yard there, where several engines and a number of cars sat parked and empty. I realized with a start that this was suddenly a very dangerous pursuit once again, for we had entered into a maze cloaked in shadows by the still, country night.

"I shall seek him to the right, you to the left," Holmes instructed. "Shout for me if you spy his form, but do not engage him, Watson, for he is death incarnate!"

I did as he directed, and was no more than ten seconds removed from my friend, when I saw spots of blood freshly speckling the gravel ahead of me. I was turning to call this fact to Holmes' attention, when from my rear, the Milanese assassin sprang from a shadow and put a blade to my throat, pulling me back to him.

I was a much larger and probably physically stronger man than my aggressor, but he was swift as a ferret, and well-practiced in his art, and instead of struggling, I froze.

"You keep tossing away the opportunities I in my mercy give you to live through this night, Doctor," he whispered in my ear, his breath warm against my flesh, the scent of blood from his arm heavy in the air. "But now I offer you no more chances, nor your friend either. And after you are both dead, know I shall strike down the family over the hillside as well."

I felt the blade move to my carotid artery, and the knowledge that for the second time in mere minutes my death was an instant away called up some instinct in me, and I drove my right elbow as hard as I could against his bullet-sheared arm, making a cry of pain erupt from the Italian, and giving me the chance to step forward while also shoving him backward, and to my surprise he actually fell, loosing hold of the stiletto as he did.

I leaped at him and we wrestled, and for a moment I thought the advantage mine, but he was trained in this skill as well, and within seconds the contest was greatly in his favor, as he kicked low at one of my ankles, connecting, and sending a river of pain up my leg and spine and into my skull, a nerve there damaged. I spilled backward into a support pole below the roof, and he drew another blade and was coiled to spring at me, when I heard a clang, and the surprise on *Il Mutaforma's* face matched my own, as we both looked down to see someone—Holmes!— had thrown a switch that controlled the movement of the tracks there in the depot, and had trapped the man's left foot forcefully between two iron rails.

The Shapeshifter cried out in pain and anger, throwing Italian oaths into the air as the great detective stepped out of the shadows and regarded his quarry with a smile.

"Checkmate, I think," Holmes said with triumph.

None of us moved then, and I noted that Holmes held a revolver in his hand, not quite pointed at his foe, but nearly so.

"Now," he began, "you will tell me some answers before anything else transpires."

"*Non sono un traditore!*"the assassin said with a savage growl, part pain, part rage.

"You are 'no betrayer'?" Holmes translated. "Perhaps that is so, but you *are* a murderer a hundred times over."

The Italian moved his hand toward his vest pocket, and Holmes pointed the pistol at his chest.

"Do not think you may draw some new weapon on me before I can fire," he said.

The killer, his fine face, feminine and masculine at once, and doubtless one which could be described as attractive when not contorted in suffering and anger as it was now, withdrew his hand and straightened up as best he was able with his foot trapped as it was.

"I shall tell you nothing," he said simply, his accent now most perfectly English.

"We shall see," Holmes answered.

There was a sound from far off in the darkness, rising almost as if in response to his boast. The masterful assassin heard it as well, and I saw he knew just as we did that it was an approaching train.

"Tell me quickly, and you shall yet live tonight," Holmes said. "Who has hired you, and what is the meaning of this streak of murders over some apparent treasure, described in a dead language? Hurry! Enlightenment me!"

The assassin turned away from us and saw it now, the headlights of the engine coming closer, a thousand yards away and moving in at a fast clip.

"Do as he asks, man!" I yelled, horrified at what was rushing into place before me. "Tell Holmes what he asks!"

But the Shapeshifter said nothing, though began to pull furiously on his trapped leg with his unwounded arm. A sound of rage now erupted from him as he realized the vice-like hold the rails had on him.

"I assure you, there is no escape," Holmes said, "lest I pull the lever and release you."

"Holmes…" I cried out, "you cannot stand there and let such a fate befall another soul!"

Not waiting for an answer, I raced forward to help *Il Mutaforma* by any means I could, only to have Holmes grab the back of my coat and pull me toward himself.

"Get within his reach, Watson," he told me, "and he gains a hostage to bargain with. He could then gain the upper hand and use you to compel me to act in any way he chooses."

I realized this was so, and that Holmes would surely throw loose the rails to save my own life, and then it was likely I, and perhaps Holmes as well, would die when the foe lashed out with his deadly speed, for I suspected he had many weapons yet undiscovered upon his person.

The train was coming closer, rushing in at thirty miles an hour, almost near to the most distant part of the yard, seconds away now.

"This is madness! Save your life!" I begged. "Tell him!"

Instead the legendary assassin locked his eyes on mine for a fraction of a second, then swept a heavy blade, like a cleaver, from his belt, and stooped to strike his own ankle a furious and precise blow that partly severed it from the leg, going mid-way through flesh and bone. He let loose a single long and terrible cry as he did, but did not halt the atrocious surgery.

With a roar of agony that vibrated off the bricks around us, he swung again and with the sound of bone shattering, his foot was cut loose and he flung himself out of the path of the train an instant before it rolled over his trapped appendage, pulping it and sending fragments of it flying, even as the man himself fell writhing onto the gravel, his blood spraying in every direction.

The train, oddly, never slowed, and I wondered if the engineer, speeding through pitch darkness, even knew what had come to pass.

I ran to our adversary, my training and oath to ever be a healer overcoming any other consideration, and pulled loose my own belt from its loops and slung it above the wound, from which blood was spurting at a level I knew would soon prove fatal, though when I cinched the would-be tourniquet, the flow reduced considerably.

"Steady, man, steady!" I cried out as I tightened the belt around the wound with all my might, making *Il Mutaforma* gasp in agony, his once-olive cheeks suddenly a dreadful, ashen hue.

Holmes began to fill his pipe as he studied our adversary, who lay on his back, panting now, releasing groans of pain through foam-slickened lips.

"He has earned his chance at a reprieve from death tonight," I called up to my companion, who merely stood above us both there on the depot floor, smoking as he stared down coldly at his foe.

"A reprieve, only, Watson," he told me, as he exhaled a great curtain of tobacco smoke, "for *Il Mutaforma* is wanted for capital crimes across the face of Europe."

The assassin seemed to re-gain a certain composure, even amid his suffering, for he looked back at the detective and declared:

"Mr. Sherlock Holmes, it would be a well-earned but tragic end to an artist such as myself, to die like a common criminal within a hangman's rope, would you not agree?"

"Indeed it would at that," Holmes concurred, "for odious though your work has been, you have spent years as the reigning master of your field, and have at times shown a degree of chivalry in your otherwise loathsome conduct."

Il Mutaforma nodded his now-pallid face, and asked:

"Will you grant me the courtesy, then, of honouring this final choice I am about to make for myself?"

"I will," Holmes said simply.

"*I miei ringraziamenti,*" the Shapeshifter said, granting his thanks.

"*Lo concedo da padrone a padrone,*" Holmes answered.

I feared I knew what this meant, but it was still a shock when the assassin reached low with his undamaged hand and loosened the belt I'd so carefully cinched around his limb, and at once blood began to pour out once more.

It was my training to want to reach forward and correct this self-destroying action, but I halted my hand in mid-motion when I saw the proud but pleading eyes of the man lying before me.

"I have chosen the hour of my death, and its cause, Doctor," he said weakly, as the crimson stain spread on the ground between us. "Please let the 'Shapeshifter' spare himself the indignity that would lie ahead if ever he fell into the hands of the police. A legend should not die in such a way, but at the hands of…a superior adversary."

I looked at Holmes, who had been expressionless and unreadable, but who now bowed his head humbly before his foe's admission of defeat. Then he gave me a single slight nod, which motivated me to retrieve my blood-soaked belt off the ground, and rise to my feet.

"You spare me an ending I have long feared might come to pass for me," *Il Mutaforma* coughed out. "To my dying breath, Mr. Sherlock Holmes, I am grateful for this kindness."

"You can re-pay this kindness by revealing to me what I seek to know," Holmes told him imperiously.

"That is true," the man gasped, his breath now failing, "but does not the greatest assassin of his age keep the secrets of those who hire him?"

"We shall tell no one concerned in this matter that the source of the revelation was you," Holmes promised. "We shall consider the debt between us—my sparing you the rope—paid in full."

"*Seek…the Order…of Saint Bacculus,*" the dying man said. He locked his eyes onto Holmes, and gave a nod.

The name was unknown to me, but I feared it contained a grave sense of portent.

"Ah, yes, of course, the Order…" it was all Holmes said, but he seemed to grasp much from the admission.

"Yes," the assassin rasped. "you understand."

Il Mutaforma laughed but a moment at this, then his head slowly lowered to the gravel, before a final shudder passed through him amid an open-mouthed gasp for breath, then there was stillness, and the light of life departed from his dark, cunning eyes.

"The Order of Saint Bacculus?" I repeated.

"Yes." It was all Holmes seemed willing to say regarding this revelation.

However, he showed his own chivalry then by kneeling beside the fallen man and crossing his arms over his chest, then shutting his eyes, and with a smoothing of his hand, erasing the pose of contorted agony that had ruled his last moments. Finally he removed a handkerchief from his pocket, and laid it almost delicately over the now-placid face.

"Come, Watson," he said, "my conscience lets me take my leave, so let us return to the third Mr. Martin Andrews, and learn of why so much bloodshed has transpired."

"But what can he tell us?" I demanded.

"Much, I am sure," Holmes replied.

We left *Il Mutaforma*, the "Shapeshifter," master among assassins, lying in the train yard, in the quiet darkness of the rural night, to be found there by whomever should next come upon him, before Holmes led us back up one side of the hill we'd climbed in our pursuit, and then down the other and into the thicket, where the Andrews family still crouched, shaken and all but undone by their fear.

The two girls were trembling in their mother's arms, while she clutched them to her, and Andrews sat on the ground, his face white, his eyes wild.

"Is he gone?" he demanded upon seeing us. "Have you got

him?"

"It is safe for your family to return to the cottage," Holmes told him. "You, however, will be taking a walk with Watson and me, so that we might have a talk about *certain matters.*"

"The killer is gone?" one of the children still persisted in asking, her voice high.

"He will not harm you anymore," I spoke up to tell her.

She fell back against her mother, limp with relief, and then began to cry.

Looking over her small golden head, Holmes locked eyes on her father, and I knew the meaning: the threat from the larger foe was not yet extinguished, and thus Holmes must learn all that the man had to tell him.

We walked back to the picturesque cottage together, and it lay heaped in shadows on this dark country night, but within a moment Mrs. Andrews was inside and a lamp was lit, and the glow from its windows was almost cheerful, despite the nature of the past hour, or the horrors of the last day.

Andrews, however, did not follow them, but had given each of the girls kisses on their brows, and had embraced his wife to him, before she had disappeared within. This done, he watched his family go into their makeshift refuge—a thing it had utterly failed to be, I reflected—then turned to Holmes and said:

"Let us walk together, we three, and I shall tell you all that I know. It may disappoint you, however, for on my oath I have obeyed the instructions my father left to me and my brothers, but as to why we laboured as we did, I have only known tiny fragments of truth."

"You have, then, served a cause with a relative blindness, sir?" I demanded.

"To a point," he said. "It was a duty into which we had been born, my brothers and I, and it came with certain financial benefits that rendered our compliance worthwhile. Besides, growing up we all acquired the notion that our tasks were somewhat ceremonial, and almost a slight joke at times, never really believing, I suppose, there was the intrinsic seriousness to them that our father impressed upon us there could be."

"So these tasks of which you speak," I said, "came down to you from your father?"

"And were handed down to him by his own father, and his father before him, going back..." Andrews tossed his hands into the air and concluded: "Going back a long way, I suppose."

"To the early fifteenth century," Holmes, who had been listening, said quietly.

"But what *is* all this?" I asked. "Why should someone send a master among killers to murder your brothers, and stalk you to this God-forsaken place in the middle of nowhere?"

"For a treasure," the man replied.

"Yes, Watson," Holmes said, "I ask you to recall that word written upon the paper, in the extinct language of Occitan."

"*Thessoaurus*," I said, remembering how I'd confused it with another word more common in everyday language. "You said it meant 'treasure'."

"A relative term," Holmes spoke up. "For what is so much fodder to one man, might indeed be treasure to another."

He looked away and added:

"Or a danger to him."

"We grew up hearing of the treasure we had to conceal," Andrews said in agreement. "As boys we imagined quite an adventure in this idea, heaps of gold coins and gemstones, and necklaces of pearl, but when we found what it really was, well, our romantic notions went out the window."

"So what *is* the treasure, and where is it?" I demanded.

"Knowledge, sir," Andrews said. "Which is mankind's greatest treasure, is it not? A small storehouse of knowledge is what we curated, so great and worthy, that he who wrote of it was killed centuries ago merely for possessing such thoughts as traveled from his brain to his pen."

"The treasure at the heart of so much death is information?" I said dismayed.

I did not know what to say, and did not know what this

meant, so I looked to Holmes, who did not glance back, but instructed Andrews:

"Reveal, sir."

Andrews drew a deep breath and shook his head, before declaring:

"So odd it feels to speak openly of this now, after keeping the secret for so long. You see, Doctor, my brothers and I were born into a family who were the guardians of the surviving writings of Ambrosius of Arden, a late Medieval philosopher, and man of great wisdom and far-thinking brilliance. He was, it could be said, our island's first scientist, for profound were his experiments, and ahead even of our own time were some of his hypotheses on the workings of the world, and the universe which surrounds us. His was a mind such as comes along once a millennium, alas, born in the worst possible era."

I had never heard of the man, but Holmes seemed well familiar with the name, for he brightened noticeably and said:

"Ah…I begin to peer into what had been only clouds and darkness. Go on, if you please, sir."

"Yes," Andrews said, "always we were taught that there is no supernatural God, which was a teaching of Ambrosius of Arden, whom we were trained to revere, a radical free thinker and skeptic in an age of extreme and unquestioned faith, and so, like him before us, we retain our doubts as to the existence of a higher being believed in by most men, and hold mankind alone responsible for its conduct, and place onto it the burden for its own salvation from itself."

I recalled that among the first facts the London-based Mrs. Andrews' had told us at the start of this case was of her and her late husband's denial of the existence of God. It was a daunting concept, man being alone and unchaperoned in the lightless void which surrounded us, all our prayers but empty echoes, all our churches but halls of folly, every miracle tale but the re-telling of coincidence, or lies. Though not a deeply religious man, I could not feel the truth in this cold philosophy.

"Our father confided all to us on our thirteenth birthday,"

Andrews revealed, "taking us to the salt cave in the mountains of Wales where the books lie hidden, and telling us how for so many generations, back to the year 1407 *Anno Domini*, our family had protected the legacy of that great philosopher and scholar, who was centuries ahead of his fellows in understanding the physical world and its intricate natural workings. Do you know he wrote of gravity two centuries before Newton, sirs? Or that he stated weather is not a localized event, but a worldwide system? The Church burned him, you see, for grasping truths about the skies and the tides and the seasons, and the place of all living things within this intricate web, and they burned his acolytes as well, only some distant ancestor of mine surviving by luck or design, to carry the remaining few volumes of his writings away and hide them in the preserving atmosphere of the salt cave, awaiting a time when man was better prepared to know of the revelations of Ambrosius."

"Fascinating," I breathed.

"There were certain benefits to the task we undertook," he continued, "for the funds of our long-ago founder had been invested over the generations, and this allowed us to live well enough in our undertaking. Always before the task had been passed from father to eldest son, but having triplet boys as he did, well, our father had no choice but to spread the job among us three."

"I don't understand," I confessed. "There were three of you, but you shared one name, and concealed the existence of the others and their families from the families of your other brothers."

"Yes," Andrews said, "for you see, the task was not the light jest we boys took it to be, with our mockery and merriment, for when we were seventeen, an assassin came, a different one than this we faced tonight, of course, acting as agent for we knew not whom, and struck down our father, and our mother too, and set fire to our house out in the wilds of Northumberland, and then hunted after us."

"Good Heavens," I exclaimed.

"Yes, we were nearly killed on two occasions within that first year, as we fled in disorganized fashion, three boys, not quite grown to manhood. We had resources, true, but how could one outrun a determined killer that only by luck we had so far stayed a step ahead of?"

"By dividing," said Holmes, wholly grasping the outcome before my mind had quite circled back to it.

"Indeed, yes," Andrews agreed. "Where our foe sought three boys, we became one man. We shed our former names and at Tobias' idea...er, you'd know him as the Martin Andrews of Newcastle, we took on the name under which we operated and by which you now know us, seeming to any who might look at us from afar to be one individual, the three distinct boys apparently vanished into thin air, and a man who had never been born entered the world. We visited one another only as needed, taking care of the business investments that had come to us by going singly to required meetings, so that none with whom we met ever suspected they were speaking to a different man on every occasion. It was rare for us to gather, but we did so every other year...this year being one, two brothers only, the third always staying away, a safeguard in case the worst happened. And so it was that Tobias from Newcastle, was in London, passing through on his way back up to Birmingham, where he was to have met Gerald, the true name of the Martin Andrews from London, and they were to have briefly gone over certain matters of business investments in the secrecy of that far-away city, where none of us had connections. We thought it a good plan, and for many years it worked, shedding three identities, and creating one."

"But it was then and there that the subterfuge that had served you for twenty years failed at last," Holmes said.

"Tobias was killed by the assassin sent by...presumably whoever it was who had struck down our father, and shortly after, Gerald as well. He returned to his home in London, and panicked upon realizing the news, I suppose, and was flushed straight into the lurking killer's hands."

"It was precisely as you say," Holmes agreed.

"Oh, my poor brothers," the man said, covering his face with his hands. "When the news reached me through the papers, I knew time was short, so I triggered the plan we had formulated long ago, and fled to the country, as you see. This cottage was to have been a gathering place for us all, but... We came alone, my family and I."

"The paintings on the walls of the studies," I noted.

"Yes, so we would recognize the place. It was acquired in our grandfather's time, and kept ever in preparation should this dread day arise. We thought, mistakenly, it now seems, we would not be found here in such isolation."

"I believe I can enlighten you as to who has sent the killer after you, both today and in the past," Holmes told the man. "It seems that though you grew up regarding but lightly the treasure you guarded—the writings of a heretic scientist and philosopher—there were those of a still-older sect, men of a repressive, orthodox bent, who instigated his execution at the stake, and so likewise have their descendants sought to stamp out any challenge to their rigid doctrines regarding the faith, which Ambrosius of Arden so offended centuries ago with his experimentations and conjectures. This group knew that by slaying the keepers of these works, they would forever silence their long-ago foe. By destroying the knowledge of where the books rested, they were putting an end to a long-ago critical voice, as surely as if they'd burned the '*thessoaurus*' itself. That would, incidentally, have been their preference, but to eliminate all knowledge of its existence sufficed as well."

"No!" Andrews exclaimed. "Then that means while I live I can never be safe...!"

"It is true," Holmes agreed, "they will not stop, nor will they be easy to locate in the shadows, operating as they do most likely from Rome itself, outside the auspices of the Church, but near its heart, striking at heretics and their works, silencing those who would unsettle the blind faith that is the hallmark of their devotion."

"It is dismal," Andrews declared, "and there is no hope for me."

"Untrue," Holmes stated, "for there is a pathway to freedom."

"What is it?" Andrews demanded, sounding like a drowning man who had spied a life preserver bobbing before him on the waves.

"The time has come," said Holmes, "indeed it is long past, for this fatal duty to be laid aside, and for your service to be brought to an end, liberating yourself and future generations of your bloodline. The writings of a man such as Ambrosius of Arden, so far ahead of his own era, belong in the hands of scholars at one of the great universities, or in a museum, where they can be read and published, and made available for all to marvel at, so they see that one man, at least, stood rooted in enlightenment even in an age of ignorance. I will gather a worthy group, and they will go to this salt cave in Wales, via the directions you will pass on to me, and all will be taken from that place, so that the knowledge shall be spread to a hundred thousand minds, defeating those who would quell science by silencing it."

"Yes," Andrews cried out, "yes, Mr. Holmes, let us allow Ambrosius his posthumous triumph at last!"

<><><><><>

And so the future unfolded just as Holmes forecast that night on the hillside when he offered his proposal.

The Andrews family returned with him to London, where he saw them placed in safe keeping, while he went to speak with scholarly men of his acquaintance, who, with enthusiasm, traveled as a group to the salt cave, and retrieved the artifacts of a scientist unjustly killed four centuries before. Within days the discovery was in newspapers across the nation, and by the end of the season, the manuscripts had been copied and set to press for reading by any who were curious as to the thoughts and theories of Ambrosius of Arden, with the original pages going on display for a month at the British Museum, before being securely stored in a vault in a sub-basement floor of the archive wing, where they remain today.

"So we are free at last?" Andrews had asked Holmes at their final meeting, held in the parlour of 221B Baker Street some six weeks after that fateful night.

"I believe you are, sir," Holmes replied, "for those who sought to kill you, however ruthless they have shown themselves to be, seem to operate under certain principles. One is they see revenge as unholy, for it places man in the rightful hemisphere of God, and usurps the justice said to belong to Him alone. The other ideal they hold is that the innocent are not harmed. Thus you and your brothers were spared when your father was targeted years ago, and the spouses and children of your late brothers were likewise left unharmed. I think they shall regard this matter as a failure on their part, and are unlikely to trouble you ever again, whatever fate they may believe awaits your heretical soul."

"But who *are* they?" I asked, seated as I was across from Andrews.

"A mysterious order, Watson, centuries old, which considers itself the arm of righteousness, moving against the enemies of faith. I fear an investigation of history undertaken with a certain insightfulness would find their dark handiwork scattered throughout the centuries, with their instigation of the arrest and burning of Ambrosius of Arden being but the merest spear-point of their intolerant campaigns of murder and intimidation of free thinkers."

Andrews drew a deep breath, and announced:

"Then at long last life is well. Alas, too late for my brothers to know this feeling of release, but I cherish it."

"What will you do now?" I asked him.

"Continue much as I have, absent the duties to the 'thessoaurus' but I shall return home and conduct my affairs, with an eye to supporting, as my means allow, the widows and children of my fallen brothers."

"I think that is a noble intent," I told him.

"Indeed," Holmes agreed, "I second Watson's sentiment, and wish you well in that regard."

When he was gone, and I was soon to be following his example and departing as well, I stood and picked up my bowler and tarried a moment, tossing a thought around in my head.

"Holmes," I said at last, "something about this does not sit well with me."

"Really, Watson?" he asked. "And I for one had thought the matter wrapped up neatly and put away on our mental shelves, like a box of old things."

"There is a matter concerning this case that still troubles me," I pressed on.

"Only one matter, my good man?" Holmes replied, his gray eyes slightly amused.

"You have said that by eliminating the brothers in their fashion, this...*Order*, should have been satisfied that it was removing the manuscripts of Ambrosius of Arden from history, yet wouldn't it have been better for their purposes had they taken one of the brothers and...well, 'compelled' him to reveal the location?"

"Oh, yes," he agreed, "far better, for the destruction of these artifacts of a Medieval dissenter would have been a far more efficient course. It would have prevented their release, as we see occurring in our own time."

Even as I stood just within the door, my exit all but at hand, I asked:

"Then why did they not?"

"Yes, I have thought on this, myself, and while I can but speculate within the known facts, I think it is because, Watson, as I said to Andrews, these are murderers who believe themselves acting within the scrutiny of God, and while the slaying of a foe of their dogmatic creed is well within bounds, perhaps the torture of a man is outside their practice."

I considered this and felt it a hollow theory, for surely a group willing to take so many lives held few morals whatsoever.

"The truth, Watson," added my friend, seeing that this matter troubled me, "is that we cannot truly know. Absent someday meeting a representative of this cult—an event I do not particularly wish to have occur—we are left with the hollow consolation of the hypothesis itself.

He then added:

"And of course we likewise have the certainty that by our actions we have served the cause of *good*."

I stood an instant longer, then nodded. If the resolution to the case of a man twice murdered had not put all things well—and how could it when two men with families had been struck down in their prime—then at least the worst had been averted, and one who had been marked to die yet lived.

All in all, in a world where man could be so inhumane to his fellow man, I supposed it was as close to a victory as life presented.

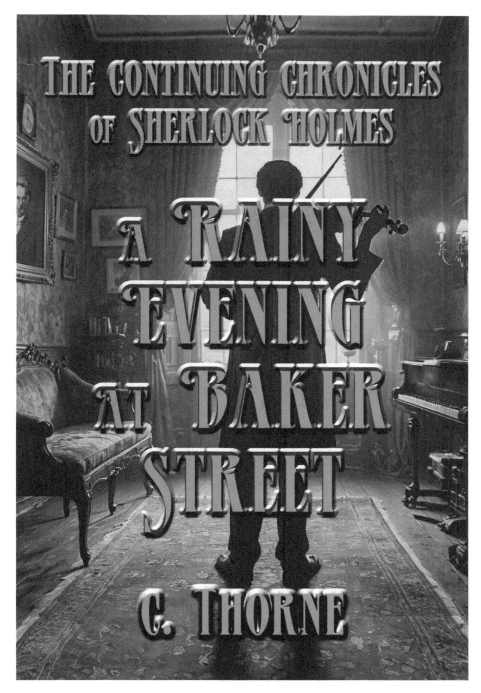

THE CONTINUING CHRONICLES
OF SHERLOCK HOLMES

A RAINY EVENING AT BAKER STREET

C. THORNE

A RAINY EVENING
AT BAKER STREET

It was a rainy evening at 221B Baker Street, and a light mist was swirling amid the rising fog outside, forecasting a night of dense, pea-soup conditions. I was back in my old lodgings along with my wife, Mary, paying a visit with Sherlock Holmes, at his invitation. My friend seemed in particularly high spirits (or else I doubt he should have issued this rare summons) and so jolly did he seem by his usual standards, that he had asked his landlady Mrs. Hudson to come up and join-in as well, as by his own hand the world's foremost consulting detective poured us all tea, and served generous slices of a walnut cake he'd acquired from a bakery before returning home late that afternoon.

The cake was delicious, the company was composed of those dearest to me, and the rainfall outdoors combined with the warmth of the fireplace to add a relaxing and settled atmosphere to the gathering. All was well that night; all was very well indeed.

Holmes had told us all of his bringing a particularly challenging case to its conclusion, one involving a Belgian criminal syndicate, intent on smuggling purloined valuables from England into Antwerp.

"They had been robbing estates, townhouses, jeweler's safes, and even museums for the past six months," he explained, "employing domestic burglars who were kept in the dark as to the extent of the operation they'd become part of, each knowing no more than his own rôle. Had those crates of ill-gotten goods left the nation, it would have been a thousand to one that their rightful owners ever again set eyes on their property."

"But you foiled them properly, I expect?" my wife spoke up to inquire.

"Every last one of the continental smugglers sits at this hour in the clink below Scotland Yard," Holmes said with a smile of gravest satisfaction, and more than a little pleasure.

"Well done, Holmes!" I cried.

"Yes, congratulations, indeed, Mr. Holmes," added Mrs. Hudson. "It's a grand gem in the nation's crown that you represent."

I knew Holmes adored praise, but he moved to hide his satisfaction in hearing us speak so well of him and his talents.

"I earned my fee in the matter, and anything less would have been shirking on my part," he replied modestly.

We sat together a while longer talking lightly, the hour not yet late, and I felt a great inner contentment right then, a happily-wed man some five months past his nuptials, amid pleasant company, and everything felt perfectly right and at peace in my world: a rare and glorious sensation that has not been entirely common in my life. I was pondering this blissful state, when I heard Mrs. Hudson asking Holmes about a matter that had been perplexing the minds of the world for over a decade, the incident of the *Mary Celeste*, an American brigantine that had been found empty and adrift off the coast of the Azores, its crew vanished, yet with the entirety of their possessions, cargo, and effects left neatly stored within the ship. Even the captain's pipe was discovered to be resting in an ash tray, as if the man had suddenly risen, mid-smoke, and left it burning, never to return. Honestly, the case had caused many a shiver in its time.

Holmes however, laughed and said:

"My dear Mrs. Hudson, I have considered the matter, and find it no mystery at all."

"No mystery?" Mary exclaimed, startled at my friend's claim. "Why, it's little less than the most perplexing maritime puzzle of our age."

"Is it now?" Holmes replied, amused.

"Well," said Mrs. Hudson, more used to my friend's grand pronouncements than was my wife, "let us have it then, Mr. Holmes, what is the solution to a fully-stocked ship hurriedly abandoned mid-journey, without a trace of the crew ever to be found?"

"The solution," said Holmes with profound self-confidence, "lies in the manifest itself, which lists a number of flammable agents stored aboard, including more than fifteen-hundred barrels of denatured alcohol, a highly explosive substance. I posited from the first that through happenstance and human error, some member of the crew conveyed a source of fire too close to the region of the hold where these volatile substances were stored, necessitating the captain to order the vessel to be abandoned. Those aboard left everything behind in their haste and took to the lifeboat, which, if you note, was listed in the official report as missing. These unfortunate souls in a slow-moving boat became separated from the much-faster ship and were eventually lost at sea, while the *Mary Celeste* herself sailed on with the currents, finally being swept along to the Azores, where a rather hollow mystery was born amid much undue sensation. Explaining it away is simplicity itself when all facts are considered."

I found I could not argue with his hypothesis, and commented:

"You make it sound so straightforward, Holmes."

"And so it is, Watson, and so it is, like nearly all mysteries, which ninety times out of a hundred have the most facile explanation at their heart. Surely you have observed this yourself from the many occasions you have ventured out with me in my work?"

"I have," I conceded.

"But there are plenty of strange things in this world, Mr. Holmes," Mrs. Hudson pressed on, "which defy ready explanation."

"Yes, 'There are more things in heaven and Earth than are dreamt of in your philosophy,'" I quoted.

"Such as?" Holmes challenged us.

"Well, in my own birth country," I said, "there is the monster of Loch Ness for one thing."

Here Holmes truly laughed, letting loose a bark he aimed at the ceiling. When he had recovered, he chided:

"Oh, Watson, come now, a lake monster?"

"Do you dismiss so much testimony as to the creature's existence?" I replied. "Remember, many of the eye-witnesses have been considered unimpeachable paragons of honesty, including Saint Columba, some thirteen hundred years ago."

"Your monster," Holmes replied, "is nothing more than large eels, salmon, seals a-float basking in the sunlight, and bobbing driftwood, all transformed by runaway imaginations into a serpent of legend, with not a little wistful fibbing added in for good measure. Let us not forget, people come to the towns along the waters of Ness to see the fabled beast…and most importantly, they spend money there. I can tell you with certainty there is no more a monster in Loch Ness than there are fairies in a vicar's garden."

"Oh, you see John, and you, Mrs. Hudson," my wife jested

lightly, "now Sherlock in his dour disbelief attacks fairies as well."

"Ah," Holmes told her, "I'd sooner believe in fairies than half the nonsense one reads of in the press these days. I espied an article last week telling of a cat the size of a bloodhound prowling the alleys of York, claiming the unwary for its prey. The disappearances of several children were cheerfully attributed to the creature."

"Those poor children," Mrs. Hudson said quietly, to which Holmes cocked an eyebrow. "If you're saying it's not such a cat, then what do you suppose it is?"

"A husky alley cat spied by some itinerate reporter, imaginatively exaggerated and linked to missing persons cases in order to sell newspapers," Holmes stated.

"But the missing children?" Mary inquired.

"If not infants who met more natural fates, then invented entirely."

"Oh, come now," Mrs. Hudson challenged. "No one would go that far."

"My dear lady," replied Holmes, "when confronted by an unlikely claim, always seek to unite it to a trail of money, for that connection explains most asinine but popularly-received tales. Even those with no interest in politics or the news of the hour might buy a paper to read of a monster prowling in their midst."

"Mankind does retain a taste for the lurid," I had to agree, thinking of how my patients always wanted to hear the goriest of details regarding obscure and disturbing diseases.

"I still say there are strange goings-on in life that defy human understanding," said Mrs. Hudson. "I'm not young, and in my day I have heard stories told to me by those I trust, telling of peculiar things that brought gooseflesh to my very arms to hear."

"Like what, Mrs. Hudson?" Mary asked.

"Like a certain empty building we all knew of when I was a little girl. We children never went near it, when abandoned homes normally drew us irresistibly to play house in them, or for the boys to make them into their forts. This house…it had a terrible feel, and many had seen strange lights moving through it at night, and even more had heard a barbaric pounding against the walls, though no one was in there."

Even from a distance decades removed from the events she described, Mrs. Hudson gave a little shiver there in the parlor of Baker Street, despite the warm fire, and the safety of good company.

"The house was no doubt occupied by tramps who had an interest in frightening away children," Holmes said easily while studying a small blister on the end of his right ring finger. I made a note to ask him later how he acquired it, and to see if it required treatment.

"You have a theory for everything, Sherlock," my wife said, "but I know of a matter not one doctor in centuries, even the most learned, ever comprehended. Remember, John, you spoke of it the other night, that unexplainable dancing mystery."

"Ah, yes, indeed," I agreed, "the peculiar Dancing Plague of 1518."

This was among the most perplexing mysteries of the health field, one studied in most medical schools, both as an exercise in theorizing, and for the odd facts concerned within it. In short, across much of western Europe around the year 1518, a strange disorder swept the countryside, seemingly infectious and progressing almost like a passing wave, causing apparently tens of thousands of all ages and stations in life to begin to fling themselves about, spinning and hopping in some madcap dance which continued for hours or days until many dropped from exhaustion, not a few falling into fatal manias. There was no seeming cause for the affliction, for it came with no other symptoms, and no cure was ever found. The episodes simply passed on their own with time, and the sufferers who survived were soon fine once again, returning to their ordinary lives as if nothing had happened. The disease had made its way across the low countries and was nearing the gates of Paris when it abruptly ceased, never, so far as we know, to return.

Holmes showed little reaction to the challenge but finally said in an almost lazy and little interested fashion:

"The field of crime is my *raison d'être*, or more specifically, the capture of criminals, and the righting of wrongs brought to my attention, yet even here I do know something of the disorder you describe."

"Then what was it?" I pressed him.

"The so-called Dancing Plague was a medical matter through and through, a form of transmissible hysteria, it has always seemed to me, and therefore it lies outside the radius of my concerns. I shall leave that to medical minds to ponder."

Hmmph, I thought, I could not let that go completely unchallenged, so I told him:

"If you had to make a judgment on the matter, though, what would you say?"

"Very well, Watson, my own thoughts," he said, "concern an ergot that has been known to infect the grain crops in particularly wet years, and when consumed will cause temporary bouts of madness, even horrific visions. It, too, is not such a mystery, nor was it a visitation by supernatural forces, as churchmen of the period claimed, it was a medical matter plain and simple, though an odd and fascinating one when studied for its merits."

"There you have my complete agreement," I told him, impressed with his theory.

There was a moment's silence then, during which the sound of the September rain rattled on the windowpanes and fell splashing into the street, while inside we were all warm and dry before the cozy little fire. It was in the midst of this brief, contemplative pause, however, that my wife seemed to hit upon an idea, for she spoke up to say:

"Well, I still think there is one mystery that even you, Sherlock Holmes, must confess defies all reason."

Here Holmes did perk up with interest.

"And, pray, Mrs. Watson, what is that?"

"The matter of the disappearance of the extended

members of the Bauer family, of Mainz, Germany, at the heights of the Rhine River in 1846."

"Ah!" Holmes cried out so suddenly that beside me Mary flinched, leaving me a trifle amused, for I knew how abruptly my mercurial friend's moods could alter. "You bring up an excellent example of why mysteries preoccupy the human mind, for we are creatures who find comfort in certainty, just as we abhor the unknown. It is, I allow you, a most excellent case to ponder, though perhaps not for the reasons you might at first suspect."

"And have you a solution to it?" Mary inquired. "If so I shall be most impressed, as it has defied all official explanation for so long."

"I have read of the matter," Holmes told her, "and am satisfied I know the answer."

"Wait," said Mrs. Hudson, her brow bearing a little frown, "I am unacquainted with this episode of which you speak."

"It is utterly mystifying," Mary told her. "I have read much about it, and knew a young woman who'd been raised by a governess from Dresden, who was obsessively captivated by the matter, since she saw it unfold in newspapers when it had just occurred."

"Yes," agreed Holmes, "as the puzzle is presented in its telling, there is much to mark it as singular, though I would stake my reputation on the fact that it has a discernible explanation, however unlikely the truth may ultimately seem to the credulous masses."

"For 'once one eliminates the impossible, whatever remains, however unlikely, is the truth', right, Holmes?" I said, calling up the maxim I had heard him invoke more than once as I accompanied him among his cases.

"That is quite correct," he agreed. "Now, if you, Mrs. Watson, would be so good as to relate the infamous account to us, I shall thereafter pierce through the unknown, and reveal the harsh truth concerning this seemingly mystifying case."

"Yes," my wife began, "well, from what my friend told me, much of it gleaned from her German-born governess, and from what I, myself, have read, it was a beautiful summer day in August of 1846, and herr Bauer had taken his household out from Mainz to the scenic heights above the Rhine valley. Being a generous man, or at least in a generous mood, herr Bauer brought along not only his wife, Lina, but their three daughters, who ranged in age from seventeen down to six, and his two sons, ages about fourteen and twelve, and also the children's governess, a Frau Mellenboek, the driver, the three housemaids, and a relative in residence, the brother of Bauer's first wife, a thirty-three-year-old simpleton called Helmet, whom Bauer had allowed to lodge in his house even after his first wife's death within a year of their marriage."

Holmes nodded encouragingly and said:

"Continue."

"They set out early in the morning," my wife said, "and before noon were at their destination, picnic basket filled, the family dog coming along, and by the accounts of those who recalled seeing the family in passing, all seemed merry. Yet just before evening, when a patroling constable came to caution those at the park that it was required that everyone vacate the setting before nightfall, not one member of the Bauer family or their servants remained to be found."

"Dear me, and where did they go?" asked Mrs. Hudson.

"No one knows," I told her.

"Yes," said Mary, "for only their picnic baskets, still laden with food, remained, as well as some cigars herr Bauer had perhaps been about to light, which were seen resting on the wooden table there. Also there were some wildflowers scattered about the setting as well, as if plucked by a child with the intention of giving them to Frau Bauer as a token. The empty carriage was nearby, the horses tethered on the grass, placid enough, but all else was strangely static, as if the family had hurriedly stepped away, leaving everything exactly as it had been an instant before. As the constable looked around, the one witness to the event came running up from out of the woods."

"There was a witness?" I questioned her, this detail

unknown to me.

"A little white terrier called Klaus," she explained, "the family dog who had been brought out from the city in the company of his masters. The poor beast was terrified and trembling."

"And what happened next?" asked Mrs. Hudson.

"Well, the constable made a hasty search of the grounds and even stepped a little distance into the woods, calling out. He testified that he had the most peculiar sense of unease, though there was still daylight and nothing menacing was about. He also said the hairs on his neck stood on end, and he felt the most curiously distinct awareness that he was being watched by someone unseen. He hurried back to town and returned with five other constables and a detective. The constables searched the woods and several went down the hills to the river, but no footprints or other signs of the family were seen. The detective, for his part, examined the food and found it had not been eaten, nor had the three bottles of wine and the one of schnapps been uncorked. If the family had disappeared, as every sign indicated, they had done so almost immediately after their arrival, before they took the chance to dine."

Holmes interjected:

"And being a far-thinking man, I believe the detective, a herr Aufenburger, took the food back to the laboratory, and surrendered it to doctors there, to be tested for poisons, of which none were found."

"Quite correct," Mary said with a smile, "that is what occurred. But before that, several hounds were brought to the scene in an effort to track the family, for by then the sun had set and it was full night. The hounds found ample scents around the carriage and at the table, but nothing else, nor did a scent trail lead them into the woods, back to the road, or down the trails to the river. It was as if the family had assembled together for their day in the sunshine of the country, and...."

"And vanished into thin air," I finished for her.

"Yes," Mary agreed, "and though the area was combed for

days by police and search parties, no trace was ever discovered, nor did any of the family ever return home. Their house was searched, herr Bauer's business records were scrutinized, family and acquaintances, even neighbours, were all interviewed, but none had motive or opportunity to do the family harm. In seven years' time courts declared them all deceased, and a cousin in Bonn laid claim to the Bauer assets, which, while a healthy sum, was far from a fortune. The family, as accounts tell us, had seemingly ceased all at once….to exist."

We sat in silence for a few seconds at Mary's conclusion, my own mind awhirl at the sheer impossibility of this infamous and oft-discussed event from the mid-century, which still managed to perplex minds in our own time nearly forty years later. It was Holmes who finally spoke out.

"A most well-told tale, Mrs. Watson, and I must salute you for the skill with which you related your account of the ill-fated Bauer household."

"Thank you," Mary said simply, though the nature of the incident seemed to distress her, and take some sense of happiness from her. It was horrific, I quite agreed.

Now Holmes took his turn, drew a breath, and began.

"In pondering the matter, I would ask each of you to consider whether one very large and significant fact rises above all others."

I admit my mind drew a blank, and as I gazed at Mrs. Hudson and Mary, I saw they were no more forthcoming than I with a suggestion.

"No?" Holmes said. "Nothing whatsoever?"

"To me the case seems absolutely inexplicable," I confessed.

"Would you then describe it as...*impossible*?" Holmes proposed.

"I would say yes to that," said Mrs. Hudson, "save that it is a well-documented event, so it *did* happen."

"Indeed?" Holmes said with a slight smile. "And how precisely is it documented?"

It was Mary who answered.

"Well," she began, "it was in a great many papers."

"Ah! Are you certain?" Holmes asked.

"Why, yes," Mary replied. "I mean…it was."

"You mean you have *heard* of it being in the papers, but did you, yourself, see it there?"

"I have seen it," Mrs. Hudson spoke up. "I distinctly remember reading of it."

"I am certain," Holmes replied, "but was this at the time of the events, in '46, or in a later retrospective of those sinister happenings?"

"Well whenever she read of it," Mary exclaimed, "everyone has *heard* of it, and there are those who remember it from the time it transpired."

"Whom?" asked Holmes.

"Well," Mary struggled, "the governess from Dresden, for one thing."

"I see. Did you meet this governess, or was she related to you by your friend, who told the story of the Bauer family to titillate her listeners?"

"I…" Mary was about to speak but instead closed her mouth and thought, then she confessed: "No, I did not meet the governess, for she was gone from my friend's life before I knew her."

"And this young friend," said Holmes, "was she normally an unimpeachable teller of truth, or was she perhaps an emerging raconteur, given to exaggerations for the sake of drama?"

Mary admitted:

"She did have a flair for the dramatic. Oh, dear…"

"Be that friend's powers of imagination as they may," said Mrs. Hudson, "this family's disappearance is a true event, as everyone knows."

Holmes let this go for a moment, then insisted:

"What if I told you, in my professional opinion the taking of an extended family, in broad daylight, as the accounts describe, would not have been a manageable deed?"

"I should, wonder how it was done then," said Mrs. Hudson.

"Maybe by a vast balloon," I posited, causing Holmes to openly smirk.

"I readily admit," Holmes stated, "that I take it as the starting point of my reasoning that it is physically impossible that thirteen people could vanish in the blink of an eye, as this tale suggests they did, and yet have the perpetrator of so colossal a crime leave behind no sign, no clue, no trace of how such a deed was done. No one, however brilliant or resourceful, could carry out such an action. Not even myself."

"But clearly, if it was, as you suggest, an abduction by a criminal element," said Mrs. Hudson, "we know it was in *some* manner achieved, for the family were no more to be found."

"Indeed?" challenged Holmes. "I for one think the facts as presented lead to two possibilities. The first that the police in Germany were so sloppy in their investigative methods as to miss all sign of a crime. I know something of the thorough nature of the Germans, particularly their police, and can tell you I find this unlikely in the farthest extreme. Which draws my mind back to the more likely explanation, indeed, the only *possible* explanation by my governing maxim Watson was good enough to quote a moment ago. The single remaining explanation is that the Bauer family never existed, and their celebrated disappearance never took place except in a widespread fiction passed off as scintillating fact."

"What?" I cried. "Holmes, as Mary and Mrs. Hudson have said, the case was in newspapers, for years, and is still discussed today. Books have been written on the matter, and individuals who knew the family interviewed!"

"Come, Watson," Holmes answered, "surely you do not think England the only nation on the planet where yellow journalism is a profitable custom? I bid you recollect the ridiculous conceit that at this very hour a gigantic cat stalks York by night."

I halted and reconsidered what I had been about to say, and Mary met my eyes, equally puzzled.

"My dear friends," Holmes spoke up, "I think the entire matter of the vanished Bauer household was a story concocted in the mind some mid-century newspaper writer, and so sensationally popular became the account, unfounded though it was, that it rapidly spread far and wide, giving rise to popular legend, and a great many outright lies, including supposed eyewitnesses coming forward, seeking to steal a moment's fame. What is remembered today is less the first reports, originating in 1846, which induced shudders of fascination across Europe, but lingering exaggerations that have grown with time until they have infected countless minds, each posing as fact."

"But surely records in Germany would testify that the family *did* exist," Mary said. "Police reports, birth records, property deeds...?"

"The Germans are great record-keepers we know, Mr. Holmes," Mrs. Hudson agreed, "it would be easy to disprove it all if it was made-up as you say."

"If one took the time, yes, I agree, but who ever has?" said Holmes. "The story sells too many papers, fills too many books written on the unusual and preternatural, it makes for far too many delicious stories to tell in the dead of night for anyone to truly root it out. But to my mind, I am satisfied that the matter was a newspaperman's hoax that has outlived its creator, and grown fat in the transmission. In fact, had I the motivation I would prove this by seeking out those same records in Germany which you cited, Mrs. Hudson."

We all fell rather quiet at this, for in disillusioning us, Holmes taken some of the fun out of a case people had loved to think on over the decades.

"Well," Mary finally said, "is there any popular legend out there you do feel might have some merit, Sherlock?"

Holmes did not need to think, but said at once:

"Czar Alexander I., Bonaparte's old foe, faked his death, and vanished from court life."

"What?" I cried.

"Oh, yes," said Holmes, "I came to see the truth of that as a boy, when first I read of his funeral, and remarked to Mycroft about certain telling details. It is obvious, and should his casket ever be opened, I am comfortable forecasting that it should be found to be quite empty."

"How extraordinary!" Mary gasped.

"Yes," agreed Holmes, "I gather the Czar, a man of almost unlimited resources and might, had simply tired of royal life, and slipped off into a quiet retirement somewhere under an assumed name. I would imagine he lived out his remaining years in happy anonymity, his work done."

"Well I never," declared Mrs. Hudson.

"It is elementary," Holmes remarked with a narrow smile

The rest of the evening slid by in short order and our little gathering broke up near to nine, Mary and I returning to our own house across town, and Mrs. Hudson heading back downstairs to her residence on the first floor.

As Mary and I settled into the waiting cab, and we both gave a wave to Holmes standing a floor above, silhouetted like a shadow against the golden glow of the lamps inside 221B Baker Street, Mary said to me:

"So tonight we learned the *Mary Celeste* mystery was not such of mystery at all, found out bread fungus made Medical peasant dance like Sufi mystics, and we had the Loch Ness monster debunked."

"Oh, I still do not agree there!" I said in protest.

"Well as a Scotsman, I believe you are required to resist all efforts to dismiss bonnie Nessie, dear," she answered, making me laugh. "And most disillusioning of all," she concluded, "we were given a lesson in the power of a legend to come alive within the mechanism of mankind's love of tall tales."

"Yes, that was unfortunate," I agreed, for I always liked the case of the disappearing Bauer household, yet, remember, we also gained the knowledge, which surely few others have, that there's an empty coffin lying somewhere in a church in Saint

Petersburg, Russia."

"The missing Czar," Mary said dreamily, as she thought on such a monumental stunt.

"All in all not a bad tradeoff for a single evening," I answered.

"He really is a most extraordinary man, isn't he?" Mary asked, as she laid her head against my shoulder.

"The most remarkable in all the world," I agreed, as we rolled along into the rainy London night, two people deeply in love, and very happy to be in one another's company.

ABOUT THE AUTHOR

C. Thorne

C. Thorne is a writer who lives in the United States, and a lifelong fan of Sir Arthur Conan Doyle's stories of the world's most famous fictional detective. He is the author of more than a thousand short stories, and nearly three-dozen books of prose and poetry, with even more tomes beneath his belt through the years as ghostwriter, and contributor to a number of college-level textbooks. The Continuing  Chronicles of Sherlock Holmes is his most recent series, and a labor of love. He hopes you enjoy these stories as much as he and illustrator L. Thorne have enjoyed producing them.

BOOKS IN THE SERIES

The Continuing Chronicles of Sherlock Holmes.

C. Thorne now presents many exciting, never-before revealed adventures of the greatest detective of all time, Mr. Sherlock Holmes. There are many more to come.
Please peruse them all!

Go to:
The Continuing Chronicles of Sherlock Holmes

Made in United States
Orlando, FL
29 June 2025

62479000R00157